DANGEROUS SECRETS

———————

(By Val Ciardullo)

Order this book online at www.trafford.com
or email orders@trafford.com

Most Trafford titles are also available at major online book retailers.

Printed in the United States of America.

ISBN: 978-1-4907-4778-1 (sc)
ISBN: 978-1-4907-4780-4 (hc)
ISBN: 978-1-4907-4779-8 (e)

Library of Congress Control Number: 2014917745

Trafford rev. 10/03/2014

 www.trafford.com

North America & international
toll-free: 1 888 232 4444 (USA & Canada)
fax: 812 355 4082

Dedication

This book is dedicated to my father. It was his illness that inspired me to pick up writing again. The distraction writing gave me was exactly the break I needed mentally to make it through my father's illness. Helping a terminally ill parent is never an easy thing to do. It weighs a lot on you. Writing became very therapeutic for me during a difficult time in my life. When I write it takes my mind off of everything around me, concentrating visually on only the scenes of the book that I am writing. I may not be a Stephen King, James Patterson or a Nora Roberts but nonetheless, I can proudly say that I am a published author and I DID IT! This is my accomplishment! I just wish that my dad were still here to see it. I think he'd be proud too.

Dad, I miss you and I love you. Rest in peace.

Special Thanks

To Sharyn: You are my mentor, my friend and my family. I have learned so much from you during the course of writing three books. Thank you so much for everything you have done for me and continue to do for me. Your devotion and time to me is priceless and is something that I will never forget. I love you always my friend. Thank you...may life always bring you happiness and health because you deserve it for so many reasons.

Chapter One

I lost my mom almost a year ago to cancer. Now it's just me, my dad Andy and my brother Joe. Joe is two years older than me. He's seventeen, soon to be eighteen in just a few months. My dad's two brothers and one sister all live within a few miles from us. We are and always have been a very close family. Uncle Michael is the oldest and was promoted from police officer to detective several years ago. My dad, who is the second oldest, owns his own construction company, Phillips Construction. Uncle Chuck is an attorney and my Aunt Dakota is a veterinarian. She is married to a really sweet guy, Jeff, who is a firefighter and paramedic.

The family has been through a lot over the years. My dad's parents, Alan and Joan, were killed in an auto accident when he was eighteen. Several years later, Aunt Dakota started dating a man that became very abusive early in the relationship. The relationship ended when my dad and uncles learned of the abuse. Then Aunt Dakota started receiving death threats; she was almost killed twice. My dad and uncles resorted to using the services of a group called "The Pack" in order to keep Dakota safe. The Pack was a club that took the law into their own hands when they felt that justice wasn't served the legal way. And, The Pack had some help, too. The Chief of police, John Franks, was not only the chief when my grandfather was on the force; he was also his best friend. He helped my family and The Pack find Aunt Dakota when the man that was threatening her abducted her. Chief John Franks has been there for my family every time they have needed him. He's like a family member to us.

My dad and uncles have always been very over protective of the girls in our family. It's the way they were brought up; they all think alike. Neither my girl cousins nor me are allowed to date until we are seventeen. I've always felt that was unfair. Why do the boys get to date sooner? A few months ago, I started dating behind my dad's back. Nobody has any idea, not even my brother.

Shawn, my boyfriend, and I are two years apart in age and have known each other for four years. We became best friends and then it turned into something more serious. My dad doesn't like me even hanging around with Shawn, says that Shawn is trouble. He thinks Shawn gets too close and friendly with me.

I have never been to Shawn's house because his mom doesn't work so she's home all the time and she can be very critical of other people. It's always been just him and his mom, not sure what happened to his dad. I was always too afraid to ask.

Both my brother and dad are at work and not expected home for another hour or so, so Shawn and I thought it would be a perfect time to be alone. We're in my bedroom, sitting on the bed talking, when we hear a knock on the door.

"Bethany?"

"SHIT!" I whisper. "That's my brother!"

Shawn whispers back in a panicky tone as he puts his shirt on. "SHIT! I thought he wasn't supposed to be home for another hour?"

"He wasn't supposed to be."

"Bethany?" Joe says again as he opens the door. "Bethany, do you want…" He's stunned as he sees Shawn leap to his feet. "What the hell?"

"Joe…"

"What the hell do you think you're doing, Bethany?"

"Joe, please." Joe grabs Shawn and throws him up against the wall. I rush to my feet grabbing Joe's arm trying to pull him back. "JOE, STOP! WHY ARE YOU ACTING SO CRAZY? PLEASE DON'T HURT HIM! HE'S MY BOYFRIEND!"

"YOUR WHAT?" He glances at me then back at Shawn.

I yell out again. "He's my boyfriend!"

Joe lets go of Shawn then threatens him. "If you ever come near my sister again, I will kill you."

Shawn gets up in Joe's face. "You better be very careful who you're threatening!"

"Get the hell out of our house!"

"You will pay." Shawn says as he points to Joe. "I'll see you later, Bethany."

"No, you won't see her later!" Joe follows Shawn out of my room making sure he leaves our house. He returns a moment later with fire in his eyes. "What in the hell do you think you're doing? You're only fifteen years old! WHAT THE HELL IS THE MATTER WITH YOU? You're not even allowed to date yet and you're having sex! If dad finds out about this he's going to flip out!"

"We weren't having sex! We were just talking! Why are you acting so crazy?"

"I'm not stupid, Bethany! He was just putting his damn shirt on when I opened the door! You are not allowed to be hanging with Shawn! Mom and Dad made that perfectly clear to you last year!"

"Please don't tell dad!"

"You have no idea what you just got yourself into dating him, Bethany!"

"What are you talking about?"

"Shawn is a gangbanger!"

"No, he's not!"

"Downstairs, now! I'm not having this conversation in your bedroom!"

"Joe…"

"NOW!"

Shit! I will be in so much trouble if my dad finds out about this. What the hell is my brother doing home early? I've never seen him act crazy like this. I follow him downstairs to the family room where he starts to pace back and forth.

"Joe, please don't tell dad that Shawn was here."

"What the hell are you thinking getting involved with a gangbanger?"

"He's not a gangbanger! Quit calling him that!"

"Did you not notice the black teardrop tattooed next to his eye?" Joe asks sarcastically.

"Yes, I did, so what!"

"So what?" Joe raises his arm likes he's going to hit me but doesn't. "Have you ever asked him why he has it?"

"No, I haven't because it's none of my business! Why are you acting so crazy? I've never seen you like act this before, Joe!"

Joe ignores my question. "If you're dating the guy then it's your business! It means that he has either killed someone or lost a fellow gang member! It's a tattoo that all gangs use! You know this! Uncle Michael tells us stories all the time about gangs! Have you not learned anything from our uncle?"

"He would have told me if he were in a gang!"

"Well, it's obvious that he hasn't been completely truthful with you! What does that tell you, Bethany? You're breaking up with him and you will NOT see him again!"

"Who are you to tell me what to do?"

Joe takes a couple of steps toward me. Not knowing what he's going to do, I take a few steps back. "You need to stay away from him! He's bad news!"

"Are you going to tell dad?"

"The way dad's temper has been since mom died? I don't want to tell him if I don't have to! We promised that we would never

8

keep any secrets from him and you've already broken that promise and now you're making me break it!"

"Please don't tell dad, Joe. You know how our family is, over protective and always up in our business and you're just like dad! Always so over protective! I can see why this family has always driven Aunt Dakota nuts! What's gotten into you, Joe?" *He keeps avoiding answering my question.*

"You're fifteen years old, dad should be all up in your damn business!"

I start crying out of fear that he's going to tell our dad. "Please don't tell dad."

He lets out a huge sigh and thinks for a moment. "You're really putting me in a tough position. You're making me break a promise to dad that we wouldn't keep any secrets from him! But today is your lucky day. I won't tell him only because of the way his temper has been lately. There's no telling what he'd do to you if he found out."

"Look who's talking about tempers? You're acting crazy yourself right now."

Joe still ignores my comments about his temper. "You're lucky I don't beat the shit out of you. This is the choice you have, either you breakup with Shawn or I tell dad."

"WHAT?"

"Break up with him and do it tonight!"

"I hate you!"

"Someday you'll understand! Get Shawn on the phone, text him, do whatever you have to do, but this relationship ends tonight!" He shakes his head in disgust. "Dad will be home any minute. I told him that I would cook dinner tonight to help him out. I'm cooking on the grill so if you would please set the dinner table I would appreciate it."

I start heading for the front door. "I need to see Shawn."

Joe instantly grabs my arm. "WHAT? What did I just say? You are breaking up with him!"

"I WILL! But I want to do it face to face and I need to hear the truth from him about the gang! I won't breakup with him over the phone!"

"Well, you're going to have to because you're not going to see him! Stay away from him!"

"Joe..."

"I'm not fucking around, Bethany! I will get dad involved if I have to!"

He leaves the family room heading to the kitchen and I head for the bathroom to wash my face so my dad doesn't see that I've been crying. *Something is not right with Joe. He's been acting really weird for the past two weeks. He's acting crazy. Dad has been working so much that he hasn't seen Joe to know that something is different about him. I wonder if I should say something to dad. But I can't...Joe will tell him about Shawn and me if I tell dad about him.*

I spend at least twenty minutes in the bathroom trying to calm myself down. When I finally leave the bathroom and go to the kitchen, I see our dad outside talking to Joe. I watch them intently as I set the table wondering if Joe's telling him about Shawn and me. They're out there for quite a long time talking. *He said he wouldn't say anything to dad as long as I do what he told me to do and breakup with Shawn.*

Dad comes into the house. "Hi, honey." He gives me a kiss on the head. "How was your day?"

"Hi dad. It was fine." *Thank god, he didn't tell dad yet. If he had, dad wouldn't be this calm and cheerful.*

"Are you okay?" he asks.

10

"Yeah, why?"

"You seem upset."

Damn, he knows me well. Apparently I don't hide my emotions very well. "No, I'm good."

"Okay. Dinner is almost done."

Joe comes in with the plate of steaks and puts it on the table. "What do you want to drink, Bethany?"

I ignore his question and grab a glass from the cabinet myself. My dad notices and looks at me then at Joe then back at me again.

"Bethany, your brother asked you a question."

"I'll get it myself, thank you."

The three of us sit down at the table and start eating. With the exception of when our mom died, I think this is the quietest dinner we've ever had. After about fifteen minutes my dad puts his fork down on his plate, leans back in his chair and places both hands on the table.

"Alright, what's going on with you two?"

"What do you mean?" Joe asks.

My dad raises his eyebrows at Joe. "Why aren't you two talking?"

"We're eating."

"Don't be a smart ass, Joe."

"I'm not trying to be, dad."

"The two of you are always chatty during dinner which surprisingly, I always look forward to. But tonight for some reason you can hear a pin drop in here, so what's going on?"

"Just sibling rivalry. There's nothing to worry about. We'll get over it." I look up at Joe and give him a dirty look. *Don't bet on it.*

"Do I need to intervene?" Dad asks.

I make no eye contact with my dad as I respond. "No, sir."

"Then I suggest that you get whatever issue you two are having worked out. I don't like it when my kids are fighting."

"Bethany and I will get it worked out. Don't worry."

I need to see Shawn. I can't breakup with him over the phone. "Dad, can I stay at Stephanie's tonight?" Stephanie is my best friend.

"Uh, no. It's a school night, Bethany. You know better. Is your homework finished?"

"I'm almost done, I was going to finish it before I went to her house. Please, dad. Tomorrow's Friday."

"I'm sorry but the answer is no. Please don't ask again."

I better send Stephanie a text to give her a heads up about what just happened between Shawn and my brother. I want to try and see Shawn tonight. She always said she'd cover for me if I ever needed her to. Maybe I can convince my dad to let me go out for a couple of hours. I grab my cell phone and send her a quick text. My dad grabs my phone from me just as I hit send. *Shit, please don't read that.*

"You know better than to have your cell phone at the table."

"I'm sorry, I just wanted to send Stephanie a quick text."

"You know better, Bethany. No cell phones at the table. That's always been the dinner table rule."

"Sorry."

After dinner I head upstairs and finish my homework. I'm working on my history paper when Joe walks into my room.

"You were trying to see Shawn tonight, weren't you? Trying to get Stephanie to cover for you?"

"I am not talking to you."

He steps further into my room and closes the door just enough so it's just barely open and starts to whisper. "You better talk to me or I will call dad up here."

"Is this the way it's going to be? You, threatening me into doing things?"

"I don't want it to be this way, Bethany. But you're not supposed to be hanging around him. He's bad news. It's not safe for you to be dating him and you are not allowed to date at your age anyways."

"Whatever."

"Bethany."

"Just get out."

"He's bad news."

"I can handle this on my own."

"You're treading in very dangerous waters, Bethany. This is serious shit!"

"He won't hurt me!"

"You don't know that! Didn't you hear him threaten me before he left? Gangs are known for retaliations! I don't want you mixed up with those kinds of people!"

"Just get out of my room."

"Bethany, we need…"

"LEAVE ME ALONE!"

He turns to leave and our dad is standing behind him. *Oh shit!*

"If you two are not back to your normal selves by tomorrow then I am stepping in, so I suggest you get your issue worked out."

He leaves the room and Joe looks at me shaking his head. "That was too close, Bethany," he whispers.

"Get out of my room."

Once I finish my homework I head downstairs looking for my dad. I find him in his office working on the computer.

"Dad, I know I can't stay overnight at Stephanie's but can I at least go over there for a little bit?"

"Is your homework finished?"

"Yes, sir."

He looks at his watch. "It's seven o'clock. I want you home by nine. No later."

"Yes sir, thank you."

The moment I walk out the door I call Stephanie and she picks up on the first ring. "Hey, girl, I got your text! I can't believe Joe caught you and Shawn together!"

"Yeah, it wasn't good. He said that he wouldn't tell our dad if I break up with Shawn. Can you cover for me? I have to be home by nine o'clock so I only have a couple of hours. I want to meet with Shawn so I can tell him in person."

"Yeah, sure. Let me know how things go if you can."

"I will, thank you."

I send a quick text to Shawn. "We need to talk. Can you please meet me at our bridge right now?" I receive a text back right away.

"I'll be there in ten minutes."

When I arrive Shawn is already there waiting for me. "Shawn!" I holler out to him. He looks up and walks toward me. "Are you okay?"

"I'm fine."

"Are you? My brother threw you up against the wall pretty hard."

"I'm fine but he's going to pay for that."

"Don't you dare lay a hand on my brother! He was only protecting me! You know my family is very over protective."

"He disrespected me in front of you!"

"Shawn, please!"

"I'm surprised he didn't tell your dad about us."

"Yeah, well there's a catch to that."

"What do you mean?"

I start crying. "I have to breakup with you."

"WHAT? NO!"

"Shawn, we have to breakup or he will tell our dad!"

"That asshole!"

"Shawn…"

"We can be more careful! No more meeting at your house. We'll just strictly meet here."

"And what? Have sex in the woods all the time? Shawn, we can't! I'm sorry!"

"Is this what you want, Bethany?"

"No, of course not! But we don't have a choice! If my dad finds out about us…"

"I know! Fuck!"

"Shawn, you'll be turning eighteen in a couple of weeks. You know that my dad could then have you arrested since I'm only fifteen."

"I know! But we can make this work!"

"It's not just my dad that you'd have to worry about!"

"Who else, your brother? Because I can handle him!"

"No, my two uncles would come after you too! And one's a cop!"

"WHAT? You have an uncle that's a cop?"

"Yes. Well he's a detective now but still."

"Holy shit! I didn't know you had a cop for an uncle! I wish I would have known that!"

"Yeah, just like I wish I would have known that you're in a gang!"

"How the hell did you find that out?"

"The tattoo on the side of your eye gave it away!"

"I've had this tattoo for a while now. Are you telling me that you're just now noticing it?"

"My brother told me!"

"Damn it! I didn't know that you have an uncle for a cop! I have warrants out for my arrest, Bethany! I could have gotten busted at your house!"

"What? What are the warrants for?"

"Burglary, drugs and I'm not sure what the other one is for!"

"Why the hell wouldn't you tell me this stuff, Shawn?"

"I want that part of my life separate from us! I don't want you mixed up in my shit! It's too dangerous!"

"How long have you been in a gang?"

"Three years."

"Since you were fifteen? Are you kidding me?"

"You're the reason why I'm trying to get out of the gang now! I don't want to be part of it anymore!"

"What do you mean you're trying? Just get out, walk away!"

Shawn raises his voice slightly. "You don't just walk away from a gang, Bethany! That's not how it works!"

"What are you talking about?"

Shawn lets out a huge sigh. "In order to join gangs there are certain things that you have to do for them to accept you and there are things that you have to do to get out."

"You need to be more specific than that."

"Every gang is different. You may have to rob a place, kill somebody or even rape someone to get in."

"Oh, my god! What did you do to get in?"

"I robbed a liquor store."

"Have you ever killed anyone?"

"Yes, I have. Two members from another gang."

"Have you ever raped anyone?"

16

"NO! NEVER! I DIDN'T HAVE TO!"

"What if they said you had to, would you have then?"

"I don't know."

"What do you mean you don't know?"

"I don't know what I would have done!"

"Oh my god, this is unbelievable. You said that you have to do things to get out. What kind of things?"

"With my gang…everybody in the gang beats the shit out of you until the leader says to stop. If you live through it and that's a big if because most don't, then you can get out. If I try walking away they would come looking for me, or worse they'd go after my mom or you if they were to find out about you. That's why I didn't tell you about me and the gang life."

"This is too much to take in, Shawn."

"I know and I'm sorry. I never wanted you to find out. I love you. I am trying to keep you safe."

"I love you too, Shawn. I asked you to meet me here because I needed to find out if it were true about the gang and to tell you in person that we have to breakup."

"NO! THERE'S NO REASON FOR US TO BREAKUP, BETHANY!"

"Please don't yell. You scare me when you do."

"You are not in any danger as long as my gang or any other gang doesn't find out about you!"

"And what if they do?"

"They won't!"

"You don't know that, Shawn! This isn't just about you being in a gang! If my dad or my uncles find out about us that's going to be the end of you! My family is very, annoyingly over protective of the girls in our family!"

"We're not breaking up! We can make this work!"

"No, we can't!" I start crying again. "I'm sorry! I have to go."

As I turn to walk away, Shawn grabs my arm in such a harsh and abrupt way that it scares me.

"I don't want to breakup!"

I scream. "LET GO OF ME!" I break lose and run from him as fast as I can. He chases me, grabs a hold of me then pins me up against a tree. I scream again and he quickly puts his hand over my mouth.

"STOP SCREAMING DAMN IT! I'M NOT GOING TO HURT YOU! I AM NOT GOING TO HURT YOU! I JUST WANT TO FINISH TALKING!" Tears are streaming down my face. "I don't want us to breakup! We will not breakup! I can't lose you! We can make this work! Please don't do this to us! I love you, Bethany! Baby, please don't do this." He stares into my eyes for a moment. "I'm going to remove my hand from your mouth. Please do not scream. I will not hurt you. I promise." He slowly takes his hand away from my mouth.

"Let go of me right now, Shawn."

"Bethany…"

"Please, Shawn. You're scaring me. I just want to go home." I plead with a shaky voice.

"I won't hurt you. I would never hurt you."

"Please, let go of me. You're scaring me."

"I'm sorry I don't mean to. I just want to talk about this!"

"There's nothing to talk about! Please let me go! I just want to go home!"

"Fine, but this isn't over! Do you hear me? This isn't over!" Shawn releases me and I run as fast as I can away from him crying all the way home. "We're not over, Bethany!"

Chapter Two

It's eight thirty by the time I get home from meeting with Shawn. As soon as I walk in the door I quickly run to the bathroom before my dad sees me and wash my face in cold water. I then go to my dad's office where he's still working on the computer to let him know that I'm home. Not wanting him to see my face, I stand at the entrance of the room instead of going inside.

"Dad, I'm home. I'm really tired so I'm going up to bed."

He looks at his watch. "It's too early to be going to bed. Are you okay?" He looks up at me and unfortunately sees that I've been crying despite my efforts to hide it. "What's wrong?"

"Nothing, dad. I'm fine."

He puts down his pen and swivels his chair around so that he is now facing me. "No, you are not fine. Come here, please." *Oh, no.* I walk up to my dad and he gently taps my chin. "You've been crying. Why? What's going on, sweetheart?"

"Nothing, dad. I'm fine."

My dad's voice becomes stern. "Bethany Ann Phillips, don't tell me you're fine. It's obvious that you're not. I want to know why you've been crying and I want to know right now."

I have to think of something quick. "I'm just upset about Joe and me fighting."

"What happened between the two of you?"

"We just had a big disagreement. That's all, we'll be fine."

"What ever the problem is, it has you in tears so I'm intervening now. Joe's not home right now so tomorrow morning the three of us are going to sit down and talk before you go to school. I want you to make sure you're up an hour earlier so we have time to talk. This fight you two are having is going to end now, understand?"

SHIT! I'M A DEAD GIRL! I have to talk to Joe! "Dad, everything will be fine."

"Don't argue with me, Bethany. I told you two that if you didn't get this worked out on your own then I was going to get involved, so now I'm getting involved."

"Yes, sir." *SHIT!* My dad taps his cheek with his finger telling me to give him a kiss. I give him a kiss and head for bed. "Goodnight, dad."

"Goodnight, sweetheart. I love you."

"I love you too, dad. Aren't you going to work tomorrow?"

"No, I'm going to work from home for the next week or so."

"But don't you have to go in?"

"I own my own business remember, I can do whatever I want. I've been working late hours at the office these last few weeks, therefore, I want to start doing some work from home and spend some time with my kids." He lets out a small chuckle. "Do you have any objections to that?"

"No, of course not. Goodnight."

My dad smiles as he swivels his chair toward his desk. "Goodnight, sweetheart."

I run upstairs and try calling Joe on his cell phone but he doesn't answer so I send him a text to call me. "Where are you? Please call me as soon as you get this message! Dad wants to know what's going on between the two of us. He wants to sit down with us tomorrow morning! Call me!"

About ten minutes later I receive a text back. "Can't talk. I'm taking care of this situation right now."

"What situation?"

"Shawn!"

"Joe, what are you doing? Please, I don't want you to get hurt! I broke up with Shawn like I said I would. I promise I did!"

Fifteen minutes goes by since my last text to Joe and he hasn't responded back. I try calling his cell phone again but it goes right into his voicemail so I leave him a message. "Joe, please call me! Don't do anything, please!"

He must have shut his phone off. Oh, my god. Joe, what are you getting yourself into? I try calling him several more times but still get the same results. By ten o'clock I must have left him five voicemails and sent him six text messages. None of which are being answered.

Maybe, I can get Shawn to answer me back. I try contacting Shawn but he doesn't answer either so I send him text messages too. "Please don't hurt my brother! I know you're upset for what he did to you but he was only protecting me! PLEASE DON'T HURT HIM! I BEG YOU! FOR ME, PLEASE!" I send several text messages like this and leave several voicemail messages and he doesn't respond either.

Do I tell my dad? I don't know what to do. What if everything is fine? I may open up a can of worms that don't need to be opened. I plug my phone in next to my bed in case one of them answers me back. *I don't know if I should tell my dad.* I lay here for several hours not able to sleep, waiting to hear something from one of them.

Chapter Three

I've been lying in bed for hours, crying and not able to sleep. I look at the alarm clock and it's now Friday, two in the morning and Joe still hasn't responded back or come home yet. *I am so scared. I have to tell my dad but he's going to flip out!* I grab my phone and decide to call my Uncle Michael instead.

He picks up right before it goes into voicemail. "Bethany, it's two o'clock in the morning, is everything okay?"

I'm crying as I answer him. "No it's not, Uncle Michael. I need you please."

"What's the matter honey, is your dad okay?"

"My dad's fine but I won't be."

"What are you talking about, honey? Why would you not be okay? Where are you?"

"I'm home. I have to tell my dad something extremely important that could possibly be life or death and he's going to flip out. I can't tell him alone. I'm scared of his temper."

"What's going on, honey? Where's Joe, is he home?"

"It's about Joe, Uncle Michael."

"I'm on my way. I'll be there in five minutes with Uncle Chuck."

I wait almost five minutes and then go and wake up my dad. I leave the bedroom door open so that the hallway light shines into his room.

I try to control my emotions while waking him up. "Dad, please wake up. I need to talk to you." I gently shake my dad by the shoulder. "Dad."

"What in the world is going on? What's the matter, sweetheart?"

"I need to talk to you. Can you please wake up?"

"What time is it?" he asks in a sleepy voice looking at the alarm clock. "Two o'clock in the morning? Can't this wait until later?"

"No, it can't. Please, dad. It's important. I need to talk to you about my fight with Joe."

He rolls over onto his back and lays his arm over his forehead. "I thought the days of you waking me up in the middle of the night ended when you were a baby."

"Dad, please get up."

"Is this going to take a while?"

"Yes, possibly the whole morning."

"You mean possibly the whole night, sweetheart. It's still the middle of the night."

"Dad."

"Okay, okay. I'll meet you downstairs in a minute. You might as well turn on the coffee maker for me. It's already set to go."

"Okay."

"Thank you." I hear my dad mumble to himself as I leave his room. "Ugh…kids, but you gotta love them."

I start crying again as I get to the bottom of the stairs then hear my Uncle Michael and Uncle Chuck now arriving.

As I let them in Uncle Michael immediately starts asking me questions. "Are you okay? Where are your dad and Joe?"

"My dad's upstairs and should be down any minute, I don't know where Joe is."

Uncle Chuck puts his hand on my shoulder. "Let's go into the family room, honey."

"I have to start the coffee for my dad."

"It can wait."

My dad comes downstairs and is surprised and confused when he sees his brothers are here. "What are you guys doing here in the middle of the night?"

My crying becomes harder as I try to talk. "I called Uncle Michael, dad."

"You did what? At two o'clock in the morning? Why?"

"Because there's something really important that I have to tell you."

"Then you should have told me instead of waking everybody up."

"But what I need to tell you is going to make you really angry with me and your temper scares me sometimes. I was afraid to tell you alone."

"What? You're afraid to talk to me?" My dad says with hurt and shock in his voice.

"Sometimes I am." He stands in front of me not knowing what more to say.

"Bethany, what's going on, honey?" Uncle Michael asks.

"I think Joe maybe in trouble and it's all my fault."

My dad's face suddenly falls and turns white as a ghost. "What do you mean he maybe in trouble? What kind of trouble? He's not home yet?"

My dad is just about to go upstairs to check and see if Joe is home when I reply quickly to stop him. "No, he's not home, dad."

My dad stops and walks back toward me. "What the hell is going on, Bethany? Where's Joe?"

I start crying heavily. "I don't know. He said he was taking care of a situation and I haven't heard from him since. He's not answering his phone or texts."

Uncle Michael grabs my shoulder turning me to face him. "What situation are you talking about, honey?"

24

Before I can start to explain Chief Franks arrives with Aunt Linda. Uncle Chuck is shocked to see Aunt Linda and my dad is shocked to see the Chief of police here.

"Linda honey, what are you doing here?" Asks Uncle Chuck.

"I heard you leave then got up to go to the bathroom and I saw your note. I got worried." Uncle Chuck gives her a brief kiss and doesn't say anything else.

Uncle Michael explains why the Chief is here. "I called Chief Franks after Bethany called me. Her call sounded urgent." He then turns his attention back to me. "What situation are you talking about, Bethany?"

I look at my dad. "I'm so sorry, dad! I'm so sorry! You're going to hate me forever for this! I'm so sorry! Please forgive me!"

My dad walks toward me so that he is now standing in front of me again. "Hate you? You're my kid. I would never hate you. I may get extremely mad at you at times but I could NEVER hate my own kid!"

"I am so sorry, dad. I am so sorry."

"Okay, Bethany, I understand that you're sorry but you need to calm yourself down and start explaining what's going on."

"Do you remember Shawn from last year?"

"The kid that I thought was getting too friendly with you?"

"Yes." I take in a deep breath and just blurt out. "I've been dating him for a few months now."

Anger now floods across my dad's face. "Come again? I told you that you were not allowed to hang with that kid anymore! And you know that you are not allowed to be dating yet either!"

"I'm so sorry!"

"Are you having sex with that boy?" I hesitate to answer until he yells making me jump. "ANSWER ME!"

In a very low and scared voice I respond back. "Yes."

25

Suddenly, my dad backhands me knocking me down to the floor. "ANDY!" Aunt Linda rushes to me, and my dad shoves her away.

"This doesn't concern you!"

Chief Franks yells at my dad. "ANDY! THAT'S ENOUGH!"

Uncle Chuck lunges at my dad but Uncle Michael stops him. "Chuck, don't do anything you may regret!"

Uncle Chuck points his finger at my dad practically putting it in his face. "IF YOU EVER LAY A HAND ON MY WIFE LIKE THAT AGAIN, IT WILL BE THE LAST THING YOU EVER DO!"

"GET YOUR ASS IN THE KITCHEN NOW!" Uncle Michael says to my dad as he and Chief Franks escort him out of the room and into the kitchen. We can hear him scolding my dad. "WHAT IN THE HELL IS THE MATTER WITH YOU? YOU ARE OUT OF CONTROL, ANDY!"

I am crying so hard that I start heaving as Uncle Chuck picks me up off the floor and holds me tight in his arms. "It's going to be okay, honey. Shhh. You're okay now." He looks at Aunt Linda. "Are you okay?"

"Yeah, I'm okay. Chuck, your brother's temper has gotten way out of control! Something has to be done about it before he seriously hurts somebody! Look at her lip! He's busted her damn lip, Chuck!"

He pulls me out of his hug to look at my face then pulls me back in again. "Michael and I have been trying to get through to him. We've spoken to him many times. He just won't listen to us. We don't know what else to do." He looks at me as I'm still heaving. "Your lip is bleeding but you'll be okay, honey. Calm yourself down. You need to take deeps breaths. Come on, take deep breaths." I take in a few deep breaths like he said. "That a girl. You're okay now. He won't do that to you again, I promise you."

"He didn't start losing his temper until after he lost Melanie," says Aunt Linda.

"I know. I really think he's still struggling with losing her."

"He has never hit his kids before, none of us do."

Uncle Chuck gives me a kiss on the head. "Honey, your dad's temper has really gotten bad since your mom died. Has he ever done this to you or Joe before?"

"No, this is the first time. He's never hit me before and he's never hit Joe either. Not that I'm aware of anyways."

"Are you telling me the truth? We can't help your dad if you protect him."

I start to panic because I don't want them to get the wrong idea about my dad. "I promise you, Uncle Chuck, this is the first time he's ever hit me! I swear to you, that's the truth! I swear!"

"Okay, honey, okay. I believe you." He looks at Aunt Linda. "If he's doing this to his kids now, there's no telling what he'd do next, especially since Joe may be in trouble. That's just going to add more stress."

"He's starting to scare me, honey."

"I know. I think it may be best if Bethany stays with us for a while. Andy needs some time alone to straighten his ass out."

"I agree, I think that would be a great idea. I'm going to get some paper towels and ice for her mouth."

She goes into the kitchen and Andy tries to apologize but she doesn't want to have anything to do with him right now. She's not interested in listening to anything he has to say at the moment.

"Linda, I am so sorry. I don't know what came over me." She grabs what she needs and leaves the kitchen without looking at him or saying a word. "LINDA!"

Chief Franks pushes on Andy's shoulder making him sit down. You can hear the furiousness in his voice as he yells. "SIT YOUR ASS DOWN!"

Michael continues to scold Andy. "What's wrong with you, bro? Did you see what you did to your daughter's face?"

"I know! It's killing me that I just did that to her! I didn't mean to do it! I've never hit my daughter before! Never!"

"You shoved our sister in-law practically knocking her down too! Chuck and I have been trying to tell you for months about your damn temper but you won't listen to us! Do you see it now?"

Chief Franks puts his finger up telling Michael to let him take this over. He then moves so that he is now standing in front of Andy.

"Andy, out of you three brothers, you have always been the one to have the most control over your temper and be the most level headed. I don't know what happened to you since Melanie died but your temper has jumped several notches! You've been flying off the handle a lot and over the littlest things and now it's way out of control!"

"I know but I'm handling it! I'm getting it under control!"

"BULLSHIT! Shoving your sister in-law and busting your daughter's lip is proof that you are NOT handling it and you are NOT getting it under control! You have crossed over the damn line, Andy! You need to control your temper! Do you hear me? If you are not going to listen to your brothers then damn it, you're going to listen to me! You are going to see Schiller tomorrow morning! He's a good friend of mine and of your family, he will get you in!"

"I'm not going to any doctor, I'm handling this on my own! Right now I need to find my son and make sure he's okay!"

Michael looks at Chief Franks then back at Andy. "You're breaking down my dear brother. Your temper is way out of control! You need to pull it together! We will find Joe but you need to deal with this temper of yours and you need to do it now not later!"

Chief Franks lets out a huge sigh. "Do you want me to arrest you for the assault on your daughter?" Michael looks at the Chief in shock but doesn't say anything.

Andy quickly looks up at the Chief in shock too. "WHAT? You're kidding me right? It wasn't like that, Chief! You know that! I didn't mean to hit her!"

"I don't know if you meant it or not." The Chief says it in a way like he doesn't know Andy anymore.

"Oh, come on, Chief! You know me better than that!"

"I thought I did. Now I'm not so sure. Andy, you need to get your temper under control before you seriously hurt somebody! The therapy sessions are only for one hour a day just like they were when you guys went after losing your parents. You can handle one hour a day. You need to do this for yourself and for your kids."

"I don't need to see a damn doctor!"

"Okay, let's go! Stand up!" Chief Franks quickly yanks Andy up out of his chair. He pulls out a pair of handcuffs and starts cuffing Andy's hands behind his back. "You're under arrest for the assault against your daughter. You have the right to remain silent, anything you..."

"WHAT? ARE YOU FUCKING KIDDING ME, CHIEF?"

"DO THESE CUFFS FEEL LIKE A DAMN JOKE TO YOU, ANDY? You have one of two choices to make here. Either your ass goes to jail or you go see Doctor Schiller tomorrow! We can't help you if you are not willing to help yourself! I am not screwing around here! This is it, JAIL OR SCHILLER? Which is it going to be? It's your choice!"

"FINE! I will go see the damn shrink!"

"Good choice! You will have an appointment tomorrow morning. Someone will take you there."

"I can handle driving myself."

"Oh, no you don't. We want to make sure you go tomorrow and every visit needed thereafter. If you miss just one appointment, just one! I will haul your ass off to jail and charge you for assault on your daughter! I WILL NOT give you any more warnings! Do you understand? Am I clear enough for you?"

"Yes! Fine! Now would you please get these damn cuffs off of me?"

As Chief Franks removes the cuffs he looks up at Michael and wipes his forehead telling him, 'whew! Thank god that worked!' Michael widens his eyes in agreement.

Chuck walks into the kitchen as Chief Franks is removing the handcuffs from Andy. "You should have left them on him." He says sarcastically.

"Chuck, I am really sorry, bro. Is my daughter okay? I didn't mean to hit her. I swear. I didn't mean to hit her or push Linda."

The tone of Chuck's response clearly shows his disappointment and anger in his brother. "Your daughter has a busted lip, Andy, no thanks to you! But she'll be fine."

"Fuck!" Andy whispers his own disappointment to himself. Then looks back at Chuck again. "What about Linda, is she okay?"

"She's fine and if you ever touch my wife like that again I will take your ass down so fast you won't know what the hell hit you! You got that?"

"Loud and clear."

"GOOD!" Chuck is so pissed off and he shows no sympathy towards Andy at all. "Bethany is going to stay with Linda and me for a while. You need some time to yourself to straighten your ass out."

Andy jumps to his feet. "WHAT? You are NOT taking my kid!"

"Watch me! Do you want to try and stop me, because that I would love to see! She needs a safe place to stay!"

"This is a safe place for her! My kid is not going anywhere! It would have to be over my dead body!"

"Well, that can certainly be arranged!"

"I WILL NOT HURT MY KID!"

"YOU ALREADY HAVE, ANDY! LOOK AT HER DAMN LIP!"

Michael intervenes by stepping in between his two brothers. "Chuck's got a point, Andy."

"I'm not an abusive father! You guys know that! She's not going anywhere! My son maybe in trouble and now you want to take my daughter from me? I DON'T THINK SO! THAT'S NOT GOING TO HAPPEN!"

Michael gets in Andy's face. "What the hell is wrong with you, man? We're trying to help you!"

Chief Franks pulls Michael back. "Let's compromise then. Andy, unfortunately, right now we don't trust your temper so it's either Bethany stays with Chuck for a while or somebody stays here with the two of you for a while." Michael wastes no time volunteering.

"I'll stay here with them or they can come stay with me. If I stay here then Tony can stay with Chuck."

Chuck responds, "That's a good idea. If I stay, I may end up beating the shit out of our brother. Tony can stay with us."

"It's your choice, Andy." Chief Franks prompts him for an answer.

"I don't need a damn babysitter! I will not hurt my daughter again. I love my kid."

"We have no doubt that you love your kids, but we don't trust your temper right now. And with Joe possibly in trouble that adds more stress to you. We're trying to help you, son."

"My daughter stays with me! End of discussion! No one is taking my daughter from me! Michael can stay here." Andy then looks at Chuck. "I didn't mean to hurt her." Chuck leaves the kitchen without saying another word to Andy so Michael replies instead.

"We know, bro. We're going to help you through this. That's what family is for. Even Chuck will be there for you."

"Am I allowed to talk to my daughter?" Andy asks very sarcastically.

"If she's willing to talk to you, sure. I'll go get her." Michael goes into the family room where Bethany is. "Hi, honey. How's your lip?"

"It hurts but I'm okay. My dad scares me sometimes."

"I know, honey. He didn't mean to hurt you."

"I know. He's just under a lot of stress right now."

Uncle Chuck immediately scolds me. "Bethany Ann Phillips, do not make up any excuses for your father. What he did to you was wrong, whether he's under a lot of stress or not. There was no excuse for it."

Uncle Michael places his hand on my back. "Your dad wants to talk to you. Are you okay with talking to him?"

"Is he calmed down?"

"Yes, he is."

"Okay, then I'll talk to him. I know he didn't mean to hurt me."

"No, he didn't. Come on, honey. Let's go talk to him."

When I walk into the kitchen my dad looks up at me and shakes his head in embarrassment and shame.

"Oh, my god. Sweetheart, I am so sorry for what I did to you. I will never forgive myself for doing that." He puts his hand out motioning for me to come closer to him. When I do he pulls me into such a huge hug that it feels like he's going to crush my ribs. "I'm so sorry, baby girl. I am so very sorry." He's practically crying in my ear.

"I know, dad. I forgive you. I'm so sorry too."

"I would never intentionally hurt you."

"I know."

My dad pulls back and looks me in the eyes with tears in his. "I am so very sorry."

"I am too, dad. Your…your temper scares me."

"I know, sweetheart. I'm going to be doing something about that."

Chief Franks motions toward the family room. "Why don't we go back into the family room? We need to concentrate on finding out what's going on with Joe." He then looks at my dad. "Are you going to control yourself now or do we have to question your daughter without your presence?"

My dad looks at me as he answers, "no, I'm fine. I will never do that again. I promise. I would take my own life first."

As they all head back into the family room, Michael pulls Chief Franks back a little and whispers, "would you have really arrested him?"

"If it meant getting through to him, yes." The Chief then proceeds to the family room.

Michael whispers to himself, "oh, shit."

Chapter Four

My dad walks up to Aunt Linda to apologize again. "Linda…"

She puts her hand up telling him to stop. "Not right now, Andy. I just don't want to hear it right now."

"Okay, I understand."

He sits down on the couch and Uncle Chuck and Aunt Linda sit as far away from him as possible. They are very angry with my dad.

The Chief takes his note pad and pen out of his pocket. "Bethany, let's start from the beginning."

"Shawn and I were sitting in my room talking when Joe came upstairs looking for me. Joe saw Shawn and before I knew it he was throwing Shawn up against the wall. He told Shawn that if he ever came near me again he'd kill him. I've never seen Joe act like that before. It was like he was a different person."

"What was Shawn's reaction? Did they fight at all?"

"There was no fight but Shawn was not happy. He told Joe that he better be very careful who he's threatening. Joe told him to get out."

"Then what?"

"Shawn told Joe he would pay for this and then he left."

"Pay for what?"

"I don't know, I guess for throwing him up against the wall."

"What else happened?"

"That was it. It was over pretty fast. Shawn has a black teardrop tattooed next to his eye. Joe said that gangs use those tattoos. Said it means that they've killed somebody or lost a gang member. I didn't know he was in a gang. I swear. I would have stayed away from him if I knew." Then I look at my dad, "which was something I was supposed to do in the first place, anyways."

My dad nods his head in agreement. "We'll discuss that later."

I continue to explain. "Shawn's a big guy so I was shocked when Joe threw him up against the wall."

Chief Franks motions around the room. "Joe's no small guy either, Bethany. Look at your family. All the men in your family are built and Joe's been working out for a couple of years. He's pretty strong. I know who Shawn is. He's not that much bigger than your brother. What did you mean when you said, 'it was like Joe was a different person'?"

"These last couple of weeks Joe's been acting different."

"How has he been acting different?"

"He's been really moody and staying in his room a lot with the door closed. He wouldn't allow me to come into his room anymore. I figured he was mad at me for something so I stopped trying to talk to him."

"Did anything else happen before this incident with Shawn?"

"No, but, after Joe kicked Shawn out of our house he started yelling at me acting all crazy like. He even raised his hand at me like he was going to hit me. He's never done that before."

My dad shakes his head as he becomes very upset but this time not with me but with Joe. "He better not hit you! Joe is not allowed to hit you, Bethany! He's not allowed to hit any female, he knows better!"

"He didn't, dad, but he almost did and I can tell that he wanted to."

My dad looks at his brothers. "That's not good. Damn it! I've been working so much I never saw anything going on with him." He looks back at me. "Why didn't you come to me right away and tell me that he was acting strange?"

"At first I thought everything would be okay. I thought he was just mad at me for something. Then this happened with Shawn. It was when Joe stopped answering his phone and my texts that I realized that something was seriously wrong. I got too scared to tell you, because I knew that I wasn't supposed to be hanging with Shawn let alone dating yet. That's why I called Uncle Michael. I thought it would be easier to tell you if somebody was here with me."

My dad looks down at the floor shaking his head, ashamed that his own daughter is afraid to talk to him.

The Chief continues to question me. "Where has Shawn been living?"

"What do you mean? I thought he was living at home."

"Have you ever been to his house?"

"No. He said he doesn't like bringing girls home because his mom can be too critical sometimes. And she doesn't work so she's always home. He never talks about his dad."

"He's been lying to you, Bethany. His mother works two jobs and hasn't seen Shawn in six months. She filed a missing persons report six months ago. As for his father, he's in prison."

"Why would he lie to me?"

"I don't know. Most gang members don't hide the fact that they're in a gang so I'm surprised he hid it from you. Shawn has a few warrants out for his arrest. We haven't been able to find him. Do you..."

"What are the warrants for?" my dad asks.

"Burglary, drug trafficking, and possible murder but we can't prove that one yet."

"SHIT!" Uncle Michael puts his hand on my dad's shoulder in an effort to keep him calm. "I'm fine, Michael. I just can't believe this is happening to our family."

The Chief continues. "Bethany, where did you and Shawn always meet up?"

36

I look at my dad almost too afraid to answer but surprisingly, he says in a very calm and controlled tone, the way he used to handle things before mom died.

"Answer the Chief's question, sweetheart."

"We'd meet here or at our private hangout." I hear my dad let out a big sigh while Uncle Michael watches him very closely.

"Where's this private hangout?" asks the Chief.

"Off of Route 7, there are some woods along the road. We have a spot inside the woods. There's a little creek back there near a beautiful waterfall. Shawn built a small bridge over the creek so we could have access to the pond and go swimming in the summer. He also built a small seating area for us. He's seems very good with his hands."

"Yeah, I bet he is," my dad says.

Chief Franks looks at my dad. "Andy, keep quiet or I will ask you to leave the room." He then looks back at me. "How long have you two been dating?"

"About four months." I look quickly at my dad. "I'm sorry, dad."

Chief Franks snaps his fingers. "I want you to talk to me, honey, not your dad. Are you telling me that you don't know where he's living or where we can find him?"

"I thought he was living at home, so no, I don't know. We've always called or texted each other to meet up."

Uncle Michael has been on his IPad looking something up. "It looks like he has his permit. Does he have a car to drive?"

"He drives his dad's old car."

"It must not be in Shawn's name because I can't find anything registered for him. Can you tell me what kind of car his dad has and if there are any distinctive marks on it? I can't find any plates registered to his dad either. At least none that are legit."

"I think it's a Chevrolet Impala but I'm not certain. It's red. It's not new I know that for sure. It has an old musky smell to it and the dash looks old. There's a dent behind the back tire on the passenger side."

He hands me his IPad. "Take a look at some of these pictures and tell me if any of them come close to what Shawn drives."

After scrolling through several pictures of Impala's I see one that looks like his. "This one looks just like his car except his car is red." I hand the IPad back to Uncle Michael.

"That's a seventy two Impala. We need to get an APB out on it. We may not have the license plate number but we have a description. There can't be too many old Impala's in this small town." He says handing the IPad to Chief Franks.

"You're not going to hurt him are you?" I ask.

"We're not planning on it, honey, but that depends on him," says the Chief. "I'll get an APB out on Joe's car too." The Chief hands the IPad back to Uncle Michael. "I'm going to head back to the station and get the ball rolling to search for Joe. Michael, while you're staying here, see if you can find any more information in the data bases on Shawn or his gang."

"No problem, Chief." Uncle Michael then looks at Uncle Chuck. "I need to grab some clothes from home. Can I trust you to play nice with our brother while I'm gone for twenty minutes?"

Without moving his head Uncle Chuck looks over at my dad and as he answers, you can hear for the first time tonight, the sympathy in his tone. "Yeah, we'll be fine."

"Thank you. Linda, do you need a ride home?"

"No, my car is here, I'll leave when Chuck does."

"Okay, I'll be back shortly."

I can feel the tension in the room after Uncle Michael leaves. "Dad, can I go up to my room now?"

"Not yet, sweetheart, we need to have a talk."

"Am I grounded?"

"Oh, yeah. You better believe it."

"I am really sorry, dad."

"What am I going to do with you girl? You disobeyed me when I said no dating, you snuck around behind my back, you lied to me and to top it all off, you're having sex already too, which really has my blood boiling."

Uncle Chuck watches closely as my dad gently grabs my hand and pulls me so that I am standing in front of him.

"I am so sorry, dad."

"I know, but unfortunately you are now grounded. You're grounded for the next four months."

"WHAT? FOUR MONTHS?"

My dad puts his hand up telling me to keep quiet and let him finish. "For the next four months, you are grounded inside the house. You're not allowed to go see your friends, and you're not to have friends over, no talking on the phone except to talk to me or other family members, no IPad, no phone…" he says as he takes my phone and IPad from the coffee table, "and no computer. You're lucky I don't take away the television too. And I want lights out by ten o'clock every night whether it's a weekend or not. Do I make myself clear?"

I look at Uncle Chuck. "Don't look at me, honey. You created this mess."

"I know I did."

"Do I make myself clear, Bethany?" my dad asks again.

"Yes, sir. I am so sorry. I won't forgive myself if something happened to Joe because of me."

He pulls me into a hug. "Let's stay positive about Joe, okay. We'll find him. It's obvious now that something was going on with him before this incident with Shawn went down. I love you."

"I love you too, dad."

"It's late. Go on and get your butt to bed."

"Yes, sir." I kiss Aunt Linda and Uncle Chuck good night then head upstairs to bed.

Andy looks at Linda and Chuck. "I can say that I am sorry until I am blue in the face but it won't change what I did. I don't know what more to say except that I'm sorry."

"I'm very angry with you Andy for what you did to Bethany and Linda. There's just no excuse for it."

"I know and again I am really sorry. I just reached my breaking point. I just lost it. I would never purposely harm my kids you both should know that. And I would never harm my sister in-law."

"We know. We'll get you through this, bro."

I tried to go to sleep but couldn't. I can't stop thinking about Joe so my dad allowed me to watch television downstairs with him, Uncle Chuck and Aunt Linda. I didn't last too long; I ended up falling asleep in my dad's arms with an afghan wrapped around me.

I wake up when Uncle Michael finally returns with a weeks' worth of clothing, then Uncle Chuck and Aunt Linda head home. Uncle Michael gets settled in the guest room upstairs and returns a few moments later. He gives me a kiss on the head then starts booting up his laptop computer.

"Bethany, why don't you head up to bed, honey. I want to have some time with your dad."

"Yes, sir. Good night." I say in a sleepy tone. I give kisses and hugs and head up to bed.

"What did I do?" Andy asks.

"Nothing, I just wanted to talk now that you're calmed down."

"I'd rather forget about what I did earlier. I have a hard enough time as it is looking at my daughter right now. I see her lip and it just reminds me of what I did. I am so angry with myself."

"I know you are."

"You know something, Michael, it didn't happen too many times but when ever mom or dad would physically discipline us, they never hit us in the face. It was always on the ass and with their hand. I don't know why I did it to my kid. Have you ever hit Tony?"

"No, I never need to, just the tone of my voice and a look is always enough to scare him. What happened to you, bro? Just like the Chief said, you used to be the one that was always in control of your temper and the most level headed one. Now you're always mad and flying off the handle."

You can hear the tears in Andy's voice as he speaks. "I don't know. Since Melanie died I've been feeling really lost. She was not only my wife but she was my best friend. She was everything to me. It wasn't supposed to be her time yet. It's just not fair. Almost losing our sister six years ago, losing my wife last year, my son is now missing and my daughter is…well, growing up way too fast. Maybe all of that has something to do with it. I don't know. Dr. Schiller helped us through the death of our parents' maybe the good doctor can help me through this too. He's pushing his seventies so maybe I should get his help sooner rather than later." Andy laughs at his own comment.

Michael laughs too. "Yeah, no shit, right. It will help. It's good to see you laugh some."

41

"I didn't think Linda and Chuck were ever going to talk to me again."

"You've got to remember that Chuck has always been the least in control of his temper and the least level headed one. He's always flown off the handle first then asked questions later. It amazes me that he's an attorney."

"This is true. He has always been that way. But why should it be any different for me then?"

"Because, that's not like you, it never has been. That's the difference between you and Chuck. When Chuck flies off the handle, it's normal because he's always been that way even when we were kids. But even Chuck has never hit his family the way you did tonight. You've never been like that until now."

"I know. I can't believe Chief Franks was actually going to arrest me."

"That shocked the shit out of me too, but I guess that was the only way he can think of, in getting through to you that you need to see Schiller."

"How are we going to find Joe? What are you guys doing to find him?"

"I've brought my computer to look into some leads on some of Shawn's connections. Maybe it can lead us to where he is. Once we find him then we'll pick him up. I don't know if he has anything to do with Joe missing but we have to start somewhere. Based on what Bethany has told us, Shawn seems to be the best lead we have at the moment. Chief Franks has everyone looking for both Shawn and Joe's cars. We're checking out some of Joe's hangouts and talking to his friends. Chuck has been calling Joe's cell trying to get a hold of him and probably will continue doing so throughout the night."

"Why aren't you out there looking for my son? You should be out there, not here babysitting me. I don't need a babysitter, Michael. I promise I will be fine. I need you out there looking for Joe."

"All efforts are being made to find him, Andy. Believe me. All of his hangouts are being checked as we speak. I am following up on other information that may lead us to Shawn."

"I don't trust anyone else but you to find him. Please, I need my son back. How would you feel if it were you going through this?"

"I would probably feel the same way. I tell you what, after Schiller's appointment tomorrow, I'll go out for a few hours and follow up on any leads out in the field if there are any. But if you feel your temper is getting out of control, you need to promise me that you will walk away."

"I promise I will walk away. Right now I need you out there looking for my son, Michael. I've lost my wife I can't lose a kid too. That will break me for sure. Right now I wish the Pack was still around."

"Are you out of your mind? It's because of that club that our sister was almost killed, twice!"

"I know but they had connections that we don't have."

"I don't care. Even if they were still around I still wouldn't take their help."

Chapter Five

It's six o'clock Friday morning; the sound of gunfire and shattering glass suddenly awaken me. I scream as I roll off of my bed and away from the window. I'm lying on the floor waiting for it all to stop and when it finally does stop, I hear the sound of tires squealing outside. Too terrified to move, I continue to lie there screaming and crying hysterically. My dad and Uncle Michael are yelling as they run upstairs to my room.

"BETHANY!"

"BETHANY, ARE YOU OKAY?"

"BETHANY!"

"BETHANY!"

They rush into my room. My dad sees me lying on the floor and quickly grabs me checking me for injuries.

"OH, MY GOD! PLEASE TELL ME YOU'RE OKAY?" he says as he and Uncle Michael check my arms, legs, back and head for any injuries.

"All she has is a bump on her head. She's going to be okay, Andy. Who ever the hell that was just messed with the wrong family!" Uncle Michael says as he runs to the window to look outside then looks around my room.

I'm still crying hysterically as my dad pulls me back into a hug that says he's never letting me go. He's practically crying as he rocks me back and forth in his arms. "Thank god you're okay. You're okay, sweetheart. You're going to be okay. Shhh, you're going to be okay."

Uncle Michael makes a call to Chief Franks and then to Uncle Chuck.

"Come on, baby girl, let's go downstairs." My dad helps me to my feet and walks me downstairs to the front room.

There's glass everywhere down here too. The television is on in the family room. Apparently my dad and uncle were in the family room having coffee, which is at the back part of the house so they were safe from the gunfire. Uncle Michael comes downstairs too.

"Chief Franks and Chuck are on their way here."

"What the hell is going on here, Michael? First Joe disappears and now my house is getting shot at!"

"I don't know but believe me I will get to the bottom of this. You and Bethany are staying with me for a while or at least until we can figure out who did this."

"What if Joe comes home and we're not here?"

"I'll keep a squad outside to watch out for him. If he comes home I'll have them bring him right to my house. It will be safer there for everyone."

"Okay."

We see red and blues lights dancing around outside. Uncle Michael opens the door to let the police in and as he does, Chief Franks and Uncle Chuck come rushing in.

"Are you sure everybody's okay?" asks Uncle Chuck.

Uncle Michael responds, "yes, we're okay."

Chief Franks starts barking orders to the police officers to check out the house down here and the upstairs and obtain any kind of evidence of bullet fragments that they can find.

"We need to find Shawn quickly, Chief," says Uncle Michael.

"Yeah, I know."

I look at Uncle Michael in shock. "You think Shawn did this, don't you? He wouldn't do this to me!"

"Bethany, let's sit."

"Come on, Bethany," Uncle Chuck says as he puts his hand on my shoulder pulling me to the couch.

Uncle Michael and my dad sit next to me while Uncle Chuck stands in front of me.

"Shawn wouldn't do this, Uncle Michael! He's a good guy!"

Uncle Chuck starts scolding me. "Bethany, you need to stop defending him! He's not good! He's robbed, he's killed, he's involved with drugs and he's only seventeen! What does that tell you?"

Uncle Michael sighs. "It may not have been him that did this shooting but I do think its gang related. Families as well as girlfriends of gang members often become targets of violence when gangs are feuding with one another. He's trouble, Bethany!"

"But he's not! He's always treated me good! He is really a good guy inside."

Uncle Michael becomes even more frustrated with me. "Listen to me! You've gotten yourself into a very dangerous and serious situation getting involved with this kid and this shooting should give you a damn good indication as to how serious!"

"He's a good…"

"I don't want to hear that come out of your mouth again! He's trouble, Bethany! He's no good! Trust me, I know his record!"

"I need to find a safe place for my daughter for a couple of hours," my dad says as he stands.

"Why, where are you going?" Uncle Chuck asks.

"I'm going to look for my son!"

Uncle Michael instantly stands grabbing a hold of my dad's arm. "No, you're not!"

"Excuse me? My kid is missing!"

"Andy, we are working on finding your son, believe me! The best thing you can do right now is stay with your daughter!"

"I'm going to look for my son!"

"Do you know where to look?"

"His hang outs!"

"Police officers have already checked his hangs outs and are going back later to check them again! Do you know where else to look?"

"No, I don't know!"

"Somebody just took shots at your house, Andy! You certainly don't need to be out driving around aimlessly in the middle of the night! That just makes you a moving target! You need to stay with your daughter! I promise you we will let you know right away if we find out anything! In the meantime you and Bethany are staying with me at my house. Okay?"

My dad thinks for a moment and nods his head. "Fine."

Uncle Michael puts his hand on my dad's shoulder. "Hang in there, Andy. We'll find your son."

My dad just nods his head again and looks at me. "Sweetheart, you're staying home from school for a few days. I am not comfortable with sending you to school when all of this shit is going on. I'll call your school first thing this morning when they open."

"Okay."

"Are you doing okay, sweetheart?"

"Yeah, I guess."

Chuck calls Dakota and Jeff to let them know about what just happened at Andy's house.

Jeff mumbles half asleep. "Hello?"

"Jeff, it's Chuck. I'm sorry to wake you up, buddy, but we've had a situation over at Andy's house."

Jeff immediately sits up in bed and looks at Dakota who's still sleeping. "What do you mean? Is everybody okay?"

"Yes, thankfully everyone is okay. There was a drive by shooting."

"WHAT?" Jeff is no longer able to keep his voice quiet, waking Dakota up.

"We think it's gang related and we think Bethany's boyfriend or his gang has something to do with it."

"Is everyone okay?"

"Yes, everyone's okay. Andy and Bethany are going to be staying at Michael's until Michael and the police can find out who did it."

"Is there anything I can do to help? Do you guys need anything?"

"No, man. We're good. Thanks. We're going to be leaving Andy's shortly. I just wanted to call you guys and let you know what was going on."

"I appreciate it."

"Try and get some sleep. We'll talk more later, right now we don't have any information as to who's responsible."

"Sure, you too. Thanks for calling. Let me know if you guys need anything at all."

"You bet. Thank you."

Dakota immediately starts questioning Jeff as soon as he hangs up. "Who was that? Was it one of my brothers? What happened? Is everyone okay?"

"That was Chuck. There was a drive by shooting at Andy's, but everybody is okay. No one was hurt."

"Oh, my god!" Dakota jumps out of bed and starts looking for something to wear.

"Where are you going?" Jeff asks as he jumps out of bed to stop her.

"I need to go to Andy's."

"Whoa! Oh, no you don't!"

"What? I need to be there for my brother!"

"They're not going to be there! Michael is taking Andy and Bethany to his house. They're going to be staying with him until they find out who is responsible for the shooting."

Dakota stops for a moment trying to think of what to do. "I've got to do something."

Jeff gently grabs Dakota by the shoulders. "Baby, there's nothing you can do. Michael and the police are right on top of this. Everybody is fine. I DO NOT want you going to Andy's house until they find the people responsible for the shooting. Okay? Please promise me you'll stay away from Andy's house."

"Why? Because I'm pregnant?"

"That's irrelevant. Whether you're pregnant or not I would not want you going to Andy's. Okay? Promise me that you will stay away from his house until this is resolved. I don't want anything to happen to you."

"I promise. I'll stay away from his house."

"Thank you. Let's go back to bed. We'll go to Michael's house a little later and see everybody."

"You promise everybody is fine?"

"Yes, I promise. That's what Chuck said and I don't think he'd lie about something like that."

"No, he wouldn't."

"Let's go back to bed for a few more hours then we'll go see them later. There's nothing we can do right now and you haven't had much sleep lately."

"Okay."

Chapter Six

It's almost five o'clock in the evening and we still haven't seen or heard from Joe since yesterday. My dad has been going out of his mind, calling all of Joe's friends looking for him. I've spent most of my day in the guest bedroom crying and listening to music on my I-pod. My dad checks on me every so often making sure I'm okay. *God, please don't let anything happen to my brother. I miss him already. Please. I'm so scared that something has happened to him. Please keep him safe. Please. This whole thing is my fault. I pray and hope that Shawn didn't do anything to my brother.*

I take off my headphones and head downstairs to see what my dad is doing. I see him toss his phone down onto the couch in frustration.

"Dad, are you okay? Have you heard from Joe yet?"

"No, sweetheart, I haven't. I'm worried about him. I wish he'd call or text, anything to let me know that he's okay."

"I miss him, dad."

He hugs me. "I do too. I love you, sweetheart. I love you very much."

"I love you too, dad. I'm so sorry for everything." I say as I start crying again.

"I know and I am sorry for hitting you. I will never forgive myself for marking your face like that. I am so sorry."

"I know you are, dad. Please let that go."

"I can't. Come on, we have to stay strong, okay? We will get through this. Joe will come home. He has to. We need to pull it together for Joe, okay?"

I nod my head as I pull away from our hug then my dad wipes away my tears. "Would you like some iced tea?" I ask. "I'm going to get some for myself."

"Now you're talking. That would be great, sweetheart, thank you."

"Where's Tony?" I ask.

"He had baseball practice today. Uncle Michael won't allow him to go to school right now either but he couldn't miss practice. He's their star pitcher. Uncle Michael picked up Tony's homework and yours already too."

"Okay. I didn't know Tony had practice. Where's Uncle Michael?"

"He's at the station."

"He's not at Tony's practice?"

"No, Uncle Jeff and Aunt Dakota are."

"Oh, I'll be right back. I'll get us some iced tea."

I head to the kitchen and start pouring some iced tea when I hear my dad click on the television. The five o'clock news is now coming on.

"The body of a young man was found in Stanley Park this afternoon by a man walking his dog. The name of the victim has not been released pending notification of next of kin. The cause of death is unknown at this time and an autopsy has been scheduled. The entire park has been shut down for further investigation. The police ask that you please stay clear of the…"

"DAD!" I scream.

I put down the iced tea and rush into the family room. My dad stands frozen staring at the television set chanting to himself.

"It's not him. It can't be him. It can't be. Please don't let…"

My dad's chant is interrupted as the front door opens. His face turns white as a ghost as panic floods over him. Uncle Michael,

51

Uncle Chuck and Chief Franks walk through the door. I look at them unable to speak and fearing the worst.

"Bethany, we need to talk to you and your dad, honey." Uncle Michael says as he puts his hand on my shoulder and guides me over to my dad. Tears start streaming down my face.

My dad turns to look at Uncle Michael, fear in his eyes. His voice quivers as he speaks. "Michael, please tell me that was not Joe's body they found in the park. Please."

Uncle Michael notices the news on the television and quickly looks back at my dad as Uncle Chuck quickly shuts the television off.

"Shit! No, Andy, it wasn't Joe! Damn the press! They wasted no time with that story! That was not Joe! That was not his body!" Uncle Michael tries to reassure us.

"Are you sure?" My dad asks again.

"I saw the body myself so I am positive that it's not Joe. I don't know who it is yet, but I do know that it's not Joe."

My dad sits on the couch as he lets out a loud sob. "Oh, thank god!" I cry in relief. My dad takes in a deep breath and looks at Uncle Michael. "Do you have any news on Joe at all? Do you know where he is? Is that why the three of you are here?"

"No, we haven't found him or his car yet. But we may know how we can find him."

"How? Do it!" He says sounding so demanding, desperate and hopeful all at the same time.

Uncle Michael sits in the chair next to the couch and leans forward, elbows on his knees. "You're not going to like it."

"How can you find my son, Michael?" He asks in a tone that says stop beating around the bush and start explaining.

Uncle Michael looks at me then back at my dad. "There's something we need Bethany to do for us."

"Bethany? What do you need her to do?"

"We need her to set up a meeting with Shawn."

My dad immediately stands and starts to pace. "WHAT? HELL NO! I DON'T WANT HER ASSOCIATING WITH THAT GANG BANGER!"

"Listen to me, Andy! I understand your concern but I promise you nothing will happen to her! We will not let her out of our sight! There will be a team there with her! I will be there too! You know I won't let anything happen to my niece! We'll be hiding but we'll be there with her!"

"Dad, Shawn has always been good to me. He won't hurt me."

"NO! ABSOLUTELY NOT!"

Chief Franks walks toward my dad. "We need her help, Andy. Please. You know that you can trust us. We'd never let anything happen to her. We promise you that. If Shawn has anything to do with Joe missing or knows anything about it then he can help us find Joe."

My dad runs his hands through his hair and paces a few more times. "What exactly do you need her to do?"

Uncle Michael points to the couch as he responds. "Sit, please." My dad sits back down, Uncle Michael explains. "Even with everything Shawn has done he's still not as bad as his father if you can believe that. Not yet anyways. But he's heading down that path and if somebody doesn't do something for this kid he will end up just like his father and soon."

"That's not my problem! What does that have to do with my son?"

"If Shawn has nothing to do with Joe's disappearance or knows nothing about it then we can use Shawn to get information for us. He can help us find Joe."

"What do you need Bethany to do?"

"Just set up a meeting with him. That's all. Once Shawn and Bethany are together and talking then we will intervene and grab him before he takes off."

"Then what?"

"Then we make a deal with him."

"What kind of deal?"

Uncle Michael glances at Chief Franks wishing that he could tell my dad what the deal will be. He then looks back at my dad.

"I have to discuss that with Shawn first."

"What the hell do you mean you have to discuss it with Shawn first? You want to use my daughter as bait and you won't tell me what the deal will be? I'm your brother!"

"It's protocol, Andy."

"Screw your damn protocol, Michael! I want to know!"

"I won't go into details with you because anything can happen in the interrogation room and the deal could change. You have to trust me on this, Andy!"

"Damn it, Michael!"

"You have to trust me on this, Andy!"

"If I allow Bethany to help you, then when this is all over with, I want Shawn completely out of her life! You got that! I want him completely out!"

"I can make that happen. I will make that happen. I promise."

My dad looks at me and lets out a huge sigh. "Fine, I'll let her help. But you better protect her!"

"I will, bro. You can count on that. You know damn well I will."

"When do you need her help?"

"Now, the sooner we do this the better it is for Joe."

My dad stands up and heads into another room. "Dad, where are you going?" I ask.

"I'll be right back." He returns a moment later and hands me my cell phone. "This is only temporary. You're still grounded."

"I understand." I look at Uncle Michael. "What do you want me to say to him?"

"Tell him that you want to meet with him at your place in the woods. Ask him to meet you in two hours. Then I want you to show us where in the woods you two meet and in what direction Shawn usually comes from. Do NOT tell him anything about us."

"You're not going to hurt him are you?"

"Don't worry about that. Just do what he says, Bethany," my dad scolds.

"We're not planning on hurting him, honey. But it will be out of our hands if he draws a weapon. If he's smart he won't put us in the position of shooting him."

I nod my head that I understand. I start my text to Shawn and notice that all previous text messages have been deleted, except the ones between Joe and I and one that apparently I received last night from Shawn. I look up at my dad and he just glares at me. *Oh, no. He must have read all of my texts with Shawn. How careless of me!*

"Shawn, I'm sorry I didn't answer back last night. My dad has grounded me and taken my phone away. I didn't know you sent me a message last night. I need to see you. Can we meet at our bridge in two hours and talk?"

Just as I'm about to hit send, Uncle Michael puts his hand out for my phone. "Don't send your message yet. I want to read what you wrote." *Wow, I get no privacy at all!* I do what I'm told and hand him my phone. He reads the message then hits the send button.

"Don't I get any privacy anymore?"

My dad answers right before Uncle Michael does. "No, you don't."

"After the shit you pulled? No." Uncle Michael responds.

Uncle Chuck responds too. "Nope."

Wow, nothing like feeling ganged up on.

I receive a message back from Shawn almost right away. "Yes, of course. Can we meet tomorrow though? I have something going on tonight so I can't see you tonight."

Uncle Michael hands my phone back to me after he reads the message. My guys have to get into position before Shawn gets there. "Tell him you can sneak out tomorrow around four o'clock in the afternoon." I type the text like he said.

"I am grounded so I will have to sneak out. I can meet you around four o'clock."

Knowing that Uncle Michael will want to read my message again I hand him my phone before sending my text. He reads it, comments and hits send. "Good job."

I receive his reply right away. "Okay, four o'clock tomorrow it is. I can't wait to see you. I told you I wasn't going to let us split up. Love you, Bethany. See you tomorrow."

After Uncle Michael reads the message he shakes his head and rolls his eyes. "You are way too serious with this kid, Bethany." I don't say anything and I look at my dad. He doesn't say anything either. Uncle Michael stands and gestures to the police officers that are with him.

"Let's head back to the station and get the details worked out. Bethany, we'll go around one thirty."

My dad stands too. "I'm going with tomorrow."

"You don't need to be there." Uncle Michael scolds.

"If I am going to allow you to use my daughter as bait then I am going to be there with you. Take it or leave it, Michael."

"I'm sorry, Andy, but this is a police investigation, you cannot go."

"The hell I'm…"

"You cannot go!" Uncle Michael repeats.

"This is bullshit!"

"I'm sorry. It's a police investigation so you cannot be there. Do you really think I would let anything happen to Bethany?"

"No, of course not," my dad says in a low voice as he looks away in disgust.

"She'll be fine, Andy. I will protect her, I promise."

My dad turns and looks at Uncle Michael as he points his finger. "You better or so help me god, Michael."

"I promise, bro. She's safe with me. You know that."

My dad lets out a sigh as Uncle Chuck places both hands on his shoulders to reassure him.

"I know. Just take care of my little girl."

"I will. I promise."

Chapter Seven

When I arrive at our bridge I notice several large blood stains on the ground and on the railing of the bridge. I look down at the water and see some blood on the rocks protruding above the water line. *Where did that come from? Why is there blood everywhere?* Suddenly, my thoughts are interrupted when I hear Shawn yell to me.

"Bethany, you beat me here!"

"Shawn! Where did all of this blood come from?"

He walks up and gives me the biggest hug and longest kiss ever. "I missed you." He looks around not sure what to say at first. "What the hell? I have no idea. Maybe an animal attacked another animal, that does happen out in the woods."

"Yeah, maybe. It's just an awful lot of blood. What happened to your face?" I ask.

"Me? What happened to your lip?"

"I fell and hit my mouth on the stairs."

"On the stairs?"

"I was running up the stairs and slipped." *Wow that was a good save, Bethany. I don't want him to know that my dad did it.*

"Oh, man. Are you okay?"

"Yes. Now tell me what happened to your face?"

"I got into a fight. It's no big deal."

"With who?"

"Don't worry about it, okay."

"Gang related?"

He pauses a moment before answering, "yeah."

"Why don't I believe you? You've never been a very good liar."

"Don't worry about it!"

58

"Shawn, with who?"

He lets out a loud sigh. "Your brother! Okay?"

"WHAT? When? Where?"

"He followed you here when we met back here that night he caught me in your room. I came back here again after you tried breaking up with me to look for my wallet. It must have fallen out of my pocket. While I was here looking for it Joe showed up."

"What happened?"

"He doesn't like the fact that you're dating a gangbanger. Told me that I had to stop seeing you. He took the first swing, Bethany, not me. I had to defend myself."

"Oh, my god. What did you do to my brother? Is that where all of this blood came from?"

"I didn't do anything to your brother! I defended myself! And I told you; this blood was probably from an animal attacking another animal! We fought, that was it. His face looks worse than mine but he's okay. Ask him yourself."

Ask him myself? That means my brother may still be alive!

I put my arms around him and hug him again. As I am hugging him I feel something under his shirt, inside the waist of his jeans.

"What's under your shirt?"

"Shit! Forget about that. It's nothing important."

"No, I want to know." I start lifting up his shirt in back and he gets defensive and pushes me away.

"I said don't worry about it!"

"SHAWN! What is the matter with you? Is that a gun?"

"I forgot to leave it at home today."

At home, you don't go home you liar! "I've never seen you with a gun before?"

"That's because I never bring it with me when I know I'm going to be seeing you."

59

"What are you doing with a gun? Can I see it?"

"Why do you want to see my gun?" he asks.

"I've never held or shot one before. Can I see it?" *I really hope I can get it from him before the cops jump him.*

"No, you can't!"

"Why not? Why do you even have it?"

"I'm part of a gang, remember?"

"Can I see it, please?"

"No! Stop asking!"

"Why not?"

"Because, one rule of thumb is you never let anyone handle your piece!"

"I'm not just anyone. Please, Shawn."

"Why are you being so persistent about my gun?"

Suddenly, several police officers rush out of the trees and bushes with their guns drawn.

"GET YOUR HANDS UP, SHAWN!" Uncle Michael yells as he points a gun at Shawn.

Shawn looks at me with shock. "You set me up? Why the hell would you do that?"

"Shawn, I didn't want…"

"I can't believe you did this to me! I thought you loved me!"

"I do, Shawn! I'm sorry, but it's not what you think!"

Shawn slowly starts putting his hand behind his back making Uncle Michael and the other officers very nervous.

"SHAWN, DON'T DO IT! I don't want my officers to shoot you but they will if they have to and you will lose! Do not draw your piece! Bethany, step away from Shawn now!"

"Shawn, please do what he says. Please don't…"

"Bethany, step away from Shawn, RIGHT NOW!" Uncle Michael yells again. "NOW, DAMN IT!"

Tears start streaming down my face as I step away from Shawn. "Please, Shawn, don't do it! I don't want them to shoot you!"

"I can't believe you would turn me in to the cops!"

"It's not what you think! I didn't turn you in! We need your help! Please! That's what this is all about! We need your help!"

Keeping his eyes on me, Shawn takes a moment to think then slowly moves his hand away from his back and places both of them up in the air surrendering. Uncle Michael rushes up to him confiscating his gun and another officer puts him in handcuffs.

"Shawn, they just need your help, that's all. I wasn't…"

"Let's go, Bethany, I need to get you home." Chief Franks takes my arm and pulls me away from Shawn.

"I'll take her home, Chief," says Uncle Michael. Once we get several feet away from Shawn, Uncle Michael turns me around to face him. "DON'T EVER DO THAT AGAIN! OR I WILL PERSONALLY KICK YOUR DAMN ASS! I PROMISE YOU THAT!"

"Do what? What did I do?"

"I told you to step away from Shawn! The next time I tell you to do something you better damn well do it immediately! I shouldn't have to tell you three times to do something! Do you understand me?"

"Fine!" *Holy crap he's pissed!*

"No, that's not the answer I'm looking for, Bethany!"

"Yes, sir. I understand."

"That's the respectful way to answer. You could have gotten yourself shot! Let's go! I need to get you home."

"Are you going to tell my dad what happened?"

He answers without looking at me. "No, I am not. Your father has enough going on. Next time, do what you're told the first time."

"Yes, sir."

"Or the next time I'll be the one reddening your ass."

Uncle Michael has never gotten that mad at me before but I know that he wouldn't hesitate to whip my butt if he felt it was needed.

Uncle Michael drops me off at his house since that's where my dad and I are staying for a few days. I walk in and my dad rushes to me not saying anything to me and hugs me tightly.

"Thank you, Michael," my dad says.

"I told you I was going to keep her safe. I need to get back to the station. I need to talk to our new friend. I'll see you later."

"Did everything go okay?" my dad asks me.

"Yeah, it did. Shawn had a gun on him but he didn't take it out. That's the first time he's ever had a gun on him while he was with me."

"Thank god that part is over with. I was worried about you."

"Uncle Michael kept me safe, dad."

My dad turns the television set back on looking for some news as he comments back, "I knew he would."

"Dad, where did Uncle Chuck and Uncle Michael take you this morning? You didn't seem to happy about where you guys were going."

My dad sighs. "They took me to see Dr. Schiller."

"Dr. Schiller? Isn't that the doctor that you said you and my aunt and uncles went to see after you guys lost grandma and grandpa?"

"Yeah, it is." My dad looks at me and notices my smirk. "What?"

"It's a good thing that you're going, dad. It's a real good thing."

"Yeah?"

"Yeah, it is. I'm proud of you."

"Proud of me, for what? Since your mom's been gone I've been, as your Uncles would say 'flying off the handle a lot'. And I hit you, which is something I will never forgive myself for."

"I know, but you're doing something about it now. You're talking to somebody. That's why I'm proud of you, dad. Mom would be proud of you too."

"You think so?"

"Yeah, she would be."

My dad gently grabs my arm pulling me toward him. "Come here, you. I love you, sweetheart. I am really sorry for what I did to you."

"I know. I love you too. I forgive you, now would you please let it go? I know you didn't mean it."

"Okay."

"I take it that…I'm still grounded?"

"Oh, you better believe it. That is not going to change." He pulls away from our hug. "You disobeyed me, you lied to me and you snuck around behind my back. That warrants grounding."

"I understand. Still four months?"

"Yep, still the four months. Longer if you don't behave yourself."

I look at my dad's wrist and notice a rubber band wrapped around it. "Why do you have a rubber band on your wrist?"

He chuckles. "It was Dr. Schiller's idea. Said that if I feel like I am going to fly off the handle I need to snap my wrist with it."

"Are you serious? What is it supposed to accomplish?"

"It's supposed to make you stop and think. Give you time to put things into perspective before loosing your temper. I don't know, they claim it works"

"That sounds like a good idea."

"I guess we'll find out whether it really works or not." I pull on the rubber band and let it snap against his wrist. "Ouch! I said I was supposed to do it, not you." We both laugh then he hugs me again.

"Dad, why aren't you, Uncle Michael and Uncle Chuck out looking for Joe? When Aunt Dakota went missing years ago, you guys went out looking for her?"

"Aunt Dakota and Joe are two totally different situations, sweetheart."

"What you mean?"

He turns the television off and looks at me. "Sit." We sit on the couch, my dad sits facing me. "In Aunt Dakota's situation, she was dating a scumbag that was very abusive to her and I do mean abusive."

"I know. I remember what she looked like after you guys found her. It was horrible."

"Yes, it was."

"You guys hired the Pack to help with Aunt Dakota. Why don't you do that to find Joe?"

"Well, for a couple of reasons. One we didn't know anything about the scumbag that she was dating. She never introduced him to any of us so we didn't know what we were walking into so we called the Pack. Turned out he was just a scumbag that we could have taken care of by ourselves. Then when Aunt Dakota started receiving death threats we hired the Pack to protect her while she still went about her daily activities until we were able to find who was threatening her."

"How is that any different than Joe's situation now?"

"Because, first of all the Pack is no longer around. We don't have anyone to call for help. Secondly, the kid you got yourself involved with is part of a gang and may be responsible for Joe's disappearance. Gangs are not groups that you want to mess around with or get involved with. They are very dangerous. Do you understand now?"

"Yes."

"Believe me, I would hire an army if I could to look for Joe." *I wonder if any of the former Pack members are still working the streets?* Andy thinks to himself.

Chapter Eight

Shawn's been sitting in the interrogation room for a little over a half hour when Michael and Chief Franks finally come in.

"What the hell, man! You bring me in here, you don't read me my rights and then you make me sit here for over thirty minutes!"

"I'm Detective Phillips." Michael says as he tosses a file down in front of Shawn. He pulls a chair away from the table, puts one leg up on it and leans in to rest his elbow on his knee.

"What's this?" Shawn asks. "Some scare tactics?"

"No scare tactics, Shawn. Just facts. This file contains the warrants for your arrest?"

"Arrest for what?"

"Don't insult my intelligent by acting like you don't know!"

"I don't know!"

"You do know but feel free to take a look to refresh your fried memory."

"Why don't you quit wasting my time and just tell me since you already know what's in it?" He says in a smartass manner.

"Those are warrants that were issued a couple of months ago for robbery, drug trafficking and accessory to murder. Ring a bell now? The murder we can't prove yet but we're working on that part of the investigation. At least they were gang members that were killed. You actually did us a favor by taking a couple of scumbags off the streets." Michael stares at Shawn for a moment. "Are you trying to spend some time with your father in prison? You can go away for a long time for what's inside that file. Plus the attempted murder on Bethany and her father."

66

"What the hell are you talking about, man? I didn't try killing Bethany and her father. Why would I do that?"

"Somebody shot up their house last night! Are you telling me that you don't know anything about that?"

"NO, I DON'T!"

"Don't play me for a fool, Shawn! You actually want me to believe that you didn't know anything about that?"

"No, I didn't! I had nothing to do with that!"

"Then maybe you know who did do it."

"If I didn't know anything about it then how could I know who did it?"

Michael ignores his question. "What happened to your face?"

"I got into a fight."

"With who?"

"Another gang member."

"I don't believe you."

"Well, that's your problem isn't it?"

"Don't get smart with me! All you have is a busted lip and a black and blue eye. Gangs do way worse than that when they fight somebody, so who did you really get into a fight with?"

"I told you another gang member."

"Shawn, don't lie to me man. I overheard your conversation with Bethany. You got into a fight with Joe the other night didn't you?"

"If you have all of the answers then why am I here?"

"Because I want to hear it from you. What happened between you and Joe?"

"He threw me up against a wall in front of my girl!"

Michael points to Shawn with anger in his face. "Don't...call her your girl."

Michael's last name now hits Shawn. "Did you say your name is Detective Phillips?"

"Yes."

"Are you related to…?"

"To Bethany? I'm her Uncle."

"SHIT! You're the uncle who's the cop!"

"Detective." Michael tries to steer Shawn's attention back to their conversation about Joe. "So Joe threw you up against the wall in front of Bethany. Your ego was hurt, is that it?"

"You don't disrespect a man in front of his girl!"

"She's not your girl! I told you not to call her your girl!"

Chief Franks says nothing as he puts his hand on Michael's shoulder telling him to calm down.

Michael takes a deep breath and continues. "What did you do with him?"

"What did I do with who?"

"Don't answer my questions with questions."

"If you would start making some sense I wouldn't have to answer your questions with questions!"

Michael starts to yell. "What did you do with Joe?"

"What are you talking about, man? I didn't do anything to Joe! Him and me fought and then went our separate ways! Call him and ask him yourself!"

Michael gets in Shawn's face. "I would love to do that but he's missing! So what did you do with Joe?"

"Hey, man, you better get out of my face!" Shawn says as he threatens Michael.

"Are you going to do something about it? Do to me what you did to Joe? Don't try and act like a tough guy in here, it's not going to get you anywhere!"

"I DIDN'T DO A DAMN THING WITH JOE! I DON'T KNOW WHAT THE HELL YOU'RE TALKING ABOUT!"

They interrogate Shawn for about two hours, and then Michael and Chief Franks leave the interrogation room. They go into the observation room where Shawn's mother stands listening and watching the interrogation.

Michael places his hand gently on her arm. "Ms. Kemp, you said that you've always been able to tell when your son was lying and you've always been right. Do you think he's lying about Joe? And please don't try and protect him. We will still do what we can to help him but we can't help him if we don't know the truth."

She looks Michael in the eyes. "For the first time in my life, I can't tell whether my son is lying or not. I don't know what's happened to my kid but I feel like I don't even know him anymore. I've never seen that look in his eyes before."

"What look is that, Ms. Kemp?"

She looks at Shawn and watches him through the one-way mirror. "The look of anger, desperation and sadness. He seems lost. I love my son but if he's done something to somebody, Detective Phillips, then he has to own up to that. For his sake, I hope he's telling you the truth."

Michael looks at Shawn through the one-way mirror too. "Me too. Okay, I will give him the benefit of the doubt here." Michael looks at Chief Franks who nods in agreement.

"Can I talk to him now?" Ms. Kemp asks.

"I'm sorry, not right now. Maybe later. We need to make a deal with him first." Michael says as he leaves the observation room and returns to the interrogation room. "I'm going to give you the benefit of the doubt, Shawn, so let's talk."

"I want a lawyer."

"You may want to hear what I have to say first before you lawyer up."

"Am I under arrest?"

"That depends."

"That depends on what?"

"That depends on whether or not you co-operate and make a deal with us."

"Man, I ain't making no deal with you."

"You may want to reconsider that decision. These warrants can put your ass behind bars for a while. A long time if we prove murder. You have two choices, Shawn. Go to jail or help us with what we need and we'll help you." Shawn says nothing and just stares at the table. "I guess you're going to be joining your father in the pen." Michael heads toward the door when suddenly Shawn panics, quickly catching Michael's attention.

"What do you want from me?" Shawn asks.

Michael turns and looks at Shawn. "Are you ready to hear my deal?"

"What do you want?"

Michael relieved that his scare tactics worked, walks back over to the table. "I want your help in finding Joe, I want to..."

"Again, for the record, I didn't know Joe was even missing."

"If that's true then help me find him."

"What else do you want?"

"I also want to know who shot at Joe's house. I want to know who the drug leader is in your gang. Who in your gang is responsible for bringing in and setting up the drug deals in the area? Who are they selling to and who's their biggest customer?"

"How are you going to help me?"

"I know you're looking for a way out of the gang."

"You're a detective so you must know how the rules of a gang work. If I try getting out their way, I may not make it out alive."

"I can help you get out alive."

"How?"

"We'll drop the drug charges and robbery charges in this file. We have no hard proof against you for the murder of two gang members. Then…"

"Why would you do that for me?"

"Because I believe that you want to better your life and I want to give you that chance. I believe that you really do want out of the gang. You just need a little help getting on the other side of the tracks. You're heading down the same path as your father, Shawn! If I can keep just one kid from continuing down that path then I've done my job."

"So you drop the charges, then what?"

"Then we will relocate you and your mother somewhere safe. We'll even help you find a job. Make an honest man out of you for once in your sorry life. We've already spoken to your mother. She would be more than willing to pick up and move if it means getting her son out of trouble."

"You want me to move away?"

"It's the safest way to get you out of the gang alive and unharmed."

"What about Bethany?"

"What about her?"

"I'm not leaving without her."

"Bethany cannot go with you, Shawn. You know that."

"Then I don't go."

You can hear the irritation in Michael's voice as he speaks.

"Shawn, are you not hearing what I'm telling you? I'm giving you a chance to start over again! To get out of the gang and to stay out of jail!"

"I love her and I'm not going anywhere without her."

Michael becomes even more frustrated and paces the room. "You are seventeen years old! What do you know about being in love? You're getting a second chance here! Not many people get that! Bethany cannot go with you! If you don't take this deal you will not get another one! Do you understand me?"

"I want to see her."

"You cannot see Bethany!"

"I want to talk to her!"

"You can't be involved with her anymore!"

Shawn yells again. "I want to talk to her!"

Realizing that he's not going to get anywhere with Shawn unless he talks to Bethany, Michael sighs and shakes his head.

"Fine, let me see if I can convince her father to allow her to talk to you on the phone."

"I want to talk to her in person."

"Either you talk to her on the phone or you don't talk to her at all. It's your choice." Michael waits for a response from Shawn who doesn't say anything but finally gestures with his hand. "Okay. I'll make a call once we're done here."

"I'm not saying anything more to you until I talk to Bethany."

"Somebody needs to knock some sense into that hard head of yours kid." Michael walks out of the interrogation room. Fifteen minutes later he returns without saying a word, and he grabs the phone sitting on the other side of the table, puts it down in front of Shawn and presses the speaker button. "Okay, Bethany. You're on speaker with Shawn."

"I want to talk to Bethany alone."

"That's not going to happen so start talking."

"Shawn, it's okay. My phone is on speaker too. My dad is here with me." My dad has been instructed by Uncle Michael to not say a word to Shawn on the phone.

"Bethany, they said they can help me get out of the gang and they would drop the charges against me but I would have to move away for it to happen."

I start crying on the phone. "I know, they told me."

"I don't want to go without you."

"I can't go with you, Shawn. I don't want to go with you."

"What? I don't believe you! Are they telling you to say that?"

"They're giving you a chance to get out of the gang, alive. If you stay here, who knows what will happen to you. I can't be with you even if you stay."

"You're the reason why I want out of the gang."

"Please just go. Take whatever deal they're offering to you and go. Please, Shawn."

Shawn thinks for a moment. "I'll take their deal but I'm coming back for you."

Just as my dad starts to say something, Uncle Michael presses the end button and the line disconnects.

"THAT'S ENOUGH! You're done with her!" Michael scolds.

"I was still talking to her!"

"You've said more than enough! Let me make this very clear to you, Shawn. Once you move away from here, don't ever come back here again!" Michael then lowers his voice so that only Shawn can hear him. "If you do, it will be the biggest mistake of your life. I promise you that. The gang will be the least of your problems. Stay the fuck away from my family." Shawn stares into Michael's eyes and realizes how serious Michael is. Michael lowers his voice a little more. "If you don't, I'll kill you." He goes back to raising his voice again. "You and Bethany are done! No longer involved! Do you got that?"

Shawn doesn't say anything as he still has plans of his own. Knowing he needs to walk away before knocking Shawn across the room, Michael leaves with Chief Franks to calm himself down.

Chapter Nine

Michael and the Chief return to the interrogation room moments later. Michael sets down a pad of paper and a pen in front of Shawn.

"I want you to write down the name of your drug leader and where we can find him, any future drops that your gang has planned and who your major buyers are."

"He's not my drug leader."

"Start writing, now."

"Then what?"

"Then you start helping me find Joe and who shot up his house."

"And how am I going to do that?"

"I don't give a shit how you do it. Just get us the information."

"If they find out that I'm helping out the cops they'll kill me!"

"That's going to be your problem if you don't come through for me."

"Am I going to be tailed? They'll find out for sure if you tail me!"

"No, I have to trust that you're going to stick to our deal. If you don't, then life as you know it will be over and you'll be seeing your father sooner than you think." Michael hands Shawn a cell phone.

"Why are you giving me a phone? I have my own phone."

"This is how it's going to work. I want you to check in with me every three hours starting the moment you're released. If you miss calling me just once, I'm coming after your ass and the deal is off. If I call you and you don't answer then I will be coming after your ass and the deal is off. Is that clear?"

"If I am with the gang I can't call you or answer your calls."

"I suggest you find a way to."

"I'm not taking this cell phone. I have my own. You just want me to take this phone so you can track me easier. I'm not stupid, Detective."

Suddenly a police officer knocks on the door then enters and whispers something in Chief Franks ear. The Chief looks at the officer stunned then nods his head and calls for Michael to follow him.

"Michael, we need to talk."

Michael looks at Shawn as he follows the Chief out into the hallway. "Keep writing." "What's going on, Chief?"

Before answering Michael, the Chief and the officer stop between the door of the interrogation room and Michael.

"They took several blood samples from the bridge where we picked up Shawn. They haven't finished testing all of the samples yet but…" He pauses. "Michael, some of it tested positive for Joe's blood."

"WHAT? Oh my, god! This can't be happening. If something has happened to Joe this is going to break my brother for sure."

"I know. This is too personal, Michael. At this point you're not going to be able to treat this kid like any other case. This is your family! I am going to have Detective Barbado take over this investigation. I'll allow you to help out with the forensics in the lab but that's it."

Michael stares at the Chief. "WHAT?"

"With this new development, I have no choice but to put you in the lab."

"Please, Chief. I promise I will keep my cool. It will be hard at times since this is my family we're talking about, there's no doubting that. But I won't get stupid with the kid. I promise."

"No, I'm sorry, Michael. Forensics is a very big part of a case like this. You know that. In cases like this, most of the time it's the forensics that solves the case. You can watch the interviews from the observation room and work in the forensics lab, but that's as close as you're going to get to working on this case. And DO NOT under any circumstances, think that you're going to go out into the field and investigate this on your own or start questioning suspects or informants. I'll suspend your ass real quick if you do. I mean it, Michael."

Shit! I was afraid of the Chief doing this. Michael throws up his hands, looks at the Chief and sighs. "Alright, fine. I understand. I don't like it but I understand your reasoning."

"Like it or not it's the way it's got to be. I'm going to talk to Shawn until Barbado gets here and find out what he knows about the blood." The Chief looks at the officer standing nearby. "Detective Phillip's is not allowed in this interrogation room with this suspect. Do I make myself clear on that?"

"Yes sir, Chief."

"I'm sorry, Michael."

The Chief returns to the interrogation room alone and Michael goes to the observation room to watch.

"When are you letting me go?" Shawn asks the Chief.

Chief Franks moves the table away from Shawn so that nothing is between them making Shawn a little nervous. "There's been a new development."

"What do you mean? What's going on? Where's Detective Phillips?"

"He has something else to take care of. Tell me exactly what happened between you and Joe at the bridge."

"I went back to the bridge to look for my wallet. It fell out of my pocket. While I was there looking for it, Joe showed up. He must have followed Bethany there. That's the only way he would have known where our spot was at."

"Then what happened?"

"He got up in my face and told me to stay the hell away from Bethany. I told him to get the fuck out of my face or I would take him down."

"So, you took him out?"

"I said take him down! I didn't say take him out! Don't twist my words! He grabbed hold of my shirt and told me that he would kill me if I came near his sister again. I pushed him away and told him that he was going to pay for disrespecting me in front of my…" After receiving a warning look from the Chief, Shawn then changes what he was going to say. "He took a swing at me and I swung back, so we fought and then he left."

"How bad were his injuries when he left?" Fearing that he will lose his own temper, the Chief takes a step back before Shawn answers.

"I'm not going to lie, there was blood."

"Was it Joe's?"

"Most of it was, yes."

Chief Franks asks again. "How bad were his injuries?"

"I don't know exactly. He's probably got a couple of black eyes, possibly a broken nose and a few broken ribs, maybe a broken hand. I did a number on him."

Chief Franks face turns red from anger. "You don't even have that many injuries! What weapons did you use on him? Who else was there with you?"

"I didn't have any weapons on me! I used my fists and it was only me and Joe there!"

"Just your fists?"

"I'm in a gang, Chief Franks! You learn real quick how to fight with your hands if you need to! He walked away! Joe was hurt, yes, but he walked away! That was the last time I saw him!"

"There was blood found on and around the bridge. It tested positive for Joe's blood."

"That's because we had a fight! He was spitting blood out of his mouth!"

Suddenly the Chief starts changing his tone from being a bad cop to now a good cop that's become your friend. "I want to make sure I understand this right. You were only angry with Joe for disrespecting you in front of Bethany, is that correct? There were no other reasons?"

"No other reasons."

"Hmm, I guess I would have to agree with you then. If somebody disrespected me in front of my girlfriend I would have probably taken a knife to him or drawn my gun too."

"I drew my knife but he kicked it…"

"You just said that you didn't have any weapons." Now he's back to being bad cop again.

"No, I said I didn't use any weapons."

"Shawn, this interrogation is being recorded. I would be more than happy to play back your own words. You said and I quote. 'I didn't have any weapons on me! I used my fists.' So which is it, Shawn? Did you use a weapon or not?"

"NO! I DIDN'T! I TRIED TO BUT HE KICKED IT OUT OF MY HAND!"

"You need to start being honest with me if you want me to help you!"

"I am being honest!"

"You just lied to me about the damn weapon!"

Chapter Ten

Detective Justin Barbado was delayed finishing another case so he couldn't make this interrogation. Chief Franks continued the interrogation for another hour and a half. Then had Shawn, taken back to a jail cell for the night. Michael headed home.

Michael walks into the house and hangs up his winter coat. He sees Andy watching television with Tony and Chuck.

"Tony, are you finished with your homework?" he asks.

"Yes, sir, I am. Have you found out anything yet on Joe?"

"No, son, I haven't. Not enough anyways. Where's Bethany?"

"She's upstairs doing her history homework," Andy replies.

Michael puts his hand on Tony's shoulder. "Tony, I need to talk to your uncles. Can you see if maybe Bethany needs any help with her homework?"

"Sure, dad."

Tony leaves the room then Andy turns the television off. *Something is wrong. I don't think Chuck came over this time to just visit with me.*

"Thanks, buddy," says Michael.

"What's wrong, Michael? I have a feeling Chuck didn't come over here this time just to visit. Do you have any news at all?"

Michael lets out a huge sigh as he sits down next to his brother. "Chuck is here for support. Chief Franks took me off the field work and interrogations for Joe's case."

"WHAT? Why the hell would he do that?"

Andy starts snapping the rubber band against his wrist and Michael notices but doesn't say anything.

Michael leans forward resting his elbows on his knees. He looks at the floor shaking his head in disgust. "I'm still working the case, I just can't go out in the field and I can't interview any suspects or informants. He has me working in the forensics lab. Keep in mind that just the forensics evidence alone solves most cases."

"Why did the Chief do that? He has known us since we were kids. He knows were all close and…"

"That's exactly the reason why," says Chuck.

"BINGO!" says Michael. "Not only are we close but we're family. That's why he did it. He doesn't feel that I would be able to treat this case like any other case and you know something? The more I think about it, the more I think he's right." Michael points to Andy's rubber band on his wrist. "I would have to be the next one wearing a rubber band around my wrist just to keep my cool. I understand why he made the change. I don't like it but I understand the reason behind it."

"What kind of evidence goes to a forensic lab?" Andy asks.

"Blood, saliva, fibers from anything, tire tracks, drugs, alcohol, paint chips even firearm residue and a hell of a lot more. You can do a lot in a lab with just the evidence alone. That's why I said that most cases are solved just by the evidence alone and not always just witnesses or interviews."

"Saliva?"

"Even body fluids, yes."

"Wow."

"Which brings me to my next thing."

Andy continues snapping the rubber band against his wrist. "I'm afraid to ask."

"You may want to snap that rubber band a little harder, buddy."

"Just tell me, Michael!"

"There is evidence that Joe was at Bethany and Shawn's bridge."

"What kind of evidence?"

"According to Shawn, he and Joe got into a fight at the bridge. Joe went there to make sure Shawn understood that he was to stay away from Bethany. Shawn's only beef with Joe was that he felt Joe had disrespected him in front of his girl."

"My daughter is not his girl." Andy continues snapping the rubber band trying to keep calm.

"Just let me finish, okay? They got into a fight and according to Shawn he said that Joe was banged up a bit from the fight but he left there alive. He walked away. There was blood found on the bridge and around it. Some of it tested positive for Joe's blood."

"Oh, my god." Andy cries out as Chuck puts his hand on his brother's shoulder in an effort to comfort him.

Michael continues to explain. "Shawn claims that the blood came from Joe's mouth and nowhere else. Said Joe left there with a couple of black eyes, probably a broken nose, broken hand and maybe some broken ribs but he was alive when he left."

"Oh my god. Do you believe him?"

"I don't know. I have the lab testing the blood for saliva now. I should have the results by Monday or Tuesday."

"Then what?"

"If the test results show saliva in the blood then that means Shawn is actually being honest with us. Chief Franks will then proceed with our deal."

"Which is what exactly?"

"He has to help us find Joe, find out who shot up your house and give up his drug leader in his gang among other things. If we get everything we want and need from Shawn then we'll drop all charges that are currently pending against him. We will then relocate him and his mother to another state for protection and give him a chance to start over with a clean slate. If he fucks up again, then that's his own problem. Then he joins his father in the pen. He's only getting one chance to straighten himself out."

"What if you don't find Joe alive?"

Chuck starts tapping Andy's back. "Let's not think like that right now okay, bro. We need to think positive that we'll find him and he'll be alive and okay. Come on, man. Mom and dad I'm sure are looking out for him right now."

Andy takes in a deep breath and nods his head in agreement. "Yeah, I'm sure they are."

Chapter Eleven

It's Monday and Michael has worked in the lab from four o'clock this morning until about six o'clock this evening, he then came home and started working on the computer. He hasn't slept much since Joe went missing four days ago. No one has slept much.

"Shit!" he says almost under his breath. He closes the lid of the laptop computer and goes to the kitchen for a drink.

Andy notices Michael's reaction and becomes curious as to why he wouldn't leave the computer open like he usually does. *He's got to be hiding something from me.* After Michael is out of the room Andy goes to the computer and opens the lid. He sees a lab report regarding Joe on the screen.

Test performed: Amylase Diffusion Quantitative or Non-Quantitative.

Results: Negative-no amylase activity is observed. Amylase, a constituent of saliva was not detected.

"What the hell? What does this mean?" Andy mutters.

Michael returns with a beer in his hand and stops when he sees Andy looking at his computer. "There's a reason why I closed that," he says.

Andy looks at him and points to the computer screen. "What does this mean exactly? Is there something you would like to tell me, bro?"

Michael sighs as he sets his unopened beer down on the coffee table. "I really didn't want to give you any information right now until we had some kind of a lead. All it's going to do is upset you more and damage your hopes of Joe coming home."

"I appreciate you trying to protect me but please don't. I need to know what's going on. Regardless of what you may or may not find, I am not going to give up on my son coming home."

"Alright, I understand. Fair enough. Amylase is an enzyme that breaks starch down into sugar and it's usually found in high levels in a person's saliva. It's also found in other body fluids as well but is normally at much lower levels. Since there were no high levels of this enzyme in Joe's blood, the results of this test mean that there was no saliva in Joe's blood found at the bridge."

"Oh, my god, so the blood was not from Joe's mouth like Shawn said?"

"No, it wasn't. I'm afraid he was bleeding from somewhere else."

"That low life, scumbag, piece of shit, gangbanging bastard! He lied!"

"Andy…"

"Don't tell me to calm down, Michael! He lied!"

"I wasn't going to tell you to calm down. I was going to tell you that I had emailed this report to Chief Franks. He's going to go talk to Shawn then he will call me."

"The Chief needs to put you back in that interrogation room with that scumbag."

"Unfortunately, that's not going to happen. And lucky for him that it won't, because at this point I would probably beat the shit out of him myself."

"I know the Pack isn't around anymore but maybe I should contact some of the former members for help."

"NO! After what happened to Dakota, I don't want us to have anything to do with any of those guys again!"

"We need help finding my son! There are a few guys that we can still trust! Bruce is one of them! We were always able to trust Bruce!"

"NO!"

"I'm done with this conversation, Michael!" Andy says as he leaves the room and heads for the guest room that he's staying in upstairs.

Michael shouts out. "Andy!" But Andy doesn't answer.

Andy closes the door to the guest room then takes out his cell phone to call Bruce. *I hope his cell phone number is still good.*

Bruce used to be part of a club called The Pack. They provided security services and sought out "justice" on those when justice wasn't served within the legal system. What the club was doing was illegal, but Chief John Franks always looked the other way. He felt the same as the club did. If justice isn't served the legal way then it needs to be served another way.

"Hello?"

"Bruce, this Andy Phillips."

"Andy? What the hell? How the hell are you, man? I haven't spoken to you since the club shut down."

"Are you still doing some work on the side, if you know what I mean?"

"Yes, but not in the way you think."

"I need to meet with you."

"You don't want to meet with me, Andy. We're not..."

"I need your help, Bruce."

"Andy, after the club shut down we lost a lot of business because of Josh. We had to pursue other activities to bring in the kind of money we were bringing in before. What we're doing now is even more dangerous and illegal. You don't need to get messed up with that."

"Who is we and what are you talking about?"

"Me, Nick, Patrick, Owen and we have a new guy, Kevin. Let's just say that we're involved with some serious shit now and it's a lot more dangerous than the things we used to do before. You don't want to get involved with us again, man."

"I don't want to know what it is you're into. I just need your help. Please. I'm begging you, man. It's about my son."

Bruce lets out a muffled sigh. "Fine, let's meet at the old barn. I don't want anybody seeing us together. When do you want to meet?"

"Now."

"It's that serious?"

"You have no idea."

"Shit. All right, buddy. I'll leave here in about ten or fifteen minutes. I'll call Nick and Owen too. Patrick and Kevin are on a job at the moment."

"Thank you. I really appreciate this." Andy hangs up with Bruce, grabs his wallet from the nightstand and heads to the other guest room where Bethany is staying. "Sweetheart, I'll be back in a little bit."

"Where are you going?"

"I have something that I have to take care of. I'll be back shortly." He heads downstairs and out through the family room grabbing his keys.

Michael sees Andy grabbing his keys. "Andy, where are you going?"

Andy responds as he walks out the door. "I have something to take care of. I'll be back in a little bit."

"Dad, what's going on, where's Uncle Andy going?" Tony asks coming down the stairs.

Michael looks at Tony and grabs his own wallet. "I don't know, son, but I have a feeling it's not good. Stay here with Bethany, please."

"Sure, no problem. I'm not going anywhere."

Michael borrows the neighbor's car and follows Andy keeping enough distance between them so Andy doesn't see him. He follows him to the bank then to the barn. Michael parks behind some bushes keeping out of sight then calls Chuck.

"Hey, Michael, what's going on?"

"Chuck, I need you to meet me on the side of the road near the old barn right away and bring your piece!"

"WHAT? What the hell is going on?"

"I don't have time to go into details. Just get here now! I think Andy maybe getting himself into some trouble. Don't drive, have Linda drop you off a little ways down the road. I'll meet up with you."

"SHIT! Alright, we'll leave right now!"

Linda drops Chuck off. Michael fills him in on his conversation with Andy about getting the former Pack members to help find Joe. They follow a trail up to the barn where they watch Andy meet with a few of the former Pack members that have arrived.

"Shit, Andy, what the hell are you doing, man? You're one stubborn ass brother!" Michael whispers.

"He sure as hell is." Chuck says. "I never thought we'd ever have to see these guys again."

"You can thank our brother for that."

Andy shakes hands and gives man hugs to Bruce, Nick and Owen. "Thank you for meeting with me. Why did you want to meet at the barn? The last time we were here we…"

"Let's not talk about that day, okay?" says Bruce.

"Yeah, good point. Sorry."

"What's wrong with Joe? You said it was something serious." Andy hands Bruce an envelope. "What's this?"

"There's fifty thousand dollars in there. I need you to help me find my son. He's been missing since Thursday night. I'll give you another fifty thousand once you find him. Will you help me?"

"WHAT? Joe is missing? Yes, of course we'll help you. What the hell happened?"

"My daughter got herself mixed up with this gangbanger. Joe found out and threatened the kid, told him to stay away from Bethany or he'd kill him. According to Bethany, the kid threatened him back. We haven't seen or heard from Joe since. I think he's involved in Joe's disappearance but I am not sure."

"This is a hell of a lot of money, Andy."

"You can't put a price on my kids, but it's what I have to give you at the moment."

"Who's the kid she got mixed up with?"

"Shawn Kemp." Bruce looks at Nick and Owen then back at Andy. "You know who this kid is, don't you?"

Nick responds, "yes we do."

"How do you know him?"

Bruce grabs Andy's hand and puts the envelope of money back in it. "I'm sorry but we can't help you after all."

"WHAT? YOU JUST SAID THAT YOU WOULD! COME ON, BRUCE! THE PACK OWES MY FAMILY!"

"The Pack is no longer around, Andy! We have our own club now and we don't owe you anything!"

Andy drops the envelope and grabs Bruce by the neck. Nick and Owen step forward to intervene. Michael and Chuck, unable to stand there and watch their brother get himself into deeper trouble blow their cover and rush in to help Andy. By the time they reach Andy, Nick and Owen have Andy pulled off Bruce and are holding him back. Bruce walks back and forth in front of Andy, contemplating whether or not to take a few punches at him for what he just did. Then just when Andy thought all was going to be okay, Bruce throws a couple of punches at Andy's stomach while the guys continue holding him.

"Don't ever try doing that again or I will kill you…old friend or not!"

"I need you to help me find my son! PLEASE!"

"We can't help you!"

"Can't or won't? I will pay whatever you want! Whatever it takes!"

Suddenly they hear the familiar sounds of guns clicking and look over to see Michael and Chuck standing nearby pointing revolvers at them.

"I suggest you release our brother and do it now!" Michael shouts.

Andy looks at his brothers stunned but at the same time feeling relieved to see them. "Michael, Chuck, what the hell are you guys doing here?"

"Saving your stubborn ass! Release him now!" Michael shouts again.

Bruce pulls out his gun and points it at Andy. "Try it and your brother is dead! Let's not go down this road, Michael. We've known each other way too long to do this."

"Release him, now! He's not in the right frame of mind right now, Bruce! He doesn't mean any harm! His damn kid is missing and it's obvious he's willing to do anything to get him back! You know him better than that, Bruce!"

Bruce looks at Andy then nods to Nick and Owen to release him. "We're not a threat to you, Michael."

"No, only to our brother."

"We're not going to hurt him."

"Really? That's not the impression we just got a moment ago!"

Bruce looks at Nick and Owen. "Put your weapons down on the ground. Prove to them we're not a threat." The three of them slowly take out all weapons and set them on the ground then moves a few steps back away from them. Bruce puts his hands up. "See, Michael. We're not here for trouble. We're here because your brother called us and asked if we'd meet with him."

Michael looks at Andy shaking his head as he answers Bruce. "Yeah, I know he did." Michael then slowly puts his gun away and nods to Chuck to do the same. "He's desperate to find his son and I can't say that I blame him. But this can't be the way to do it. Apparently Andy feels differently at the moment, but Chuck and me, we don't trust you guys. Look what happened to our sister!"

Bruce points to himself and the other two guys standing there with him. "That was not our fault! We had nothing to do with any of that!"

"That might be true, but you were still a part of the club at the time so that makes you responsible too!" Chuck says as he picks up the envelope full of money and peeks inside. Shaking his head he hands it back to Andy. "I promise you, bro, we will find Joe but we have to do it without these guys."

"What would you do, Chuck, if it were one of your kids missing? Wouldn't you call them too?"

"No, I wouldn't. I would find another way."

"Yeah, well, you'd be surprised what you'd do when you're desperate."

Bruce takes a step toward Andy. "I'm sorry that your son is missing and I am sorry that we can't help you."

"Can't or won't?"

"We can't!"

"You were going to help me until I mentioned Shawn's name to you! What is it about that kid that makes you not want to get involved?"

"I told you, it's not that we don't want to, we can't! I'm sorry!"

"We're not taking your help regardless! Let's go, Andy!" Michael says as he turns Andy around forcing him to leave with him and Chuck.

As they're walking away, Andy grabs the gun out of the back of Chuck's pants and rushes back towards Bruce and the guys.

"ANDY!" Chuck shouts.

"ANDY!" Michael shouts too as they both run after Andy.

Andy reaches Bruce and puts the gun to his head. "Tell me what you know about Shawn, or I swear I'll kill you! Why can't you help me? Does he have something to do with my son's disappearance?"

Nick and Owen immediately draw their guns too, and Michael now has his gun out pointing at them. Guns are pointed at everyone.

"ANDY, WHAT THE HELL ARE YOU DOING?" Michael yells. "HAVE YOU LOST YOUR FUCKING MIND?"

"He knows something, Michael! He knows something about that kid Shawn!"

Chuck pleads with his brother. "Come on, bro! Please don't do this! He's not worth it! We will find Joe! We promise you we will find him! Just put down the damn gun! Please!"

92

"Do you know something about Shawn and Joe?" Michael asks Bruce.

"I know Shawn personally, but I didn't know Joe was missing. If you don't get Andy to lower his piece this whole situation may become a blood bath."

Andy shoves the gun harder against Bruce's temple and says through gritted teeth. "I'm not lowering anything until you give us the information we need."

Michael pleads with Andy again. "Come on, Andy! Give Chuck the gun back!"

"NO! He knows something and he's either going to tell us or he's going to die!"

"NO! Nobody needs to die today! Andy! Not today! Come on, man! We promise you we will find Joe! Give Chuck the gun back!"

"Bruce, so help me god, you better tell me what you know about Shawn and my son or, as god is my witness, I will take your ass out right now!"

"Shawn's a gangbanger. That's all I know and I don't know anything about Joe!"

"You're a liar! You just said that you knew Shawn personally! You know more than you're telling me!" Andy cocks the gun.

Suddenly, Michael and Chuck start to panic.

"Andy, don't do it, man! Please!" Chuck pleads.

Michael pleads too. "ANDY, DON'T!"

"Come on, man! Think about your daughter, she needs you right now, man!" says Chuck.

Michael lowers his gun and takes a step closer. "Andy, please don't do this! Think about Bethany."

"Think about your daughter!" Chuck yells again. "She still needs you, man!"

Michael takes one more step toward Andy. "Andy, please put down the gun! Don't do this! Think about Bethany!"

Andy starts thinking about Bethany. *They're right. My daughter still needs me.* He pushes Bruce away and starts lowering the gun, but not before putting two bullets in Bruce's left kneecap.

Suddenly they hear another shot ring out and Andy falls to the ground. Bruce yells to Nick. "CEASE FIRE, NICK! CEASE FIRE!"

"DAMN IT, ANDY!" Chuck rushes to Andy to see if he's okay, Michael takes the gun from him.

"You have lost your fucking mind! You know that!" Michael then checks Andy's shoulder. "Fuck! He shot you good!"

Bruce motions to his guys to stand down. "Put your weapons away! Now!" He looks at the three brothers. "I am giving you guys one chance to get the hell out of here! Don't ever call us again! Or the next time, you guys may not be walking away!" Bruce says as he holds his knee in pain.

Chuck and Michael grab Andy's arms helping him to his feet and escort him to his car. Michael shoves Andy in the front passenger seat and then gets in the back while Chuck jumps in the driver's seat.

Chuck then continues scolding Andy. "Damn it, Andy! You could have gotten yourself killed!"

"I just want my son back!" Andy replies.

"I know you do, man! But calling on the former Pack members is not the way to do it!"

Chuck drops Michael off at the car he borrowed from his neighbor. "I'll call Jeff and ask him if he can treat Andy at my house. I really don't need Chief Franks getting wind of this one." Michael says in a pissed off tone as he gets out of the car.

Jeff is their brother in-law and he's a paramedic and firefighter. Michael has known Jeff since before Jeff met his sister.

Chapter Twelve

Jeff is already at Michael's house when they arrive.

"I'm no doctor, Michael, but I'll do what I can." Jeff says as he helps bring Andy into the house and lays him down on the couch.

While Jeff washes his hands and prepares Andy's shoulder for treatment, Michael and Chuck continue their tirade.

Chuck is the first to start. "What the hell is wrong with you? Are you trying to get yourself killed? We said we would NEVER do business with those guys again!"

Andy looks at Chuck with tears in his eyes. "I'm desperate to find my son! I cannot lose my son!"

Chuck lets out a huge sigh realizing that he understands and suddenly feels the hurt and fear that his brother is feeling. In a calmer voice he continues to scold Andy. "I know, bro. I can understand that but Bruce and his guys? We said we'd never hire them again!"

"I cannot believe you just did that, Andy! You must have a death wish! Think about your damn kids!" Michael says as he takes his gun and holster off putting them into the safe.

"I was thinking about them! I'm trying to find my son!"

"And we will find him but we…"

Suddenly, they are interrupted by a creak on the stairs. They turn to see Bethany and Tony standing at the bottom of the steps watching and listening.

Chuck points to the upstairs. "Go back upstairs, please."

"What's going on?" Tony asks as he continues to walk toward them. "What happened to Uncle Andy? Did he get shot?"

Michael yells at Tony. "Tony, your uncle just asked you to go back upstairs!" Tony immediately retreats back upstairs.

Bethany sees her father lying on the couch. *Oh my, god! DAD!* "Dad, are you okay?" Bethany asks as she tries to run to her father but Uncle Chuck stops her.

"Yes, sweetheart. Do what your uncle asked of you and go back upstairs."

"Dad, you're hurt! What happened to you?"

"Come on, honey. He's going to be okay. I promise. Go back upstairs please." Chuck says as he walks Bethany back to the bottom of the stairs. She too now retreats back upstairs. Chuck looks back at Jeff. "Andy is going to be okay right, Jeff? I hope I just didn't promise something to my niece that isn't true."

"Yeah, he's going to be fine." Jeff cleans up the wound so he can see and starts extracting the bullet from Andy's shoulder. "This is bad, Andy. It's deep. Shot you at close range?"

"Yeah."

Michael pours a glass of whiskey for the four of them and hands one to Jeff as he continues to scold Andy, but Jeff refuses the drink. "I promise you, Andy, we will find Joe if it's the last thing we do. But we will NOT take Bruce's help in doing it! We can't! What if I didn't follow you? They could have killed you!"

Michael then hands Andy a glass of whiskey. He takes it, chugging the entire glass at once then hands it back to Michael right away. Jeff tries to take the glass from Andy but it's too late. He'd already finished the drink.

"Andy, you shouldn't be drinking alcohol right now, it will make you bleed more." Jeff scolds.

Andy ignores Jeff and addresses Michael. "I'm sorry, but I am desperate. I don't know what else to do. I feel so helpless, like I should be out there looking for him, doing something! I've tried calling all of his friends and they don't know anything and haven't heard from him either." Andy starts snapping the rubber band against his wrist. "Not knowing where he is or if he's okay is just driving me crazy. I'm thinking the worst here! I can't eat, I can't sleep, and I can't focus! Every time I hear the phone ring or I hear the door open I think it's him calling or coming home! What am I going to do if something has happened to him?"

"I know it's hard but you have to think positive right now. We have no hard evidence yet that Joe is not coming home. How much money is in the envelope you tried giving to Bruce?" Chuck asks.

"Fifty thousand dollars."

"WHAT?" Jeff responds to what Andy said.

"Holy shit!" Chuck says in shock.

Michael looks at Andy in shock too. "JESUS!"

"I told him that if he finds Joe I would pay him another fifty."

Chuck plops down on the chair next to the couch feeling stunned. "One hundred thousand dollars…you have officially lost your fucking mind. They could have easily taken your money and run and then you would still have been without Joe!"

Andy looks at his brothers. "You guys know Bruce better than that. He wouldn't do that."

"Are you kidding me? We haven't seen or talked to them in six years. Who knows what they've been up to and what kind of trouble they get themselves into now! That's a lot of money, Andy!"

"I told you, Chuck, I am desperate to find my son! I will do whatever it takes!"

"We can clearly see that, bro, and we are doing everything we can to help."

Jeff starts stitching up Andy's shoulder as they hear the doorbell ring. "That should be Brian. He said he'd snag some pain meds and antibiotics from the rig at the station." Brian is Jeff's best friend and is also a firefighter that works with Jeff. Michael answers the door letting Brian in.

"Hey, man, thanks for coming." Michael shakes his hand.

"You're welcome." Brian gives Jeff the supplies he asked for. "It's all legal and good. Chief Davis signed off on it and said it will stay between us."

"WHAT? You told Chief Davis?" Chief Mark Davis is their Chief in command of the firehouse.

"He caught me taking the supplies out of the rig!"

"SHIT! I am so sorry! I hope I didn't get you into any trouble."

"No, you didn't. I thought quick on my feet and told him that I was taking the supplies to show him what I needed so I can get approval and explained to him what happened. Once he heard about Andy he was fine with it."

"Whew! Nice save."

"Yeah, thanks. He let me take some antibiotics and extra bandages but would only allow me to take a few pain meds."

"He was actually cool with it?"

"Yeah, he was. I was surprised too."

"Thank you. I've got a sling and some bandages but he's bleeding pretty badly. I've removed the bullet, I'm just in the process of stitching him up now."

Brian leans over to take a look. "Nice job."

"Thanks." Jeff glances at Andy while bandaging his shoulder. "You guys sure know how to get yourselves into some rough situations."

Andy chuckles a little. "Yet, you still became a part of our family. Ouch! That's a little too much pressure."

"Sorry." Jeff laughs too. "What was I thinking?" he says jokingly.

The doorbell rings again. Michael looks at Chuck and Andy. "Who the hell is that this late at night?" He answers the door and it's Chief John Franks and he does not look happy. *Oh, shit! What's the Chief doing here? This is not good.* "Chief Franks." Michael says in shock.

The Chief practically pushes Michael out of the way as he walks into the house and goes to Andy to check on him. "Don't try and keep me outside, Michael. I already know about Andy. Is he okay?"

"He's going to be, yes. How did you find out?"

"Chief Davis called me! What the hell is the matter with you people! What did I tell you, Michael, about investigating this outside the lab? I told you I would suspend your ass if you did!"

Andy immediately comes to Michael's defense. "Chief, Michael was not investigating, it was me, he was just saving my ass!"

The Chief turns and looks back at Andy. "You? What the hell are you talking about?"

"I called up Bruce and asked him to meet me. I asked him for his help in finding Joe. Michael and Chuck followed me."

"Bruce from the old Pack? Hasn't your family had enough of those guys?"

"I called him, yes."

Chief Franks lets out a frustrating sigh then looks at Jeff and Brian. "Don't worry, I'm the only one that Chief Davis told. He was concerned about Andy. He's not reporting this to anybody else." He then looks back at Andy. "Out of all the stupid stunts your family has pulled this has to be right near the top of the list! Your father would kick your ass if he were still around!"

"My father would have done the same damn thing and you know it!" Andy yells back.

The Chief doesn't argue back, figuring that Andy may have a point. After all, the sons did learn from their father. "What happened?" Everyone fills him in, telling him their part of the story. Once they're finished he looks at Jeff. "How bad is his shoulder?"

"The bullet was pretty deep since he was shot at close range but he should be fine. I was able to extract the bullet. It doesn't look like there was much tissue damage. He got lucky."

The Chief shakes his head then starts scolding all three brothers. "Michael, I will make this clear one more time! Forensic lab is the only job you have on this case! The next time, whether you are doing the investigating or not, I will pull you off of this case completely and suspend your ass! So you may want to make sure your brothers stay out of it too! Andy, Chuck, if you interfere with this case again, I will have you arrested! Andy, if Bruce knows or has anything to do with Joe's disappearance then you may have just seriously jeopardized this case!"

Andy frantically tries to sit up but Jeff won't allow him to move yet. "WHAT? No! I was just trying to get some help!"

The Chief raises his voice slightly. "I am doing everything in my power to find Joe! I have a team of eight working on this case and on different leads! Stay out of the investigation or you may not get Joe back at all if he's even still alive! I will keep you informed of any new developments, I promise! Just stay the hell out of the investigation before you jeopardize everything if you haven't done so already! I will NOT warn you guys again!" Chief Franks storms out of the house slamming the front door.

Jeff widens his eyes and raises his eyebrows in shock. "Holy shit, I have never seen Chief Franks so pissed off."

"I have, just not with any of us. He's not one that you want to piss off either." Michael says as he stands staring at the front door.

"Yeah, well we've pissed him off now," says Andy.

Michael turns and points to Andy. "No, let's keep the record straight, you pissed him off and just got the rest of us in trouble with you."

"Yeah, I'm sorry about that."

Michael's cell phone rings. He takes it out and looks at the caller I.D. "It's Chief Franks. Is he not done yelling at me yet?" Michael says in a sarcastic tone.

"Hey, Chief."

"Michael, I just received a call from Detective Barbado. They found Joe's cell phone."

Michael walks into the other room to talk. "That's not good, Chief. So far we haven't received anything positive telling us that Joe may still be alive."

"Yeah, I know. But this still doesn't mean that he's not."

"Where did they find his phone? At the bridge?"

"No, they found it down by the docks."

"The boats docks?"

"Yes. Detective Barbado is going to be asking Jeff if he and his dive team will do a search and hopefully rescue mission."

"Shit! He's good, Chief. Jeff's good. If Joe is in that lake Jeff will find him."

"That's why he's going to be asked to lead the search."

"Can we go down…?"

"I know what you're going to ask and the answer is no!" The Chief says cutting Michael off.

"Chief…"

"Michael, stay away from the docks and the lake. I mean it!"

Michael sighs, "yes, sir."

102

"I'm going back to the station to have a chat with our friend Shawn. You can observe if you want to but that's it."

"No, actually I think I am going to pull Shawn's cell phone records. I want to know who he's been in contact with and when. Please keep me updated on what you find at the docks."

"I will. Michael, let's keep this between us. Don't say anything to Andy about this. It may destroy his hopes all together in finding Joe. I don't want him worrying about something that may turn out to be nothing. Detective Barbado knows that Jeff is at your house with Andy. When he calls Jeff he will tell him to be discrete about it too."

"Okay."

"I'll talk to you later."

Michael goes back into the family room. "What's up with Chief Franks?" Andy asks.

"Just making sure I understand the rules."

"Rules?"

"Sticking with the forensic lab."

"Oh."

Jeff's cell phone rings. "Hello?"

"Jeff, this is Detective Barbado. I know you're at Michael's with Andy so I need you to be very quiet about this and not lead on that anything is up."

Jeff turns on the outside light then walks out the patio door. "Yeah, sure. What's going on?"

"Has Chief Franks spoken to you yet?"

"No, he hasn't."

"They found Joe's cell phone down at the docks. I need a dive team to do a search. You're very experienced in this type of search and rescue missions. Will you do it?"

"Yes, absolutely!"

"Okay, great! Thank you. I'll meet you down at the docks."

"Actually, I'll meet you down at the fire station. All of my equipment is there. Brian is here with me, I'll have him be the first diver tender."

"A dive tender?"

"A first dive tender is responsible for monitoring the safety and health of the divers in the water. He'll monitor the diver's breathing rate, air supply, location and depth in the water. He will also be responsible for staying in verbal contact with the divers in the water. He'll listen for any distress calls from the divers and provide instructions if needed. He's good Justin, don't worry."

"Whatever you need. We are at your disposal. I'll meet you at the station."

"We're on our way."

Jeff hangs up and looks in through the family room window. He sees Brian looking at him and motions for him to come outside.

"What's going on?" Brian asks as he comes outside.

"Close the door please, we need to keep this quiet and we can't let Andy know what's going on. They found Joe's cell phone down at the boat docks."

"Oh, my god."

"Detective Barbado called me and asked if me and my dive team would do a search. I'd like you to be my first dive tender."

"I would be more than happy to assist. Who do you have in mind for the two standby safety divers? We need guys who are prepared to respond immediately to a distressed diver that is under the water and to check the divers' equipment prior to the diver jumping into the water."

"I was thinking Alexander and David. They're also paramedics so they would be good for that. We need to head to the station first to get the gear and the boat. Detective Barbado is going to meet us there."

"Let's go get this done and hope that we don't find anything."

"Yeah, this family has been put through enough over the years." Jeff says as they head back into the house. He looks at Michael. "We just got called in for an accident. They need our help. Andy, keep that shoulder covered. I'll be by again to check it." Michael discretely nods his head telling Jeff thank you.

"Okay, thank you, Jeff, for the help. Stay safe out there," says Andy.

"Thanks and you're welcome."

Right after Jeff and Brian leave, Tony walks half way down the stairs and calls for his father. "Dad?"

"Tony, stay upstairs please."

"Dad." Tony calls out to him again.

Michael looks at Tony again and this time Tony is waving for him to come upstairs. "I'll be right back Tony needs me." He meets Tony at the top of the stairs. "What's wrong?"

Tony says in a low voice. "Bethany is very upset. She's in her room crying. I tried talking to her but she wouldn't answer me. It sounds like she's heaving or something."

"Okay, I'll go check on her, you go get your Uncle Andy."

"Okay."

Uncle Michael rushes into the bedroom. "Honey, are you okay?" I don't answer. "Bethany?" I'm sitting on the floor leaning up against the bed with my face buried in my knees. He kneels down in front of me and gently rubs my back then grabs my arm. "Honey, what's wrong? You're hyperventilating, take some deep breaths."

"My...dad!" I say through tears trying to catch my breath.

"Your dad? He's going to be okay, honey. Calm yourself down. You've gotten yourself worked up. Take in some deep breaths."

I try but it makes me cough. "I don't...want to...lose my dad... too!" I continue to explain between breaths. "I lost my mom...maybe...my brother." I struggle to continue talking.

"Honey, you really need to breathe. Stop trying to talk and breathe."

"I can't lose...my dad too!"

Uncle Michael gently grabs both of my shoulders making me look at him. "Calm yourself down. Breathe."

Suddenly my dad rushes in with Uncle Chuck and kneels on the floor with Uncle Chuck's help. "Sweetheart, what's wrong?"

Uncle Michael explains. "She's afraid of losing you."

"What? Sweetheart, hey, you're not going to lose me. I'm okay. I'm not going anywhere. Listen to me." He takes my chin in his hand and turns my head so that I am looking at him. "You need to calm down and take in some deep breaths. Come on. Breathe. You're hyperventilating, sweetheart. Breathe."

As I'm crying I do want he says. I cough a few more times before it finally becomes a little easier to take a breath.

"You were shot...weren't you?" I ask through more tears as I look back at my dad.

"Keep breathing, come on. You're getting yourself too worked up. I'm going to be fine. I promise. Yes I was shot but it was my own fault. Okay? I'm going to be okay. It was just my shoulder."

"It could...you could have died."

"Stop, okay? Sweetheart, I'm fine. Look at me." I look at my dad as he forces my chin up again. "Do I not look okay to you? Huh? I'm sitting here with you talking, breathing and moving just fine with the exception of my shoulder. Okay? I promise you I'm fine." He kisses me on top of my head while pulling me into a hug with his good arm and holds me as tight as he can. "I'm going to be okay."

"I love you, dad." I wrap my arms around him and hold on for dear life.

"I love you too, sweetheart. More than you know. Come on, keep breathing."

Uncle Michael leaves the room looking for Tony and finds him in his room on the computer. "Hey, buddy. Stop what you're doing for a moment. I want to talk to you."

Tony stops and swivels his chair around. "Yeah, dad?"

"With everything going on I just want to make sure you're doing okay."

Tony shrugs his shoulders and becomes a little teary eyed. "I'm close to my cousins, the girls are like my sisters and the boys are like my brothers so it's a little hard not knowing if Joe's okay or not."

"Yeah, I know. It's hard on all of us. Are you doing okay though?"

"Yeah, I guess."

"I want you to come talk to me if you start having a hard time with any of this, buddy. Okay? I mean it. No secrets."

"I will, I promise."

Michael nods toward the computer. "Okay. I thought you were finished with your homework?"

Tony swivels back toward his desk. "I'm am. This is just a little project that I'm working on."

Michael leans in to take a closer look. "What are you working...fliers for Joe?" Suddenly Michael becomes impressed when he sees what's on Tony's computer.

'****MISSING**** JOE PHILLIPS, 17 YEARS OLD.'

"Yeah. I feel like I have to do something to help find him. I decided to make up some fliers so we can either hand them out to people or put them on the trees and cars around town."

"That's really awesome of you, son. I'm proud of you. Thank you for doing that. It looks really nice."

"Thanks. I have a couple of different styles that I'm working on. I want something that will catch people's eye."

"Did you ask Bethany if she wanted to help you?"

"I was going to but I didn't know if it would upset her more."

"I think it would help her. It would make her feel like she's doing something too. Why don't you ask her to help you? I think it would be good for her."

"Sure, if you think she'll be okay with doing it?"

"I think so. Come on, let's go ask her."

"Okay."

I'm sitting on the bed with my dad talking when Uncle Michael and Tony come into my room. I look up at Tony feeling bad. "I'm sorry, Tony, if I freaked you out. I didn't mean to."

"Nah, I was just worried about you. I'm making up some missing person fliers to hand out around town for Joe. Do you want to help me make them?"

"Really? Yes, I would be happy to help. Thank you for doing that for my brother."

My dad looks at Tony stunned. "Fliers? Really? Tony, that's an incredible gesture. I don't know what to say. I can't thank you enough, buddy."

"You're welcome. I've got to do something to help."

"If you make them up, I'll take them to the local printers and have copies made."

"Okay. Come on, Bethany. Let's go work on them."

Once they leave the room Uncle Chuck taps Michael on the back. "You did good raising him. He's a good kid and will grow into a good man."

"Chuck took the words right out of my mouth, Michael," says Andy.

"Thanks guys. But I had some help. My family has always been there for me and I appreciate it."

"That's what we're supposed to do," says Chuck. He then looks at Andy. "I think it would be a good idea if Bethany talks to Doctor Schiller too. She needs help getting through this as well."

"Yes, I agree. I was thinking about that earlier. Who knows, maybe she's having a hard time with the loss of her mom too. She hasn't said anything but that doesn't mean she's not having a hard time. I'll bring her with me to Schiller's tomorrow."

Chapter Thirteen

When Jeff and Brian arrive at the fire station Detective Barbado and Chief Franks are already there.

Jeff and Brian jump out of their trucks and rush into the station for equipment. Chief Davis follows them trying to help.

"What do you need help with, Jeff?"

Jeff points to the back room. "I need all of those lights in the back room that are on charge. There should be about fifteen of them. Most divers usually have their own diving equipment but I always bring along a little extra just in case somebody forgets something or something stops working."

"No problem!" Chief Davis motions to a few other guys in the firehouse to follow him and help him with the lights while a couple of other guys hook the boat up to the rescue truck.

"Detective Barbado, how many divers are available from my group other than Brian here?" Jeff asks.

"All but one so I have eleven meeting us at the docks with their gear."

"I need an even number of divers. Can you find me another one? They need to have nighttime diving experience."

"I'll see what I can do."

"Alexander and David are experienced too. They're off today but I know they won't mind coming out and helping. Can you contact them too, please? We'll meet you at the boat ramp."

"Sure thing."

"I'll be right back, Brian. I have to call Dakota and let her know that I'll be home late."

"Okay, sure. I should probably call my wife too."

Jeff quickly calls his wife Dakota. "Hi, honey." Dakota answers.

"Hi, baby. I am going to be late tonight."

"Okay, let me know when you're on your way home and I'll make sure your dinner is warmed up by the time you get here."

"I think it's going to be very late by the time I get home. Don't wait up for me, okay?"

"Okay. Is everything okay?"

"My dive team and I have to do a search."

"Please be careful."

"I will. I love you, baby. Get some rest and I'll see you in the morning."

"Okay. I love you too. Bye."

All divers including David, Alexander and a few extra volunteers are waiting at the shoreline near the boat ramp when Jeff and Brian arrive with the boat. They lower the boat down the ramp and into the water then tie it down so that it doesn't float away.

Jeff puts his hands up in the air. "ALRIGHT! EVERYBODY, LISTEN UP! LISTEN UP!" Everyone stops what they're doing giving Jeff their full attention. "I see a few new faces but I'm pretty sure everybody here knows me but for those of you that do not, I am Lieutenant Jeff Cartrite from Fire House 16. I am also the Dive Team Leader for this search and hopefully rescue operation. First of all, I want to thank everyone for coming out today to help. I do things slightly different than most search and rescue teams so just bear with me. We are looking for a seventeen-year-old boy by the name of Joe Phillips. If you see anything at all that you think may be of importance to this kid's disappearance, I want you to put a marker light next to it. If you need to send something up, make sure you use your ChemLight so we can see it when it comes to the surface." Jeff stops talking as he suddenly focuses on one of the volunteers that is not from his group. He calls out the volunteer's name. "You're Jensen, is that correct? You're from my daytime dive and rescue classes?"

Jensen steps forward. "Yes, sir?"

Jeff gives Detective Barbado a dirty look then looks back at Jensen. "I appreciate you being here but you have no experience in nighttime search and rescues. I need you to stay up top with me and have somebody else take your place." Jeff motions to an off-duty paramedic that he works with. "Ryan, would you please step in and take over Jensen's spot."

"No problem," Ryan responds.

Jensen doesn't look happy with Jeff's decision to pull him from the dive. "With all due respect, Lieutenant, I am sure that I can handle it down there. I'm a good diver."

"Jensen, nighttime search and rescues are very dangerous, you know that. And with it being wintertime right now, that is not going to help this operation at all. This water is sixty-five feet deep and the visibility is going to be zero. You've taken my search and rescue daytime courses but you have never signed up for the nighttime courses. You must have training and certification in the nighttime search and rescues before actually doing one. I'm sorry. I haven't lost a diver yet and I am not about to start now. I can use your help up here. Please step aside and let Ryan take over."

"Yes, sir." Feeling like Jeff may send him home if he doesn't do what he asked, he decides to step aside and let Ryan take over his spot as one of the divers.

Jeff focuses back on the divers waiting to go into the water. "Alright, it's been awhile since we've had to do a live search and rescue in the wintertime let alone at night. However, we've all been practicing every month for it. Let's just be grateful that this lake has not iced over, as that would make this mission even more difficult and dangerous for us all. Due to the temperatures of the water we will be switching divers every five to six hours if not sooner if we're out here that long. We're going to have a buddy system so choose somebody that you trust with your life. The two of you will be responsible for checking each other's equipment and watching each other's backs while down in the water." Jeff puts his hand on Brian's shoulder. "Brian here will be the first Dive Tender. You must stay in communication with Brian the entire time! He will give you instructions if needed and he will be listening for any distress calls from you." Jeff then points to David and Alexander. "David and Alexander will be the standby safety divers. They will be the ones to jump into the water and assist you should you get into any trouble down there. Your buddy will be your primary equipment checker; however BEFORE you jump into that water you must see Alexander or David to have your equipment double-checked. This is just for your safety. This is where I do things differently than other dive teams. Any questions so far?" Jeff waits for any replies.

"How much distance are we covering?" asks one diver.

"Good question. That depends on what we find if anything. We're going to cover small areas at a time. Since it's wintertime this water is going to be colder than usual, I would rather you guys not be down in the water for too long at a time."

The diver nods his head. "Thanks."

Jeff continues. "Keep the radio airway open at all times. Only talk on it if you're in trouble or if you find something. Again, this lake is sixty-five feet deep and has zero visibility at night. Because of that, you will need to make sure that you use your lights for signaling and communicating with your buddy. Even though there will be a lot of flashlights down there you still will not be able to see hand signals unless you're right next to each other. If you don't remember what those signals are, come see me BEFORE jumping into that water! There's going to be one bright white light and one red strobe light on the boat, which is going to be the command base. This is for when you come up to the surface you'll know where to swim. I do not want you going out too far. This is for your safety. You will be hooked to a tether just like we've practiced. You must have two dive lights with you. You are to swim side by side with your buddy. Not one behind the other. If something happens to the guy behind you, you may not know it, so it's important to swim side-by-side so you'll know where everyone is at, and you won't get separated. We're going to split up into four groups. Two groups will dive now and the other two will relieve. For the two groups that are diving now, one group will search out this way and the other group will search near the break wall. If you have any problems with any of this, now would be the time to tell me." Jeff waits to see if anybody speaks up but no one does. "Excellent! Let's go look for Joe. Be very careful down there!"

Mitch, one of the firefighters that Jeff works with who also volunteers in search and rescuer missions walks up to Jeff.

"Lieutenant, I apologize but the only signal I don't remember at the moment is the okay signal with the flashlight."

Jeff takes out his flashlight, turns it on and faces it down toward the ground moving it around in a circular motion. "Don't apologize. It's okay. Always face the light down otherwise you may end up shining it in your buddy's face and blinding him. Who's your buddy?"

"Thanks. It's Thomas." Thomas is another firefighter that Jeff works with.

"Excellent pair up." Jeff looks back at the divers as they're putting their gear on. "Just a reminder, have your equipment checked and double checked. I can't stress that enough!"

The divers have been in the water for several hours when Jeff notices Brian becoming concerned.

"Brian, what's the matter?"

"This monitor says something is wrong with Mitch's tank. This is Brian from command base calling Mitch." Mitch doesn't respond. "This is command base calling Mitch! Answer me, please!"

"This is Mitch, go ahead command base."

Brian and Jeff let out a sigh of relief when they hear Mitch's voice. "Mitch, something is wrong with your tank. Return to command base immediately! I repeat, something is wrong with your tank! Return to command base immediately!"

"Copy that, command base. Returning to base now."

"What's wrong with his tank?" Jeff asks.

Brian points to the monitor. "This monitor shows Mitch's air level is almost empty but that can't be. These tanks hold more air than that and it looked fine before he dove into the water. His gauge said it was full. He should still have a long way to go before running out of air."

"We'll take a look at it when he comes up. It may have sprung a leak. How's everybody else doing?"

"Everyone else is fine."

Once Mitch and Thomas are on board Alexander immediately checks Mitch over, making sure he's okay, while Brian looks at the gauge on his tank. "This is strange. Your gauge on the tank still says it's full but my monitor says it's nearly empty."

"I thought it felt a little light," Mitch replies.

Jeff becomes angry with Mitch as he lifts up the tank to examine it. "Next time stop what you're doing down there and check it!" He immediately feels how light it is. "You're almost out of air in this tank! He then hands the tank to David. "Do me a favor. Turn the valve on and put it down in the water with the mouth piece above the surface."

David turns on the valve then lowers the tank into to the water. "It's making bubbles, it's leaking air, Jeff. His gauge must be broken."

"That's what I thought. Mitch, you need to pay more attention to your equipment when you're down there otherwise you're going to get yourself killed!"

"I definitely will in the future," says Mitch.

"We've been out here for several hours, let's bring everybody back up and head home for the night. We can't see much down in the water right now anyway and it's getting colder." Jeff looks at his watch. "We'll meet out here again at ten a.m. that will give everybody a few hours sleep. Everyone, expect to be back in the water no later than eleven in the morning."

Chapter Fourteen

By eleven a.m. the divers are back down in the water searching for Joe. They have been searching every inch of the waters for nearly five hours when suddenly Mitch radios in.

"Command base, this is Mitch. Thomas and I are coming up."

"Mitch, this is command base. Is everything okay?" asks Brian.

"We found something."

"That's not what I wanted to hear." Jeff mutters.

Ten minutes later Mitch and Thomas arrive at the surface of the water, not far from the boat. Once they reach the boat Alexander and David helps them out of the water.

"What did you find?" asks Jeff.

"I don't know if it has anything to do with Joe but regardless, it's not good either way. I hate to ask this but do you happen to know Joe's license plate number or the description of his car?"

"You found a car?" Jeff questions with disbelief."

"Yeah, we did."

Chief Franks responds immediately. "I have his license plate information and car description."

"Where did you find it?" Jeff asks.

"Twenty yards out from the break wall and twenty one yards down. We couldn't tell if anyone was in it. We're going back down to check it out some more."

Jeff grabs some diving gear. "Thomas, I'm going with you this time. Brian, I want you to radio the other divers and give them the location of the car. Have them do a search around that area. Chief Franks..."

"I'm on it," says Brian as he immediately gets on the radio to the other divers and gives them the coordinates of the car while

David and Alexander help Jeff put his diving gear on and check his equipment.

Jeff looks over at the chief, and the Chief cuts him off knowing exactly what he's going to ask. "I'll have my guys check the top of the break wall for any tire tracks or evidence of a car going over the wall."

"Thanks, Chief."

The Chief leaves on a smaller boat with his team and heads for the break wall.

Jeff says a prayer to himself as he dives into the water behind Thomas and Mitch. *Please don't let Joe be down here. In my heart I am hoping for the best but in my head I fear the worst at the moment.* Once he's fully submerged he can feel the coldness of the water through his diving suit. The only thing he can hear is his own breathing through the regulator of his tank. As he sinks deeper into the murky and muddy waters he can no longer tell which way is up, it's like being up in the dark and cloudy skies at night. It's a scary thing to feel and perhaps one of the scariest parts of being a search and rescue diver. He can't see anything in front of him except his light and the lights from the divers that he's following. He sees seaweed, branches and a few fish here and there as he passes by them. He relies on his hands and the lights to guide him through the cold dark waters. Praying that he doesn't brush up against a body or worse, that one doesn't pop up in front of him. He bumps into something and becomes nervous that it may be Joe, but thank god, it's not. It's just a large piece of boat that looks like it's been down here for years. Suddenly, Thomas turns motioning with his light to swim in the direction ahead of them. It's the car, it's upside down and by the looks of it, it appears it hasn't been down here for very long. He continues to approach the car as his heart races with anticipation that it might be Joe's. *Please don't let this be Joe's car.* He swims around to the rear of the car and reads the license plate, then yells into the microphone of his headset. "SHIT! It's his car! It's Joe's car!"

Brian immediately tries to keep Jeff calm. "Take it easy, buddy. Just take it easy, it doesn't mean that Joe is inside it. You know that, just stay calm my friend."

"God, let's hope not. Our family has been through enough," Jeff responds. *Oh, my god, Joe. Please don't be inside this lake.*

Jeff swims to the floor of the lake to get a look inside the car and report back to Brian and the other divers. "It looks like the windows are still rolled up and I don't see any broken."

"Windows are closed here too. Everything is intact," Thomas reports to what he sees on his side of the car.

"The car has been down here long enough so the air pressure has equalized by now. Try and open the doors," says Jeff.

It's a four-door car so Jeff, Thomas, Mitch and Ryan each take a door to open.

"The door is locked!" says Thomas.

Jeff responds. "Mine is too."

"So is mine," Mitch replies.

"Break the windows. We need to check this car." They break the windows and they each check their part of the car for a body.

"From what I can tell it's clear here!"

"Clear!"

"Clear!"

"Clear here, too!"

After Jeff returns to the boat the divers search around for about forty-five minutes for Joe. Jeff receives an update from all other divers searching the area. No one has found any bodies. Then suddenly, Ryan yells over the radio. "I just ran into a body!"

"WHAT?" Jeff yells.

Once they've pulled the body out of the water and onto the boat they're relieved to see that it's not Joe.

"It's one of the local gang members," says Jeff. "But I don't remember his name."

Within minutes of finding the body, Thomas radios in. "This is Thomas to command base!"

Jeff immediately responds back. "This is command base. Go ahead Thomas."

"Jeff, I found another body!"

Jeff looks at the Chief who has now joined them at the command base. "What in the hell is going on? What's your location...?"

"I've got his location on the monitor." Brian says as he cuts Jeff off. "He's near the dock over there." Brian points to the dock area.

Jeff motions to Brian to send down a few volunteers that are warmed up and waiting for something to do.

"You six swap with the divers coming up." Brian says as he points to the divers. "This is command base to Thomas. I'm sending a few guys down now to assist you and Mitch."

"Copy that, command base."

Jeff looks at the Chief and nods at the body that was pulled out of the lake. "Hey, Chief. I know this guy is from one of the local gangs, but don't remember his name."

The Chief looks at the body. "That's Arturo Rodriguez. Shawn's gang."

After about fifteen minutes they finally pull the second body out of the water. Jeff's the first one to take a look at the face.

"This isn't Joe either, thank god." He motions to everyone to gather around. "Everyone, listen up! I appreciate your hard work and I know that you are all very tired and cold and you're running on little sleep. However, now that we've found two bodies we have to continue searching for more. Those of you who have been out of the water for a while and warmed up, I want you diving. Give these other guys a break. Then we'll switch off again in a little bit."

The Chief looks at Jeff. "It's another gang member. Shit! This is Jose Shepherd. I can't believe somebody was able to take this guy out! So far we have two dead gang members and Joe's car. What in the hell did this boy get himself into?"

"Something is off, Chief," says Jeff.

"What do you mean?"

"All windows on Joe's car are up. None, not one was even partially opened so you know there were no attempts to get out. All doors were closed too and the stranger thing is they were locked. How is that even possible? Most cars, and Joe's is one of them, the doors lock automatically when it reaches a speed of ten miles per hour. Which tells me that this car had to somehow be driven off that break wall at a speed of at least ten miles per hour or faster but the question is, how? There's nobody inside that car and every thing is locked up tight and you have two dead bodies not far from it. I don't get it."

"The other question is, if Joe was in that car how is it that his cell phone was found on the dock and not on the break wall and still in working order?"

Mitch calls to Jeff. "I would like to go back down, Jeff."

"No, not right now. You've been down there for along time. You need to rest up."

Chief Franks points toward the break wall. "We saw two different sets of tire tracks up on the break wall and some skid marks. Detective Barbado is doing an impression of all the tracks before the tow truck destroys any evidence."

"Have you called Marcus out yet?" Marcus owns the towing company that the police and fire departments frequently use.

"Yeah, he should be here any minute."

"Why don't we head up to the wall and wait for him?" Jeff suggests. He turns to Brian. "I'm going to the break wall with the Chief to meet Marcus. I'll have my radio on. If you need anything let me know."

"Okay."

Jeff then jumps on the smaller boat with the Chief and they head up to the break wall. Shortly after, Marcus arrives with his large tow truck that he calls the 'Great White' and brings along a slightly smaller truck that Roberto; his right hand man is driving. Marcus jumps out of his truck and greets Jeff.

"Hey, man, how are you holding up?"

"Better than my family is, thanks." Jeff says as he shakes Marcus's hand. "Why two tow trucks? You don't normally bring two for jobs like this."

"This is deeper water than we usually pull from. I learned the last time that it's easier with two trucks. When we start dragging that car toward the break wall it's going to bring the lake floor with it too making it harder to pull the car. It's less stress on my truck if I use both trucks to get the car to the wall then use the Great White to pull it up."

"Makes sense."

"Where's the car's location?"

Jeff points in the direction of the car. "Twenty yards out from here and twenty one yards east."

"What's the position of the car?"

"The rear of the car is facing toward the break wall and it's upside down."

"On it's roof?"

"Yeah."

"Oh, this is going to be fun. I don't get too many of those under water." Marcus says sarcastically.

"You won't need two trucks."

"I'm using two anyways."

"You won't need two."

"I'm using two anyways." Marcus replies in an irritated voice. Marcus doesn't like it when Jeff tells him how to do his job. Because most of the time, Jeff is right and that pisses Marcus off.

"Okay, okay." Jeff puts his hands up in retreat.

Marcus looks at Jeff as he and Roberto start getting the chains into position to send down into the water. "Alright, well, you and I have done enough of these together, you know what to do."

"Yep. I'll let you know when we're all hooked up."

Jeff returns to the boat that takes him back to the command base. "What's the game plan?" Brian asks as Jeff comes aboard.

"Marcus has both tow trucks here. He's going to use them both to pull the car toward the break wall."

"I don't think he'll need both trucks," says Brian.

"I know. I tried telling him. Once he has the car near the break wall then he'll pull the car up with Great White. I want Thomas, David, Mitch..." Jeff pauses and looks at Jensen as he sighs, "and Jensen to take the chains from the tow trucks and hook them up to the rear axle of the car. I want those guys over there to be their standby divers under water." Jeff points to a group of six guys sitting and chatting while waiting for instructions.

Jensen pops up out of his seat when he hears his name. "You're going to let me dive?"

Jeff turns and looks at Jensen. "I need four guys hooking up. Those chains are going to be heavy and a bitch to carry under water. I want two guys on each chain. You stay near the buddy Brian pairs you up with. Do everything you are told. Follow their lead and you'll be fine."

"Yes, sir. Thank you for letting me help."

"Thank you for volunteering. Get signed up for my nighttime course then I'll let you do more nighttime dives."

"I will this week," replies Jensen.

Jeff taps Brian on the back. "I'm going back up to the break wall. I'll be listening to the progress below. Please let me know if you need anything over here."

"Absolutely." Brian rallies up the divers as he points to the group of guys. "Listen up! You six guys come over here. David, Mitch and Thomas, I need you guys over here too."

The divers all gather around Brian for their instructions.

"What do you need us to do, Brian?" asks David.

"David, I want you paired up with Jensen. Mitch and Thomas, I want you two guys to stay paired up. You four are going to be responsible for hooking the tow truck chains to the car. Marcus is going to use both trucks to pull the car near the break wall. Once the car is close enough we will then unhook the smaller tow truck, leaving the car hooked to the larger truck only. Does everybody understand what they need to do?" Everybody nods their head yes. "Let me know once you guys have the chains hooked to the car."

"What do you need us to do?" asks Max, one of the divers from the group of six.

"Max, I need your group to be their backup divers under water. Stay out of their way unless you need to assist them or if something happens. All of you check your buddy's equipment before you guys dive back down into the water." Brian points to David, Thomas, Mitch and Jensen. You guys remember to turn on your lights on your helmets. Try not to blind each other too, okay?

You won't be able to carry your flashlights and the chains at the same time. Keep the radios clear of chatter! Be careful down there! Okay, let's do this! It's getting late and the longer we're out here the colder it's going to get!"

Once David, Thomas, Mitch and Jensen are in the water then the backup divers follow in after them. The four guys swim to the break wall and grab the chains that Marcus is lowering down. They carry the chains down through sixty-five feet of ice cold water. David and Jensen work on chaining up the driver's side of the axle while Mitch and Thomas work on the passenger side of the axle. Once they're finished hooking the chains up to the car they check each other's work then David radios back to Brian.

"Command base, this is David."

"This is command base, go ahead, David."

"Car is hooked up and ready to go."

"Copy that."

Jeff immediately gets on the radio with the guys down in the water. "Divers, this is Jeff. I want you guys to stay clear of those chains! If one breaks or comes loose it won't be a situation that you want to be in!"

David responds as he motions to the other divers to move back. "Copy that, Jeff. We're moving back."

"My chains will hold, Jeff. They're strong enough," says Marcus heatedly.

"I'm not taking any chances with my guys."

"As long as your guys did their job right the chains will hold."

"My guys are good, it's the chains I'm worried about."

"They will hold." Marcus repeats. Jeff just gives him a dirty look but doesn't say anything in return. *Strong or not, I'm not taking any chances with my guys.*

It takes about twenty minutes to carefully pull the car near the break wall. Jeff turns to Roberto. "Roberto, we need some slack in your chains for my guys to unhook!"

"You got it, Jeff!"

Once the chains from the smaller tow truck are loosened up Jeff radios to the divers below.

"This is Jeff. David and Thomas, unhook the chains from the car for the smaller tow truck. Please be careful!"

"Copy that, Jeff." David replies. He and Thomas swim to the car. The car is facing down with the back end of it barely out of the water. David and Thomas work together to unhook the chains from the car. "Jeff, this is David, smaller tow truck is now unhooked."

Jeff responds. "Copy that. Great job guys! Everyone move away from the car immediately!"

Once the divers are at a safe distance from the car, Jeff motions to Roberto to bring in the chains that have been unhooked. Roberto retracts the chains back onto the smaller tow truck and moves his truck out of Great White's way. Everyone stands nearby watching Great White pull Joe's car out of the lake.

Since the diver's could only look into the car through broken windows, Jeff and a few other firefighters use the Jaws of Life to open all doors, checking the car again, for any bodies, and as they do water, clay and silt rush out of the car.

"No one's inside." Jeff reports. He then uses the Jaws of Life to open the trunk. Shocked at what he sees, he stands staring at the inside of the trunk. "You have got to be kidding me!" Jeff says as he looks at yet another body.

Chief Franks walks to the car since it is now safely on the break wall. "That is George Desoto."

"Let me guess, also a gang member?" Jeff asks.

"You nailed it."

"Are all of these dead guys part of Shawn's gang?"

"Yes, they are. All three of them."

David, who has now joined them up on the break wall notices something with Joe's car and yells out. "I think I know how he got out!"

Jeff and Chief Franks rush over to see what David is talking about. David points to the roof of the car.

"Of course, I forgot that Joe had put a moon roof in his car," Jeff says.

"Had a moon roof, its no longer there," responds David.

Jeff looks at Chief Franks. "I know the car is evidence but can I check out the moon roof?"

"Yeah, go ahead."

Jeff climbs inside the car and inspects the inside of the roof. "This window has been popped out," says Jeff.

"I'd like to know how they did that. It's not easy popping these things out. Do you think that's how Joe got out?" Chief asks.

Jeff comes out of the car and looks at the Chief. "I don't know. Moon roofs are easy to kick out if they're already partially opened."

"I wonder if that's how Joe got out…if he was even in it."

"That's your job to figure out," says Jeff as he smacks the back of the Chief's shoulder. "I've got to get my guys out of here and back into their warms homes. Let me know if there's anything else you need. We'll be back out here again tomorrow during daylight and do another search."

Before Jeff has a chance to walk away, an officer hollers out to the Chief. "Chief Franks, you may want to take a look at this. I have a feeling this isn't good."

The Chief and Jeff exchange glances as they walk to the passenger side of the car.

"What did you find?" asks the Chief.

The officer hands a very well preserved package to Chief Franks. "I have some water in the trunk of my car, I'll go get it so we can rinse some of this silt and mud off," says the officer.

"Okay."

A moment later the officer returns with a gallon size container of water. He and Jeff carefully rinse the package as best as they can then gently dry it off.

"I can't see much through the plastic bag," says Jeff.

The Chief motions to Jeff. "You can go ahead and open it up."

Jeff hands the package to the Chief. "No thanks. This could be evidence. I'll let you guys open it."

"Good point." Chief Franks opens the first zip lock baggie only to find another one inside. He opens that one and finds a third zip lock baggie and then a fourth. "Wow, he's really got this thing very well packaged, it's closed up tight." He pulls out a case and walks to the hood of a nearby police car placing the baggies and case on the hood. He reads what's written on the baggie. "Dragon?" He looks at Jeff confused.

"Holy shit!" Jeff comments.

"That doesn't sound good, Jeff. I've never heard of 'Dragon', what is it?"

"Chief, the name Dragon is a new name for heroin out on the streets. How could you not know this?" asks Jeff as he slides on a glove and opens the case revealing several syringes.

"Drugs? In Joe's car?"

"I'm afraid so."

"Oh, man. This is a new one on me and here I thought I knew all of the names of the street drugs out there." Chief Franks looks at the officer standing with them. "Officer, get a test kit please."

"Yes, sir."

128

Jeff picks up one of the syringes as he explains to the Chief what they're looking at. "The liquid inside these syringes has solidified. These are preloads."

"DRUGS? In Joe's car?" The Chief repeats in shock.

The officer returns with the test kit then pulls out a few already preloaded hypodermic needles taking the plunger out of one of them. He tests the contents and waits for a few moments. "Jeff's right, Chief. It's heroin."

"SHIT! How I do I tell his family? How many syringes are there?"

"There are six." Jeff says as he lays them out on the hood of the police car.

"Have you guys found anything else in the car?" Chief Franks asks the officer.

"Just a knife."

"Okay, make sure you bag it and get everything processed and take this car down to the evidence garage. I want every part of this car torn apart and searched."

"Yes, sir. I'll have Marcus take it there now."

Jeff decides to have the divers search for another two hours then finally calls the search off for the night and sends the divers home until the next day.

Chief Franks walks up to Jeff just as he finishes cleaning up their gear. "If you don't mind, Jeff, I need to go to Michael's and talk to Andy. I would appreciate you coming with me. They may have questions about the search or the car that I can't answer yet."

"Sure." Jeff looks at Brian. "Would you mind finishing up here, Brian?"

"Not at all. Go do what you have to do. We'll see you out here in the morning."

"Thanks."

Chief Franks follows Jeff to the station to get his truck then to Michael's house as he calls Chuck.

"Hello?"

"Chuck, this is Chief Franks."

"Hey, what's going on?"

"Where are you right now?"

"I am getting ready to go to Michael's for a late cook out. Why, what's up?"

"Jeff and I are on our way to Michael's. There are some things we have to talk to you and your brothers about."

"Is it about Joe?"

"Yes, it is."

"Did you find him?"

"No, not yet, but there are other developments that you guys have to know about. It's not good."

"Alright, I'll see you there shortly."

Jeff and Chief Franks arrive at Michael's at the same time Chuck and his family does. As Michael answers the door, he's shocked when he sees Jeff and Chief Franks with his brother.

"Did you guys find Joe?"

"No, is Andy around?" asks Jeff.

"Yeah, We're in the family room watching movies with the kids while we were waiting for Chuck and his family. What's going on?"

"Jeff and I need to talk to you and your brothers. It's very serious," says Chief Franks.

Once in the family room Michael grabs the remote and turns off the movie and the television. "Tony, please take all of the kids upstairs."

"Is everything okay, dad?" asks Tony.

Chief Franks responds before Michael can. "Uncle Jeff and I have to talk to the adults privately for a little bit."

"Okay." The kids head upstairs, giving the adults privacy to talk.

"Have you found my son?"

"No, Andy, I'm sorry we haven't found Joe yet but we do have other developments to tell you about and you're not going to like them."

"Okay, go ahead." Andy says quietly as he starts snapping the rubber band around his wrist. Chuck sits down next to Andy.

John starts to explain what's going on. "Shortly after I left here last night I received a call from Detective Barbado advising me that they found Joe's cell phone down at one of the docks." He then motions to Jeff to continue the explanation.

"Detective Barbado then called me asking if I would lead the dive team. They…"

"Dive team?" Andy asks as he swallows hard.

Jeff continues to explain. "Since Joe's phone was found near the lake we needed to do a search just to make sure Joe wasn't in it. My dive team just completed an eight-hour plus search looking for Joe. They have not found him yet."

"I feel a, but coming on," says Andy.

"We didn't find him but we found his car."

"Where exactly?"

"We found his car in the lake, Andy. Sixty-five feet down."

"Oh, my god!" Andy runs his hands over his head and takes a deep breath. "Could you tell what kind of condition the car was in?"

"It was upside down on the bottom of the lake when we found it. All windows were rolled up and all doors were still locked. Whoever was in that car when it went over the wall must have gotten out through the moon roof because the moon roof was kicked out. I called off the search for the night but we're going back out again in the morning."

Andy takes in a deep breath trying to compose himself. "Since we are in the middle of winter, if he were in the water, how long would he have to survive?"

"Don't do this to yourself, Andy."

"Damn it, Jeff! How long?" Andy yells.

"The water temperature right now is twenty-nine degrees, which means he would have less than forty-five minutes."

Andy starts yelling at Jeff. "Why the hell aren't you out there looking for him then? Why did you call off the search? You should be looking for him right now, not tomorrow!"

With a calm voice Jeff continues to explain. "Andy, it's the dead of winter out there. The water is ice cold..."

"I DON'T GIVE A SHIT! YOU SHOULD BE OUT THERE LOOKING FOR MY SON!" Michael immediately puts his hand on Andy's shoulder in an effort to calm him down and let Jeff finish.

"Andy, as much as you are not going to like hearing this and as much as I hate having to say it, I have to look out for my divers. It's my job to keep them safe. Diving operations are very dangerous to do and even more so in the wintertime. The visibility in that lake is zero especially at night. The water is ice cold so cold, that we're lucky the lake has not started to freeze over yet.

Thankfully the lake is large enough that we haven't had enough of these cold temperature days for the lake to freeze. The car was sixty-five feet down." Andy just stares at Jeff. "I have to look out for the safety of my divers. If I leave them out there all night looking for Joe, I'll start losing divers. I haven't lost a diver yet and I'm not about to start now. We're going back out again tomorrow." Jeff then motions to Chief Franks to take over.

John sits in a chair near Andy. "Andy, I'm not sure what Joe has gotten himself into but I can tell you that it's pretty damn serious."

"What you mean?"

John lets out a loud sigh. "There were two bodies found not far from where Joe's car was found. Both bodies are local gang members."

"You think Joe was involved with a gang? There's no way, Chief!"

"Andy, listen to me, son. After we pulled Joe car's from the lake, we found a third body…inside the trunk of Joe's car."

"WHAT? I don't believe this! There's got to be some kind of mistake!"

Chief Franks now turns the floor back over to Jeff. "I really wish that we didn't have to tell you this." Jeff glances at the Chief then continues. "We found six hypodermic needles filled with a drug called the 'Dragon', inside the glove compartment of Joe's car."

"What the hell is a Dragon?" asks Andy.

"It's another name for heroin."

Andy starts snapping the rubber band harder against his wrist. "You're out of your damn mind if you think my son is on drugs! Or involved with them in anyway!"

"Andy, it was in Joe's car, inside his glove compartment," Chief Franks reiterates.

Andy quickly stands and starts pacing back and forth while rubbing his face with his hands. "No, no…this can't be happening! My son is not on drugs damn it! There's no way! I would know if he was!"

Chuck stands, trying to calm his brother down. "Andy, listen…"

"No, Chuck! There's no way! He can't be!" Andy suddenly grabs his keys off the coffee table and storms out of the family room.

Everybody quickly follows him. "Andy, where are you going?" Chief Franks asks.

Andy ignores the Chief's question and hollers for Bethany upstairs. "Bethany! Bethany!"

Bethany immediately comes to the top of the stairs. "Did you call me, dad?"

"Yes, I'll be back in a little bit, okay? I want you to stay here."

"Okay. Where are you going?"

"I have to run home for a bit. I'll be right back." As Andy says that Jeff rushes outside to his truck knowing exactly what Andy is going to do.

Andy leaves the house with everybody following him, except Linda, she stays behind with the kids.

Chapter Fifteen

Andy runs into his house and up to Joe's room then starts tearing it apart. Jeff immediately tries to stop him.

"ANDY, STOP! ANDY! YOU NEED TO STOP!" Jeff grabs Andy's arm to stop him and Chuck and Michael do the same. "Andy! You cannot go through this room like an F5 tornado! If Joe is really into drugs then there's no telling what's in this room! If there are needles in here and you get stuck with one you could become sick!"

With his breathing rapid, his heart racing and eyes wide open with panic and anger, Andy stares Jeff in the eyes. "Let go of me."

Jeff squeezes Andy's arm harder, "not until you calm your ass down. Andy, I promise you we will search this room from top to bottom if it takes us all damn night to do it. But we have to do it carefully or somebody can get hurt. You cannot tear through here like a madman. Calm your ass down. Understand?"

Andy let's out a huge sigh. "Yeah, fine."

"Okay? You good?"

"Yeah."

When Andy started to leave Michael's, Jeff knew what he was going to do so he grabbed several pairs of gloves and a test kit from his truck. He starts handing the gloves out to everybody including Chief Franks.

Michael takes a pair and puts them on. "We need a place to put stuff if we happen to find anything."

Andy walks over to Joe's dresser knocking everything off and onto the floor with one swipe of his arm. "There, now you've got a place."

Michael raises his eyebrows and nods. "That'll work," he says quietly.

They search Joe's room for about three hours checking every nook and cranny they can find. Once finished, they all stand staring at Joe's dresser unable to believe what they have found, eight hypodermic needles already prefilled, tie-offs that drug addicts use for tying around their arm, paper towels and rubbing alcohol.

Shaking his head at the drug paraphernalia, Jeff starts performing a test on each of the syringes. "He couldn't have been doing this for very long."

Chuck takes a step toward the dresser to get a closer look. "Why do you think that?"

"I've seen a lot of drug addicts in my time and from my experience, somebody whose been doing this for a while will have more than just prefilled syringes and tie-offs. They would have spoons for cooking it, lighters, cotton balls for straining it and more than that if they're sniffing it."

"What are you doing?" Chuck asks watching Jeff.

"These packages say Dragon on them which is another name for heroin. If it's truly heroin then the test will turn purple. This is what we call a presumptive test, which only gives us an indication of which type of substance is present in these syringes. Michael will still need to do a confirmatory test in the lab but these presumptive tests are usually pretty accurate."

"I can't believe my son is doing drugs and he brought it inside my house! INSIDE MY DAMN HOUSE! AND WITH HIS SISTER HERE! WHAT THE HELL WAS HE THINKING?" Andy leans up against the wall and slides to the floor with his arms on his knees.

Everyone waits for Jeff to complete the tests on each syringe. "I'm so sorry, Andy. These syringes are filled with heroin just like the ones found in Joe's car."

"God damn it!" Andy drops his head onto his knees. "That's why Joe has been avoiding you, Jeff, and Michael too. He wasn't mad at you guys, he was afraid you guys would figure out that he's doing drugs."

"Andy, are you…"

"Just leave me alone right now, Chuck. You guys please…just go home." Andy says in a choked up voice.

Chuck motions to the others to go downstairs. "We'll wait downstairs but we're not leaving." Michael and Jeff grab all of the hypodermic needles and paraphernalia from the top of the dresser.

"What are you going to do with that?" Andy asks.

"You heard Jeff. I have to do further testing on these in the lab then I'm going to dispose of it." Michael replies.

"I'd rather keep it in case Joe does come home. I can talk to him about it."

"Then I'll take pictures of it on his dresser and give you the pictures. Since I'm part of law enforcement, I can't legally leave this stuff here."

"Fine, do what you need to do." Andy puts his head back down on his knees.

"I need to go to the station but if you guys need anything at all, please don't hesitate to pick up the phone," says Chief Franks.

Chuck and Michael share a brief man hug. "Thanks, John."

"I'm heading out too. I have to meet my dive team…" Jeff looks at his watch. "In six hours."

Andy sighs while looking at the floor and asks Jeff and the Chief. "Is there anything else I should painfully know?"

"That's all the information we have right now." Replies the Chief.

Andy shakes his head. "I think it was more than enough."

"I know, I understand."

Andy looks up at Jeff. "I'm sorry, Jeff. Thanks for everything you're trying to do. I really do appreciate it."

"I know you do and you're welcome. You guys try and take it easy. If you need anything at all, you've got my number."

Michael shakes Jeff's hand and gives him a man hug goodbye too. "Thanks."

Jeff turns to John. "Chief, do you mind giving me a ride back to Michael's so I can pick up my truck?"

"Sure, no problem."

Once downstairs Chuck says to Michael. "Our kids are close cousins. They spend a lot of time together...all the time."

"I know. Maybe we need to have a chat with our kids too. Make sure they're not into this shit as well."

Chuck plops down on the couch still stunned. "This is a blow that Andy didn't expect."

"Yeah, none of us did. I need to use the bathroom, I'll be right back."

Michael quickly goes into the bathroom and closes the door. He splashes cold water over his face several times then stands with his hands on the sink, staring at himself in the mirror. *I can't begin to imagine what my brother is going through right now. I know what I'm going through and Joe's not my son. I'm a detective, yet I feel so damn helpless. I'd be going out of my mind too if it were my kid. Shit! Damn you, Joe! What the hell were you thinking?* Michael hears loud banging snapping him out of his trance. He splashes his face once more, dries it then leaves the bathroom to see what's going on.

Michael and Chuck look at each other then rush upstairs as Chuck asks, "what the hell is he doing up there?"

"Whatever it is, it can't be good," Michael replies.

When they reach Joe's room, they see Andy sitting on the turned over mattress leaning forward, elbows on his knees, and his knuckles bleeding on one hand. Then they notice the numerous holes in one wall.

"Looking for drugs inside the walls, are we?" Michael says sarcastically.

Andy responds without looking up at his brothers. "Where did I go wrong? What signs did I miss? We are so damn close to our kids. I shouldn't have missed the signs. I shouldn't have been working so much!"

Chuck squats down in front of his brother. "What are you talking about, man? This isn't your fault, bro. You're a great hard working father."

"We've all had our kids in sports their whole life to keep them out of trouble. My son came to me and asked, 'Dad, can I stop taking sports? I'd like to enjoy my last year of high school'. I say, 'yes you can, go ahead and enjoy your last year', instead of saying no. I should have just said no."

Michael sits down next to Andy. "Andy, this is not your fault. All we can do is teach our kids to the best of our ability and hope that they retain what we've taught them. You know that. As much as we'd love to, we can't watch them twenty-four seven."

Chuck sits next to Andy too. "We have to trust they'll do all the right things just like we taught them. Are you going to be okay?" Andy doesn't say anything. "This isn't your fault. You're a working father. What are you supposed to do, stay home and babysit your teenagers? You shouldn't have to. At some point you had to trust him."

Andy looks at Michael and Chuck. "Don't take this the wrong way, but since our kids hang out so much together and they're close cousins with one another, I think you should sit down with

139

your kids and talk to them. I'm going to with Bethany. I need to make sure she's not involved in drugs too."

"Yeah, Michael and I were discussing that downstairs a few minutes ago. We'll talk to our kids too. Come on, we'll help you clean this mess up."

"No. Leave it just the way it is. It'll serve Joe right." Says Andy. "If Joe comes home I want him to see what he just put his family through. I want him to know how much he just hurt everyone around him and I want him to know that we found his stash."

Chuck raises his hands. "Alright, man. We'll leave it alone."

"I am so angry with my son right now. I can't even begin to explain how angry. If he were here right now, I don't know if I would be able look at him. We promised not to have any secrets. Not to lie to one another. Now I find out he's been keeping a dangerous secret."

Michael taps Andy's back. "Come on. We haven't eaten anything. Let's go back to my house, grab a bite to eat and talk some more."

Chapter Sixteen

Andy and Chuck are at Doctor Schiller's for Andy's therapy session. Chuck sits out in the waiting room as he usually does when he takes Andy and works on cases on his computer. Just as he finishes writing notes about a deposition a client gave, the door to Schillers office opens.

Chuck stands. "All finished?"

"Yep," replies Andy.

"Nope," replies Doctor Schiller.

Andy looks at the doctor confused. "What do you mean 'nope'? It's been an hour."

"There's one thing I want to add to today's session."

"What's that?"

"You'll see." He then looks at Chuck. "Would you be up for a ride along?"

Chuck looks at his watch. "Umm, yeah sure. I'm not due in court for another three hours."

"Excellent. This won't take long. We'll take my car."

"Where are we going?" Andy asks.

"I told you, you'll see."

Andy and Chuck look at each other and shrug their shoulders. About twenty minutes later they arrive at Durango Island Cemetery. You can tell that Andy is becoming very angry and nervous at the same time.

"What in the hell are we doing here, Doctor Schiller? This is where my wife and parents are buried."

"I know it is," he replies, as he pulls up in front of the row that Melanie is buried in. "Andy, I didn't tell you that I was going to take you here because I knew that you weren't going to come otherwise."

"You're damn right I wouldn't have. I'm not ready for this, Doctor Schiller."

Chuck keeps his mouth shut and just watches and listens feeling stunned, himself that Doctor Schiller pulled this little trick on Andy.

"Yes…you are, Andy. You said yourself that you're afraid of seeing her name written in stone. You need to see it sometime. You have not been to your wife's grave since the day you buried her. It's been almost a year. You haven't even been to your parent's grave because it reminds you of losing Melanie. You need to do this. This is part of your therapy. Don't talk about your kids. This is about you and her. You can tell her about the kids at a later time. You need to talk to her. Scream, yell, get angry, cry, do whatever it is that you have to do. But you need to get it out and face this. Melanie being gone is not going to change."

"Shit, Doctor Schiller," Andy sniffles a little. "I'm not liking you very much right now."

"I know."

"You're a crazy old man," Andy scolds.

"I've been called worse. Come on, Andy. You can do this. Chuck and I will be right here if you need us." Andy sits staring in the direction of Melanie's grave. "Go, Andy." Doctor Schiller prompts.

"We will be right here for you, buddy," Chuck, says giving his support too.

Andy finally gets out of the car and walks toward the grave gently rubbing his hands together and sticking them in his pockets.

"I can't believe you're doing this to him so soon. It just seems so extreme." Chuck says to Doctor Schiller as they watch Andy walk toward Melanie's grave.

"It's not that extreme but unfortunately, it's something that has to be done. He won't deal with her death otherwise. Seeing her gravesite will finally make it reality for him."

They sit and watch Andy approach Melanie's grave but can't hear what he's saying. He stands staring at it for the longest time then suddenly drops to his knees and cries. Chuck starts to get out of the car but Doctor Schiller stops him.

"Leave him alone, Chuck. He needs some private time. This is something he has to do by himself."

Chuck stays inside the car but keeps the car door open.

Andy tries to talk through his sobs. "I'm so sorry I haven't been here to visit you, honey. I've been having a really hard time dealing with the fact that I lost you. I miss you so much. I love you so much. I know it's not your fault but there's a part of me that's so angry with you for leaving us. It wasn't your time, honey. It wasn't supposed to be your time yet." Andy traces the letters of Melanie's name on the tombstone with his finger. "We were supposed to grow old together, honey. Watch our kids have kids and watch our grandkids grow." Tears continue to roll down his cheeks. "Damn you for leaving us!"

Doctor Schiller can tell that Chuck is getting antsy. "Chuck, stay inside the car. You have to let him do this on his own."

"I don't like seeing my brother like this."

"I know, Chuck, but he has to work through that pain to get through his loss. You know how this works. You, your brothers and sister went through it when your parents died."

"That was a totally different relationship. This is Andy's wife we're talking about. You're never closer to anyone than you are your spouse or kids."

"That may be true but the grieving process is still the same. It's just some may hurt more than others."

Andy continues talking to Melanie. "Kids are okay but I have to tell you…I need you so much right now. I love you, honey. I miss you so much." After a half hour, Andy tries to gain control of his emotions and compose himself as he clears his throat. He wipes the tears from his face and stands. "I have to go but I promise I will be back again soon." He kisses the top of the tombstone. "I love you."

As Andy walks back toward the car Chuck looks at Doctor Schiller. "Now can I get out?"

"Just stand outside the car. If he wants comforting, he'll come to you."

Chuck gets out of the car and stands there like Doctor Schiller said but can't resist saying something to Andy as he walks up.

"Are you okay?"

"I'm fine. Can we just get out of here now?" Andy answers in a very clipped tone.

Chuck opens the car door for Andy. "I guess that's up to Doctor Schiller."

Once inside the car Doctor Schiller takes a moment to observe Andy. "How are you doing, Andy?"

"What do you think?"

"I asked you."

Andy swallows hard as he plays with his wedding ring that he's still wearing. "I'm angry with her. I know it's not her fault. But I'm angry with her for leaving us."

"That's all part of the grieving process."

"I miss her so much. It's so painful to think about her being gone."

"What did we talk about back at my office, Andy?"

"Don't focus on her being gone. Focus on the moments that we were together."

"Exactly. As I was just telling your brother, I know it's a different relationship but the grieving process is all the same as it was when you lost your parents. The only difference is, this was your wife and that makes it a lot harder. I want you to come back here again this week but by yourself."

"Do you want to visit mom and dad while we're here? You haven't seen them either since Melanie died," asks Chuck.

"No, you can. Maybe I'll come out here later by myself to visit with them."

"Okay."

Chapter Seventeen

Jeff walks from the bow of the boat to the stern where Brian is currently monitoring the divers down in the water.

"Hey, Brian."

"Hey, buddy, what's up?"

"How are these guys doing?" Jeff points to the divers that are sitting on the boat chatting and warming up.

"They're good, they're warmed up and rested some."

"Good, call the other divers back in and send these guys back down again for another hour or two. I want to search a little farther down the lake then we'll call it quits indefinitely."

Brian looks at Jeff. "What? Jeff, I am not sending these guys back out again."

"Excuse me? This search is not over unless I say it's over! It will only be another hour or two then I'll call it off."

"We've been searching for three days! Joe is not in the water! That is a good thing! I will not send these guys back down again!"

"Yes, you will!"

"No, I won't! They've had enough!"

"You said they were warmed up and rested."

"Not rested enough for more diving! You asked me to be the Diver Tender of this operation, which means I am responsible for their health and their safety! When I tell you they need to stop you are supposed to listen! We need to call this search off! Joe is not down in the water! If he were, we would have found him by now! These divers are worn out, Jeff!"

"I want these divers down in the water in fifteen minutes! End of discussion!"

"I will not send them back down and I will not let you send them back down again and if you try sending them I will make sure that they refuse to go."

"Why are you defying me all of the sudden, Brian?"

"Because this time, you are not making the right choice! I have never gone against ANY of your directions before because you have always been smart about your decisions, except for now! The divers are worn out! If you send those divers down again you will be putting their safety at risk even more than it already is and I just can't let you do that!"

"Then I'll go by myself."

"The hell you will!"

"You cannot tell me what I can or cannot do!"

"You know how dangerous it is going by yourself! Think about your wife and kids! What if something happens to you?"

Jeff starts picking up some diving gear as David grabs his arm. "I'm with Brian on this one, Jeff. I can't let you do that either. Your safety is just as important as anyone else's here."

"What the hell is the matter with you two? We are looking for a missing kid! Get the hell out of my way, David!"

David puts his hands on Jeff's chest to stop him and Brian grabs Jeff by the arm as he scolds him some more. "Jeff! Just stop and think about this for a moment! You're not using your head, man! You cannot go down there by yourself! I know this is a family member missing but even your family wouldn't want you to put your life at risk like this!"

Jeff looks at Brian and David. "We are firefighters, we put our lives at risk every time we go into a burning building or come into contact with hazardous materials! How is that any different than diving down into the water?"

Brian looks at Jeff. "Did you really just ask us that? It's not any different! We don't go into a burning building without backup! Just like diving, you don't do it without backup! You would NEVER let a diver go down by himself so why would you do it! I'm sorry but as your best friend, I can't let you do this by yourself! You know damn well that it is not safe for any diver to do alone, especially during the wintertime and at night!"

Jeff stares at Brian and David. "Shit!" He sighs as he drops the equipment and leans up against the railing of the boat rubbing his face with both hands as Brian continues.

"We have searched a huge part of this lake already, Jeff. Not finding Joe is a good thing. It means he may still be alive. These divers need to go home, take a nice long hot shower and spend time with their families. They're tired and worn out and some of them are volunteers so they aren't even getting paid to do this. They're here because they wanted to help, don't take advantage of that. This search is over, Jeff. Joe is not down there."

Jeff throws his hands up. "You guys are right and I know that. I just hate giving up, especially when it involves a kid, whether it's family or not."

"We gave this search our two hundred percent so we are not giving up. We did what we could. We searched everywhere down there. We cannot continue looking for something that is not there," says David.

"I know! I know! You guys are right." Jeff shakes his head as he lets out another huge sigh. "I'm sorry. Let's get the other group of divers out of the water and send everybody home."

"Okay, now you're talking," says Brian.

Chapter Eighteen

When Jeff arrives home he puts his coat away and immediately peeks in on Dakota to make sure she's sleeping, then checks on Adam, their three-year-old son. He gives Adam a kiss on the head, adjusts his blanket then starts to leave the room.

"Daddy?"

Jeff stops and turns around. He walks back toward Adam. "Hey, buddy. What are you doing awake?"

"I missed you."

"I missed you too, buddy," he says as he sits down on the bed next to Adam.

"Is it story time?"

Jeff puts his index finger to his lips. "Shhh, keep your voice down or you'll wake up mommy. No, it's sleepy time. Come on. Go back to sleep. Okay? I'll tell you a story tomorrow night."

"Okay. Love you, daddy."

Jeff grins from ear to ear as he kisses Adam again on the head. *I never get tired of hearing that.* "I love you too, buddy. Now, go back to sleep."

"Okay." Jeff sits with Adam until he falls back to sleep then goes out to the family room.

He's been sitting on the couch with the light dimmed low for about an hour when Dakota wakes up and comes looking for him. Leaning up against the family room wall she calls out startling him.

"Jeff?"

"Shit! You scared me. Baby, what are you doing up?"

"I'm sorry I didn't mean to scare you. I got worried when I woke up and didn't see you lying next to me." She walks toward him and sits down next to him. "Why are you sitting in the dark?"

"I'm sorry if I woke you up."

"You didn't. I haven't been able to sleep very well because of this whole thing with Joe. Are you okay?"

"I have to tell you something, baby." He grabs one of her hands and holds it tight. "The search that me and my dive team had to do down at the lake…it was a search for Joe."

"Oh my god!" Her other hand instantly covers her mouth.

Jeff tightens his grip in assurance. "We did NOT find him. We've been searching for three days. If Joe were in that lake we would have found him by now. But we did find his car in the lake."

"In the lake?"

"Yes. We also found three bodies, one of which was in the trunk of Joe's car. All three bodies found were gang members."

"Oh my god!" she says again in shock.

"Baby, I really hate having to tell you this but we also found heroin inside the glove compartment of Joe's car."

Dakota shakes her head in disbelief. "I don't believe it. It couldn't have been Joe's. Are you…?"

"I know what you're going to say and yes we are absolutely sure that it belongs to Joe. I know this is hard to believe and hard to take in, baby. I'm so sorry. After our search last night, Chief Franks and I went to Michael's house to talk to Andy and your brothers."

Tears are streaming down her face. "How did Andy take the news about the gang members and the drugs?"

"Not well at all. He took off like a bat out of hell for his house and once he got there he started tearing apart Joe's room like a bad tornado."

"Was he looking for more drugs?"

"Yes. All of us started searching Joe's room."

"Were there any drugs found in his room?"

"Yes, unfortunately we found eight preloaded hypodermic needles and very little drug paraphernalia."

"Oh, shit. Oh my god. I can't believe this." Dakota starts to cry harder. "Why didn't you tell me this sooner?" She puts her face in her hands as she cries.

"I wasn't sure how to tell you. I knew this was going to be hard for you and your family."

"Is that why you're sitting in the dark? You were trying to figure out how to tell me?"

"Yeah, but then realized that there was not going to be an easy way to tell you. From what we found in Joe's room I believe that he is very new to using drugs."

"What makes you think that?"

"There wasn't nearly as much drug paraphernalia and drugs in his room as there would normally would be if he were an avid drug user. If a person is a heavy drug user and has been on it for quite a while you would find a lot more drugs and paraphernalia than what we found."

"That's good news isn't it?"

"Yeah, baby, it is. It means that if they find Joe alive it may be easier to get him off of that shit. That's if he hasn't been hitting it heavy."

"I would like to go to Michael's and see Andy. I want to be there for him."

"Okay. We'll go tomorrow. I'm off for the next couple of days. First I want you to try and get some sleep. You're sleeping for three now you know." He says in a cute way as he taps Dakota's chin.

"Yes, I am." She smiles back. Did you see Adam when you got home? He kept asking for you when I was trying to put him to bed. He refused to go to sleep until he became too tired to fight it anymore."

Jeff smiles. "Yes, I did. I checked in on him when I got home."

"Okay, good."

Chapter Nineteen

Michael arrives at the break wall, where the Chief is already waiting.

"Is this where Joe's car went off the wall?" Michael asks as he gets out of his car.

"Yeah, it is. I want to bring you up to speed on Joe's case."

"I appreciate that."

"I had Ralph in the lab do the tire impressions and compare them with Joe's car."

"Were you able to figure out where Joe's car went off?" Michael asks.

"It went over the wall over there." Chief Franks points toward the tracks. Michael starts leading in that direction as the Chief follows and continues to explain. "There are skid marks and long ones."

"Skid marks from Joe's car?"

"No, we believe they're from the other car."

Michael stops and stares at Chief Franks. "Are you saying he was run off the break wall?"

"That's exactly what I'm saying." The Chief takes out some photos of Joe's car after it was retrieved from the lake and hands them to Michael. "The evidence garage took these photos. What do you see on the back of Joe's car?"

"There's a lot of red paint on the bumper."

"Yeah, and Joe's car is white. I don't know if that red paint was previous to this incident or due to this incident."

Michael raises his eyebrows. "That would be something to ask Andy. I don't think Joe has ever been involved in any accidents."

"That's what I want you to find out. I just hope Andy knows the answer. If it wasn't there before, then that means we need to start looking for a red car." Then Chief Franks says sarcastically. "That narrows it down."

"Yeah, you're not kidding. Talk about trying to find a needle in a haystack but it's a lead. One we didn't have before. Is there anything else?"

"No."

"Do you mind if I take these? I'll go talk to Andy right now and call you or send you a text."

"You can have those copies, I have more. Let me know what he says."

"I will."

When Michael arrives home, he finds Andy in the kitchen working. "Working from home again?"

"Yeah. I want to stay close to Bethany."

"I think that's a good idea." Michael reaches in his pocket for the pictures of Joe's car. "Andy, I have to ask you something about Joe's car."

Andy takes off his reading glasses and sets them down on the table. "Sure, what about it?"

Michael hands the pictures to him. "These pictures were taken of Joe's car after it was pulled from the lake. Look at the photo that shows the back of the car."

Andy flips a couple of pictures in to find the photo Michael is referring too. "Okay, what am I...where did this red paint come from?" Andy immediately notices the red paint marks on the bumper.

"I was hoping you would know."

"I have no idea. Joe is on my insurance so he would have told me if he had gotten into an accident. This wasn't there before."

"Are you sure?"

"Yeah, Michael, I'm positive. I helped him with his car a couple of days before he disappeared."

"What do you mean you helped him with his car? How?"

"Joe decided to wax his car for the first time and as a first timer he did what most guys do…"

"Keep the wax on for too long?" Michael says as he chuckles lightly.

"Exactly. He came into the house upset because he couldn't get the wax off of the car. He thought he ruined his car. Come to find out, he waxed it out in the sun in the driveway and then let the wax sit for about an hour. I had to buff his entire car out for him, so I know for a fact that this red paint was not there."

"And when did you say this was?"

"A couple of days before he disappeared. Why do you ask?"

"Because it could mean one of two things. One, he had gotten into an accident with someone or something and didn't get a chance to tell you, or somebody who owns a red car ran him off the break wall."

"Didn't Bethany say that Shawn has a red car?"

"Yeah. Chief Franks is talking with Shawn now."

"If that son of a bitch has anything to do with…"

"Andy, don't jump to conclusions yet. We don't know for sure it was Shawn who did it. I need to call the Chief and let him know that this red paint wasn't here before so we need to look for a red car."

Chapter Twenty

Detective Barbado enters the interrogation room with a file containing pictures as Chief Franks watches from the observation room. Without saying a word, he lays the pictures out on the table. Once he's finished he waits and watches Shawn's reaction.

"Why do you have a picture of my watch?" asks Shawn.

"Good, that means I now have two confirmations and the description on the watch to prove it's yours."

"Where did you find it?"

"In Joe's car. How did it get there, Shawn?"

"I don't know how it got there! Maybe he stole it from me."

"You know damn well he didn't steal your watch! How did it get there?"

"I don't know!"

Detective Barbado slides a picture in front of Shawn showing the red paint on Joe's back bumper. "Look familiar to you?"

"No, should it?"

Detective Barbado's cell phone rings. He looks and sees it's Chief Franks. *Why is Chief Franks calling me from the observation room?* "This is Detective Barbado."

"I just got word that they found Shawn's car. It's at the evidence garage. They're checking to see if the paint or tire tracks are a match."

"Okay, thanks." Barbado hangs up his cell phone and looks at Shawn. "To answer your question, yes, it should! It's paint from your car on Joe's back bumper! It got there when you ran Joe's car off the break wall!"

"WHAT? Man you're out of your mind! My car never touched Joe's car!"

"We've impounded your car, Shawn, so it would be in your best interest to start talking before we…"

"Look over my entire car, search my entire car, I don't give a shit, because there's no red paint missing on it! I never ran anybody off the break wall! I don't know what the hell you're talking about! I didn't do it!"

An hour later there's a knock on the door then Officer Stewart enters and whispers something in Detective Barbado's ear.

"I'll be right back, Shawn," says the detective.

Detective Barbado steps out of the interrogation room to find Michael standing in the hallway with Chief Franks. "Michael, what's going on?"

"As much as I would love to nail this kid, I can't nail him for Joe's disappearance. Not yet anyways. The other tire tracks we found at the break wall did not match Shawn's car. The paint was extremely close but it didn't match either."

"WHAT? So we're now looking for a different red car?"

"Yeah, I'm afraid so."

"Shit! Could this get any worse? We still don't know how or why Shawn's watch ended up in Joe's car." Just as Detective Barbado says that a man dressed in a suit carrying a briefcase walks up and addresses Detective Barbado and Michael. "It just got worse," whispers Barbado.

"Detectives," says the well-dressed gentleman.

Detective Barbado is the first to shake his hand. "Attorney Cesar Layton, what are you doing here?"

"I am representing Shawn Kemp. His mother hired me to take his case. I believe you're working on the case that he's a suspect in?"

Michael responds. "There is no case against Kemp. We're just asking him some questions."

"Well, now you can ask him some questions in the presence of his attorney."

"We can go into the observation room and fill you in," says Michael.

"That's quite alright. I'm up to speed on the case already. I would like to see my client now."

Chief Franks opens the door to the interrogation room. "Right this way, sir."

"Thank you, Chief. Oh and, Michael. I'm surprised you're working this case. Since it is a conflict of interest and all. Joe, the missing teenager, isn't he your nephew?"

"Yes, he is. I'll admit it, Cesar, I so badly want to get the son of a bitch that is responsible for my nephew's disappearance, but I am NOT willing to pin it on just anybody. That's not how I operate. I want the true perpetrator that's responsible for this just like you do."

"With you, I can truly believe that."

"Somebody is working closely with Michael." The Chief immediately comes to Michael's defense. Layton nods his head and says nothing more as he enters the interrogation room.

Michael looks at Barbado and Chief Franks. "This attorney is good, real good. He doesn't miss a beat and he is very, very thorough. Shawn's mother hired a good one. We have to release him. We have no hard evidence to hold him."

You can hear the frustration in Barbado's voice as he responds, "what about his watch being found in Joe's car or Joe's blood found at the bridge? Shawn admitted fighting with Joe."

"You know as well as I do, that is not hard evidence. It helps but it doesn't build a case. So he got into a fight with Joe, unfortunately it's not proof that he has anything to do with Joe's disappearance. And as for Shawn's watch, you know they could argue that part of it and say that Joe and Shawn were friends and that Shawn dropped it in Joe's car one night when they went out. We've got nothing to hold him on. I don't like it anymore than you do."

Barbado shakes his head. "I think he knows more than he's telling."

"I think he does to, but his attorney is involved now so it's going to be harder to get it out of him," says the Chief.

"I know I'm not working outside the lab on this case, but if you two don't mind, since Layton and I have such a good rapport with each other, when he comes back out I want to throw that deal we first offered to Shawn at him. Maybe we can put Shawn back out on the street and use him as an informant."

Barbado and Chief Franks look at each other and agree. "That's fine with me." "Maybe that would be a good idea."

"What do we have…?"

Michael is interrupted when Layton comes back out of the interrogation room. "That was quick," says Chief Franks.

"I told you, I'm up to speed on this case already. All I had to do is talk to my client and make sure he agrees with the decision of me defending him and get a little bit of information from him."

"And does he agree?" Michael asks.

"Yes, he does."

"Good, then I have something to share with you." Michael hands the file that he's holding to the attorney. Feel free to take a look." *This will prove to him that I can be unbiased in this case even though it involves my nephew.*

Layton opens the file and seems relieved at what he sees. "Lab results. Extra tire tracks found at the scene are not a match to Shawn Kemp's car."

"Read further, Cesar. Neither does the paint," says Michael.

Cesar Layton continues to review the files. "Hmm, paint comparison is extremely close but doesn't match Shawn's car either." Layton hands the file back to Michael with a raised eyebrow and an impressed look. "Since you have nothing against my client then I suggest you release him immediately."

Michael gestures toward the observation room. "Not so fast, Cesar. That boy still has warrants for his arrest that are unrelated to this case. There's nobody in the observation room let's go talk in there." Barbado and Chief Franks stay behind allowing Michael to negotiate with Layton alone.

"I have a deal that I would like to offer. Actually, it's something we offered Shawn when all of this started but he never gave us an answer."

Layton leans up against the wall intrigued to hear what Michael has to say. "Okay, I'm listening."

"Shawn may not have anything to do with Joe's disappearance but we think he knows something about it. Call it instincts if you will, but he knows something. We are willing to work with him on the warrants if he helps us."

"That's going to depend on what it is that you want him to do."

"Help us find Joe, give up the name of his drug leader in his gang. We have proof that his gang is the biggest drug cartel in our county. If we can nail the ringleader and actually catch them making a deal, then we can crack down on a huge amount of drug trafficking in our town. We want their biggest customer and the name of the person who shot up my brother Andy's house the night Joe disappeared."

"That's a lot you want from him."

"Come on, Cesar. Shawn has a warrant for drug trafficking, armed robbery and accessory to murder, although we can't quite prove that last charge yet, but he can go to jail for quite a while just on the first two charges alone. Those we do have hard evidence for."

"My understanding is, he was more like a witness to murder, not an accessory to murder. What makes you think that my client can find Joe or help you find who shot up Andy's house?"

"He's a gangbanger, Cesar. Gangbangers know more of what is going on out on the streets than the cops do and if they don't know they have ways of finding out. I should know, I used a few gangbangers as informants when I was a cop and as a detective I still do on occasion."

"If he gives up the name of his drug leader or any other information they'll kill him for sure or worse his mother. What are you going to do to ensure that doesn't happen?"

"His mother has already agreed to relocate to another state and change her name if she has to if it means getting her son back on the right track again. He'll get a fresh start then it's up to him to keep his ass out of trouble. If he doesn't then he's on his own."

"What about his warrants?"

"I told him we'd drop all charges for the drug trafficking and the robbery but if he ever comes back into our town again we will arrest him. Once he leaves this town, there's no coming back here again."

"What about the accessory to murder charge. Neither one of us can prove anything on that one either way, you know that. Drop that charge too, since we have no hard evidence, and then I'll consider the deal."

Michael thinks for a moment. "No, if I do that then you'll take the deal and get your client to take it too, but it's only because we have no hard evidence against him for it."

"Fair enough. Do you have a game plan as to how you want him to help you?"

"Regarding the drug leader and biggest customer, he can tell us that now and we'll take it from there. If he doesn't know who shot up my brother's house or where Joe is then he needs to discreetly snoop around and find out. If he doesn't find out the correct information then we have no deal. We won't wire him. If they find a wire on him they will kill him for sure. We will put a GPS chip in his phone and track him so we will know where he is at all times. We're not going to tell him about the GPS chip otherwise he may either leave his phone behind or destroy it. He would have to check in with Detective Barbado every three hours starting from the time we release him until midnight. Then he has to check in by seven in the morning and every three hours from there, until midnight again every day. The first time he misses calling Barbado or doesn't pick up if Barbado calls him, we will pick his ass up and the deal is off. We don't trust him, Cesar, but we have to trust him if that makes any sense."

"Yes, it does make sense. What if he's with his gang then he can't call or answer his phone?"

"Then he better find a way to communicate back to us. By text if he has to. I don't give a shit. Every three hours, one way or another he better contact us. We will not budge on this part of the deal, Cesar."

Cesar nods his head in agreement. "Okay, seems fair enough. I'll put it out there to him and see what he says. I'll try to convince him that taking this deal would be in his best interest and his mothers. I'll push him but I'm not making any promises, Michael."

"I know. Thank you. But I'm not too worried about him not taking it. You're pretty good with convincing your clients to do the right thing."

"My files show that Detective Barbado is leading this investigation and you're strictly labs, is that correct?" The tone of his voice gives Michael the feeling that Layton doesn't trust him.

"Yes, that's correct. What, you don't trust me with the evidence?"

"Oh, on the contrary, Detective, I would trust you with my life. You're a good detective and one of the most honest detectives I've met. I'm just making sure that's where you're at with this case. This case is so personal to you that I can't see you being unbiased out in the field with suspects."

"Other than making deals with you, unfortunately, the lab is as far as the Chief is willing to allow me to go on this."

"Yes, detective, it is unfortunate. It's unfortunate that the victim in this case is your family member. You would have been good out in the field for this case. You know, I kind of like you. I have to say that you've never thrown ridiculous deals at me. They've always been fair."

"And you've always been reasonable enough to accept them and most of the time, get your clients to accept them to and I appreciate that."

"You are one of the very few that do. Stay out of the observation room. I want some privacy to talk to my client."

"You got it."

They shake hands and leave the observation room. Layton returns to the interrogation room while Michael fills in Barbado and Chief Franks.

"What's the word?" Barbado asks.

"If Shawn agrees to help us find Joe, the shooter responsible for Andy's house and gives us his drug leader and biggest customer then we'll drop the charges against him for his warrants. If he doesn't know the information then he has to get it for us."

"Even the accessory to murder charge for the gang members? Do you think that's wise?"

"We have no hard evidence either way to prove he was involved. We have evidence that shows he was there at some point but nothing proving that he did it or was an accomplice to it. He could have showed up after the fact like he said he did. With that being said, yeah, I think we should relinquish him of all three warrants if it means getting what we need. It would be huge for us if we are able to bust the biggest drug dealer in town and their biggest customer."

"You're right, it would be. That would be really good for our town."

"If Shawn accepts the deal will you write it up since technically I'm not supposed to be working this part of the case?" Michael glances at Chief Franks knowing that the Chief has allowed him to step out of bounds this one time.

"Yes, of course. What else did you guys agree on?"

"We would relocate Shawn and his mother to another state of their choosing and change their names if they want them changed."

"Kind of like a witness protection program."

"Something like that, yeah. Every day he has to check in with you by phone or text by seven a.m. in the morning and every three hours after that, starting from the time we release him. If he misses

164

just one check in time or he doesn't pick up just one of your calls, then we will pick his ass up and the deal is off. Which means the charges will stick. I told him that we wouldn't budge on that part of the deal. Layton feels the deal is good and fair. He's talking to Shawn now to see if he'll take it."

Barbado turns to the officer standing outside the interrogation room. "I'll be in my office, please let Layton know where I am once he's finished in there."

"No problem, detective."

Barbado shakes Michael's hand. "I'll call you as soon as I know if Shawn's accepted the deal or not."

"Great, thank you, I appreciate that." Barbado walks away leaving Chief Franks and Michael standing in the hallway. "I have to get back to the lab."

"What are you working on?" the Chief asks.

"There were several blood samples taken from the bridge the day we arrested Shawn and so far none of them matches Shawn's blood type. One matched Joe's now I'm trying to figure out who the others belong to."

"Great, what did they do, have a shoot out over there?"

"I don't know but I think Layton needs to ask his client more questions about the night Shawn fought with Joe. Maybe there were more guys involved. I don't know."

"I'll send some guys back out to the bridge and comb over that area again."

"Sounds like a good idea. I'll talk to you later."

"Alright, talk you later."

A couple of hours later Michael hears his cell phone ring so he looks to see who it is.

"Detective Barbado, what's the word?"

"Michael, Shawn took our deal. He gave up the name of the drug leader in his gang but said he's not sure who their biggest client is. Says he hasn't gone on too many deals with them to know but says he'll find out for us."

"Excellent! Layton is very good at talking his clients into taking deals."

"Chief Franks released Shawn a half hour ago."

"Who's tracking the GPS in his phone?"

"Officers Welch and Brown are assigned to his surveillance."

"Good, let's hope Shawn comes through for us and finds some answers."

"He says he doesn't know who shot up Andy's house but may have an idea who did. Says he'll find out for us. He also claims that he doesn't know anything about what happened to Joe other than the fight he and Joe had. I don't know how much of that I believe."

"I don't believe much of that either. Can you please keep me updated on everything? I have some things to finish up here then I have a stakeout tonight for another case."

"Absolutely. Stay safe tonight."

"That's the plan. Thank you."

"You bet. We'll talk again soon."

"Bye."

It's about nine thirty at night and Michael has finished getting ready for his stake out tonight. He grabs his keys and wallet from the coffee table.

"I've got to get going. I'll see you in the morning."

"Be careful out there, okay?" says Andy.

"I will."

Andy sits watching television when a commercial about lawn care comes on. They're showing a family running and playing in nice green soft grass. Suddenly, Andy grabs his cell phone and calls Chuck.

"Hello?"

"Hey, Chuck."

"Andy, it's late. Is everything okay?"

"Yeah, it is. I'm sorry to call you so late but I have a favor to ask."

"Sure, what's up?"

"Can you come to Michael's and stay with the kids for a little bit?"

"What are you up to, Andy?"

"It's not what you think. There's some place I need to pay a visit to."

"Where?"

"I'll tell you once you get here. It's all good, bro."

"Okay. I'm on my way."

"Thank you."

Chapter Twenty-One

It's early in the morning and Andy is standing in the sunroom watching the sun come up over the horizon. Michael grabs a couple of cups of coffee and joins him.

"Here, it's a good thing this sunroom is heated." Michael says as he hands Andy a cup.

"Thank you. Yes, it does stay nice and warm. You don't have to keep checking up on me. I'm doing okay."

"I'm not. I didn't know you were out here until I came out."

"Hmm, so you always walk around with two cups of coffee in your hands."

Michael smirks as he answers. "All right, you got me on that one." Andy smirks back. "You seem pretty mesmerized by the sunrise. Do you want to share what you're thinking?"

Andy continues staring toward the sunrise. "Yes actually, I do. There's something I want to talk to you about. I've already spoken to Chuck about it last night." Andy turns and looks at Michael. "You're probably going to think I'm nuts."

Michael nods his head. "You are, but we're okay with that." He says as he chuckles to keep things lightened up. Andy smirks too. "Seriously though, what's on your mind?"

"I went to visit mom and dad's graves last night."

"Taking notes from our sister I see. Didn't she pull a late night visit once too?"

"Yes, she did."

"You really went to the cemetery?"

"Yeah. I was talking to mom and dad telling them about Joe.... when something really weird happened and I would have never believed it myself if I hadn't seen it with my own eyes."

"At the cemetery? Now you've got me curious. What happened?"

"I asked mom and dad for advice on something, then told them that I wish they could give me some sort of a sign if they felt it was a good idea. All of the sudden, a freaking rock landed by my foot."

"A rock? You're right, you are nuts."

"I knew you'd say that."

"There are no rocks in that cemetery or at least no where near mom and dad."

"I know. That's what's so weird about it. I don't know where it came from. There was nobody else in that cemetery but me. No one! And it landed right next to my foot after hitting the tip of my shoe. It freaked me out at first but then I took it as a sign that mom and dad were answering me. I know it sounds crazy but that's what happened." Andy turns back to look at the sunrise.

"What advise did you ask mom and dad for?"

Andy becomes choked up as he responds. "If Joe's found...." Michael nudges Andy with his arm making him change his wording. "When...Joe's found...I want to put him into a drug rehabilitation facility. I was asking mom and dad if they thought that would be the right thing to do. I took that rock as a sign that they agreed. It would really tear me..."

"Yes it would be the right thing to do, absolutely."

"So you agree too?"

"Whether it's my nephew or my own kid, I think that is the best decision. You need to nip that drug problem in the ass now before it becomes worse. Is that what you spoke to Chuck about last night? If he thought it was a good idea too?"

"Yeah."

"Knowing the way Chuck is, I think you already knew what his answer was going to be. Hell, he may even drive Joe to the center himself."

"He agreed too. It will tear me up, to do it but I think it has to be done. I'm just afraid of doing more harm than good if I lock him up."

"You wouldn't be locking him up. You'll be trying to help him. He may not understand why at first but in the long run he'll understand why you did it."

"If he's suffering from depression then putting him into one of those centers may just depress him even more."

"They will help him with any depression he may have."

"If he is depressed, I don't want my son medicated. I want him to be able to deal with his depression and get through it without medication."

"Andy, he may have to be put on medication for depression at first. Sometimes that's the only way to get a patient to talk. If you can bring down the depression they may be more likely to want to open up. Then the therapist can help him."

"I don't know, Michael. I don't want him on antidepressants for the rest of his life. I don't want that for him."

"He may not have to be and I don't think he will be. I think whatever it is he's going through has a lot, if not everything to do with losing his mom. He was fine before she passed away. If he is depressed and you don't allow them to put him on medication for it then you WILL be doing him more harm than good."

"Yeah, I've thought about that too."

"I have an idea. Why don't we talk to Jeff? In his line of work he has a lot of connections with different centers. Maybe we can tour a few of them and you can see for yourself how the staff interacts with their patients. You can ask them questions about how they handle a patient with depression. Chief Franks is a firm believer of surprise visits. He believes that if they're doing something wrong they can't hide it if they don't know you're coming. So we won't call, we'll just show up."

"I think that is a great idea. Thank you."

"You're welcome, I'll call Jeff."

"Okay. What's on your agenda for the day other than the lab?"

"I'm going to work on my other case for a little bit this morning then go to the lab for little while this afternoon."

"Is the lab regarding Joe's case?"

"Yeah."

"I know you can't tell me a whole lot about the other case you've been working on, but how is it coming along? How did your stakeout go last night?"

"I'm very close to busting this case wide open."

"That's awesome, Michael. You've been working on that case for a few years now."

"Yeah. This may be my biggest bust of my career."

"Proud of you, man. You've really done great for yourself and for Tony."

"Thanks, but don't forget I had some help with Tony from family too. You need to get ready. Chuck will be by to pick you up soon."

"You guys really don't need to keep driving me to Schillers. I can drive my self and I will go. I'm too afraid of what Chief Franks may do to me if I don't go." Andy chuckles.

"Chuck and I are only doing what Chief Franks said we had to do. I'll call the Chief later too."

After Andy leaves the sunroom, Michael takes out his cell phone and calls Chester Brantley, a detective that's working with him on another case.

"Hello?"

"Hey, Chester. It's Michael."

"Hi, Michael. I received your message about the stakeout last night. Do you really think the gang's biggest buyer is that group?"

"Yes. I really do think it's them. We weren't able to see their faces last night but something seems very familiar with two of the guys they were meeting with."

"That seems really hard to believe though."

"Yeah, well. My gut strongly says it's them. If it really is who I think it is, then we have to be extra careful because those guys are extremely smart and quick. They don't mess around."

"What do you want us to do now?"

"Bring in our two biggest informants and find Shawn. I'll meet with them before I go to the lab. We need to find out what their alternate meeting locations are and what their usual meeting times are."

"Alternate?"

"I told you, these guys are smart. They may set up a meeting in one place but then at the last minute they'll change it to another location, which is why they haven't been caught yet."

"Okay, we'll pick up the informants and find Shawn. We'll see you later," says Chester.

Michael responds, "see you later. Keep me updated."

"I will."

Chapter Twenty-Two

Andy is at Schillers' for his session and Michael is preparing to head to the station then to the lab.

"Bethany?"

"Yes, Uncle Michael?"

"Tony is coming with me to the station and then to the lab. Even though you and your dad are staying at my house for a while, don't forget that you are still grounded and not allowed to leave the house."

"I know, Uncle Michael. I haven't forgotten."

"I'm just making sure. Your dad and Uncle Chuck should be back from Doctor Schiller's in about an hour."

"Okay." Bethany gives Michael a hug and kiss goodbye.

"We'll see you later."

Three hours later, Michael's, cell phone rings. "Hi, Chief."

"Hi, Michael. Are you still at the lab?"

"Yes, I am."

"How's it going? Find anything yet?"

"I'm working on the rest of the blood samples and fingerprints that were taken from the bridge. I have three sets of prints other than Joe and Shawn's and two other different blood types that were lifted off of various things around the bridge. I'm in the middle of entering two of the prints now into the NCIC system. Hopefully the combination of prints and blood types will match somebody or at least a match to the prints would be nice."

"How many people were at the bridge?"

"Well, we've obtained Bethany's, Joe's and Shawn's prints and ruled those out. So if you count them out, that means there were at least two more people that have been at that bridge."

"Joe's? How did you get his?"

"I lifted his prints from his bedroom."

"No, shit. That was a good idea. But I thought Shawn said nobody knew about his and Bethany's secret place until Joe followed her there?"

"Maybe somebody followed Joe or Shawn there. I don't know. But there were definitely other people there."

"Hmm, I'm curious now as to who those other people are. Let me know what you find out."

"I will. I'll talk to you later, Chief."

"Okay, bye."

Michael was very happy and very willing to bring Tony along to the lab, hoping that maybe it will become a career choice for Tony once he's out of school. Although, in order for Tony to go to the lab he had to promise not to touch anything and to keep everything he sees or hears confidential since Michael is working on a case. Michael inputs all of the information he has for two of the fingerprints and blood samples into the system as Tony asks questions.

"Dad, what's NCIC?"

"It stands for, 'National Crime Information Center'."

"What does it do?"

"We input fingerprints, tattoos or even dental records into the system, if there's a match it tells us right away who they are and where their last known address was."

"Can you run just blood types alone?"

"No, you can't. You can be 'A' positive and I can be 'A' positive, that's not going to help somebody find us. Fingerprints, dental records and tattoos are always the best way to find

174

information on somebody. You can use blood types but you need something else to go along with it to get a positive match."

"Like fingerprints, tattoos or dental records?"

"Yep."

"Wow, that's pretty cool."

"Yes, it is." Michael says as he turns to grab another fingerprint sample.

"Dad, the screen is flashing the word 'MATCH'."

"What?" Michael turns around immediately and looks at the screen. "I'll be damn, we have two matches."

"Who are they?"

"Both gangbangers, Tony. One is George Desoto and the other one is Jose Shepherd. It even shows their pictures." Michael quickly enters a third print into the system but comes up empty. "Well, two out of three isn't bad."

"They even look like gangbangers, dad."

Michael laughs at Tony's comment. "Yes they do, buddy."

"What are you going to do with the information now?"

"Well, since I'm not working out in the field on this case, I'm going turn the information over to Detective Barbado and he'll share the information with Chief Franks."

"Cool," says Tony. "It's amazing the things you can do in the lab."

"Yes, it is."

Michael picks up the phone and calls Barbado. "Hello?"

"Justin, I've got a match to two of the three prints from the bridge."

"Really? Whose are they?"

"George Desoto and Jose Shepherd."

"Local gang members. The same ones found in and near Joe's car."

"Yep, I think Shawn has more explaining to do. I don't think he's been completely truthful about Joe. Has anyone found Shawn yet?"

"No, they're still looking for him."

"Good, we really need to get Shawn back into that interrogation room again."

"Let me call Layton now and I'll follow up with Chief Franks too."

"Okay. Thank you."

"You're welcome. I'll keep you informed."

"Thanks."

Chapter Twenty-Three

I am sitting on the couch watching television wondering where my dad is. I turn down the volume and grab my cell phone to call him.

"Hi, honey."

"Hi, dad. Where are you guys? I thought you were coming right home after Schillers."

"We had to make a couple of stops. We'll be home in a few minutes."

"Okay, see you when you get home."

"Is everything okay?"

"Yeah, I was just wondering where you guys were at?"

"Okay. We'll see you in a few minutes."

"Okay, bye."

I hang up the phone and turn the TV volume back up, when suddenly somebody puts a hand over my mouth.

"Please don't scream. I won't hurt you, you know that." *Oh my god, that's Shawn's voice!* "I'm going to remove my hand. Please do not scream. Nod your head if you understand."

I nod my head yes and he removes his hand then walks around the couch so he's standing in front of me.

"Shawn, what are you doing here? How did you get in here? My Uncle and dad will be back soon."

"I know. I came in through the back door. I've been watching the house so I know what time your dad's appointments are in the morning. I was waiting for you to be alone. I was just running late getting here."

"You were watching the house? How did you know about my dad's appointments? How did you know where my Uncle lives? Did you follow somebody here?"

"You make it sound so creepy."

"That is creepy, Shawn! I believe they call that stalking."

"Call it what you want I don't care but you're coming with me. Grab your coat and gloves. They've impounded my car so we'll have to walk," he says as he grabs my arm.

"I can't leave the house. I'm grounded!"

"Not anymore you're not." Shawn pulls me up to my feet.

"Where are we going?"

"We're getting out of this town."

"Shawn, let go of me! I can't go with you!" I yank my arm out of his grasp.

"Bethany, I love you and I am not leaving without you. You are in a lot of danger. I need to take you somewhere safe."

"Why am I in danger?"

"My gang found out about you. I don't know how. I don't want to take the chance of them coming after you. They were responsible for shooting at your house."

"Oh my god! What about the deal you made with the lawyers?"

"I just told them what they wanted to hear and gave them false information so they'd release me. We have to go now, come on!" He pulls on my arm trying to make me follow him.

"Stop it! Let go of me! I don't want to go with you!"

He grabs my coat and hands it to me, then stops and looks at me. "What? I thought you wanted us to be together?"

"Not anymore. The whole time we were together you kept secrets from me and lied to me, Shawn. You even tried lying about the fight you and my brother had. When it comes to my family, I draw the line. You don't mess with my family, Shawn! I can't trust you."

"I told you that I didn't want you mixed up in my gang life and that's why I didn't tell you about it! And your brother, like I told you, he came at me! I am not leaving this town without you!"

"Let go of me!"

Just as he pulls me toward the front door, it opens. *Oh, thank god! It's Uncle Chuck and my dad!* They suddenly stop just inside the doorway. My dad makes eye contact with Shawn and says in a very controlled voice.

"Sweetheart, are you okay?"

"Yes, dad. He hasn't hurt me."

"Good. If you harm just one hair on my daughter's head, I swear to god I will kill you."

I notice Uncle Chuck sneaking his cell phone out of his pocket as my dad is speaking to Shawn.

Shawn responds as he tries to convince my dad that he means no harm. "I am not going to hurt Bethany, Mr. Phillips. I love her."

Michael's cell phone rings but since he's right in the middle of placing another sample of something into the NCIC system he has Tony answer it.

"Hey, buddy. Would you see who that is that's calling me?"

"Sure, dad." Tony leans over and looks at the caller I.D. on the cell phone. "It's Uncle Chuck."

"Okay, put it on speaker."

Tony presses the speaker button. "Okay, it's on speaker."

"Hey, Chuck, what's going on?" There's no answer. "Chuck? Hello?"

Suddenly, he hears voices in the background.

"If you love her then you'll let go of her," says Andy.

"She's coming with me. We're getting out of this town."

"You'll have to get past me first. Nobody is taking my daughter anywhere. That includes you."

Looking confused, Michael turns and looks at the cell phone as he whispers. "What the hell? Are you sure that's Uncle Chuck?"

Tony picks up the cell phone and shows his dad. "Yeah, see it says, 'Chuck'. What's going on, dad?"

"Shhh." Michael puts his hand up telling Tony to keep quiet so he can listen.

I see Uncle Chuck glance down at his phone then he starts asking Shawn questions. "Shawn, how did you know that Bethany was staying here?"

"I followed you guys here yesterday."

Michael looks at Tony and says in a low voice. "They're at our house."

"Shawn, please let go of me. You're hurting my arm." I plead hoping that he'll listen to me and let me go.

"Why, so you can run from me? I told you that you're coming with me. We're supposed to be together."

"I don't want to go with you Shawn. Please! Let go of me!" I try breaking loose from his grip but he's holding me too tight.

"Shut up!"

My dad becomes angrier. "You better watch how you speak to my daughter! Let go of her! She doesn't want to go with you!"

"I'm trying to protect her! She has to come with me, now!"

"Protect her from what?" Chuck asks.

Michael looks at Tony and whispers as he takes off his gloves. "I'm going to call Chief Franks from the lab phone. Send Uncle Chuck a text telling him that I'm on my way."

"Okay, dad."

Tony types a brief text and hits send. "I'M ON MY WAY. CALLING CHIEF FRANKS TOO!"

Luckily Shawn doesn't hear it but I do, I hear the sound of Uncle Chuck's phone quietly vibrate. He glances down and suddenly looks relieved. Shawn starts walking us backwards still holding me tight.

"Shawn, please let go of me."

Shawn kisses the back of my head, which makes my dad's face turn red in anger.

"Bethany, you're coming with me. It's safer for you this way."

"Shawn, if you leave here with Bethany then you'll be charged with kidnapping too. Let her go. You're already in enough trouble as it is. You'll get more jail time if you take her." Uncle Chuck says trying to remind him to do the right thing.

"They'll have to catch me first."

Uncle Chuck puts his arm out in front of my dad to keep him from approaching us. "Where are you going, Shawn?" he asks as he discreetly slides his cell phone back into his front pocket.

"I told you. Bethany and I are getting out of this town."

"You're not taking my niece with you."

I start crying. Suddenly, Shawn pulls out a switchblade and holds it in front of my neck but doesn't touch me with it.

"Do you want to try and stop me? Because it seems to me that I'm the one in control here, not you."

You can hear the fear in my dad's voice as he pleads with Shawn. "Please don't hurt my daughter."

"He won't hurt her, Andy."

"I don't want to but I will if I have to," says Shawn.

"No you won't. You love her too much to hurt her. You don't hurt the ones you love. Even you know that."

"You don't know shit about me." Shawn walks us a few more steps back.

"Shawn, please don't hurt anybody. I'll go with you." I plead as I continue crying and keeping my eye on the knife in his hand.

"Don't play games with me, Bethany."

"I'm not playing games, Shawn. I promise."

My dad looks at me. "Sweetheart, what are you doing? Don't give in to him."

"Dad, I don't want anybody to get hurt."

"Honey, don't make promises to Shawn that you can't keep. You're not going with him." Uncle Chuck says shaking his head.

"I have to go with him."

"You're not going with him," he repeats again as he takes another step toward us.

"Stop walking toward us! I don't want to hurt her but I will if you force me too."

"Okay, okay." Uncle Chuck puts his hands up. "We're staying right here."

"No, you're not. Close the front door. Then I want you two to sit on the couch. Now!"

My dad immediately closes the front door then he and Uncle Chuck sit down on the couch.

My dad's voice becomes angrier. "So help me god if you hurt Bethany, I promise you that I will find you if it's the last thing I do and when I do I will tear you apart, limb by fucking limb."

"You'll have to find me first."

"Oh, make no mistakes about that. I will find your ass."

"Andy!" Uncle Chuck scolds trying to tell my dad to keep quiet.

Shawn points to my dad's shoes. "Take your shoelaces out of your shoes."

"What?"

Shawn becomes irritated. "Are you hard of hearing? I told you to take your shoelaces out!"

My dad is dressed in jeans, T-shirt and gym shoes and Uncle Chuck is dressed in a suit since he has court in a few hours. My dad does what he's told and removes his shoelaces.

"Now what?"

Shawn points to Uncle Chuck. "You…take one of the shoelaces and tie his hands together. Don't get stupid about it. Tie it tight!" Uncle Chuck does what he's told. Shawn then walks us over to the front of my dad and Uncle Chuck. "Bethany, I want you to take the other shoelace and tie your Uncle's hands together."

"Shawn…"

"Do it!" Still holding the knife near my neck he yells making me jump.

Tears flowing down my cheeks, I grab the other shoelace and apologize as I tie his hands together. "I'm sorry, Uncle Chuck."

"Don't be, honey. This is not your fault. Just do what he says. You're going to be okay."

I finish tying Uncle Chuck's hands together then Shawn takes us a few steps back. "Say goodbye to your dad because this is going to be the last time you will see him."

"I love you, dad. I'm so sorry for everything. Please forgive me. I love you."

"I love you too, baby girl. Like Uncle Chuck said, this isn't your fault. You haven't done anything wrong."

"Say goodbye to your Uncle," he whispers.

Before I have a chance to say anything, Uncle Chuck says first. "I'm not saying goodbye, because you're not going anywhere with her."

"You seem so sure about that. I don't see you doing anything about it."

Michael and almost the entire police force pull up outside the house. Michael looks at Tony as he gets out of the car.

"Stay put inside this car, understand? I want you out of harms way."

"Yes, sir."

Chief Franks is the first one to rush to Michael as he gets out of his car. "Have you heard anything more from Chuck?"

"No, I haven't."

"We need to figure out where in the house they are and get the snipers in place."

"Chief, with all due respect, I don't mean to tell you how to do your job but we need Shawn alive. As much as I would like to see his ass taken out, we need him alive. Based on the lab evidence, I think he's our link to finding Joe."

"How would you suggest we do this then?"

"I know this is my family, Chief, but let me help. I know my house better than anybody here."

"You've got a good point there. All right. But when you see Shawn, you don't do anything and you let Detective Barbado talk to him. Understand?"

"Completely."

"Okay. I think we still need to put one sniper in the back of the house and one in the front just as precaution. But we will try and use Tasers first choice if possible."

"Fair enough. I'll have Detective Barbado, Officers Welch, Smith and Reed come with me around to the front of the house. We'll have Officer Lackett and a few others go around back."

"Sounds good. I'll come with you too." Chief Franks looks around at the officers standing nearby. "Everybody get your ear buds in for communication." Chief walks over to a group of officers and detectives and fills them in on a game plan.

Michael's group sneaks around the front of the house as Officer Lackett and his group sneak around the back.

Michael hears Lackett reporting in his ear. "Michael, the back of the house is clear. I'm looking through the window but I can't see anybody. The lock on your back door has been broken."

"10-4. Standby for further instructions," says Michael.

"Copy that."

Detective Barbado takes a sneak peek inside the front window. He holds his fingers up indicating total number of people inside then suddenly jumps back. Michael points toward the ground for them to squat and talk.

"There are four people?" Michael asks.

"Yes. Shawn, Andy, Chuck and Bethany. Chuck and Andy are tied up. Shawn has a knife to Bethany's neck. He's facing our direction. He'll see us before we even have a chance to get through the front door."

"Shit!"

Chief Franks whispers, "let's send Lackett and his group in through the back."

Michael nods his head. "They can get his attention while we sneak in the front. He'll be surrounded then."

"Exactly," says the Chief.

Michael whispers back to Lackett. "Lackett?"

"Go ahead, Michael."

"They're in the front room facing our direction. We won't be able to enter the house without Shawn seeing us first."

"Tell me what you want us to do."

"We need you and your group to enter through the back. Get his attention so we can sneak in from the front."

"Copy that."

"Once you get inside the door you'll be inside the kitchen. There will be a narrow alcove off to your left. It's deep enough for one person to fit into. You can hide in there and still see a small portion of the front room. Inside the kitchen there is an opening in the wall so you can see from the kitchen right into the front room. It's a big opening so be careful so Shawn doesn't see you."

"Copy that. I'll send you a beep once we have Shawn's attention."

"This is my family, Lackett. Please be careful."

"They're in good hands, detective."

Michael and the rest wait patiently for their queue to enter the house.

Officer Lackett and his team quietly enter through the back door. Officer Lackett hides inside the alcove that Michael mentioned and has a perfect view of Shawn, but not of the others. He motions to the other officers to take a look from their positions.

One of the officer's stands off to one side as he peeks around to get a good look. He has a clear view of everyone in the front room. He looks over at Lackett and gives the signal they use to communicate that, suspect has knife to hostage's neck.

Officer Lackett slowly moves out of the alcove and down the mini hallway until he's at the opening of the front room. With his piece drawn, he speaks slowly and softly trying not to startle Shawn.

"Shawn, I'm Officer Lackett. I'm here to help you. Put down your weapon, son."

Shawn immediately turns us around. "What the…? How did you get in here?"

"The same way you did, Shawn. Through the back door," responds Lackett.

Shawn then notices the officers in the kitchen with their guns drawn pointing at him. "This doesn't concern you guys. You can go, everything is fine here." Shawn says, trying to convince them to leave.

Officer Lackett hits a button on his radio that sends a beeping tone to Michael. Michael and his group quickly enter through the front door.

Officer Lackett shakes his head. "We can't go, Shawn. Everything is not fine here. You're holding Bethany hostage. That's not okay."

"I'm not holding her hostage. She's already said that she's coming with me and willfully."

"If that's true then let go of her."

"No."

"Shawn, you're surrounded. You can't go anywhere. Let her go, Shawn," says Barbado.

With his arm still around my neck, Shawn turns us around and sees Detective Barbado, Uncle Michael and other officers pointing guns at him. He becomes confused, not sure what to do. He has guns pointing at him from all directions.

"Shit!" Shawn whispers to himself.

Barbado begins pleading with Shawn. "Shawn, man what are you doing? Why did you have to go and do this? We made a deal. We were going to get you and your mother out of town safely."

"I found out that my gang knows about Bethany and they were the one's responsible for shooting at her house. I need to take her somewhere safe."

"She is safe, Shawn."

"No, she isn't. If I can find her, then so can they."

"Shawn, come on buddy, put down the knife. These officers won't hesitate to take you out or Taser you. I don't want to see that happen. Shawn, I can see that you love Bethany a lot. You have deep feelings for her don't you?"

"Yes, I do."

"Then do the right thing, Shawn, and let her go. We'll keep her safe. We promise. No harm is going to come to her."

"I don't know."

"Shawn..."

"Bethany." Detective Barbado interrupts me putting his finger to his lips. "Shawn, we know how much you care for Bethany. We can see that, but this isn't protecting her. You're threatening her by holding a knife to her."

"You're going to take her from me then I'll never see her again."

Detective Barbado tries to avoid that topic of conversation. "Shawn, listen to me son. I believe that you love Bethany and you want to protect her. I believe you but these..." He motions to the other detectives and officers surrounding them as he puts his gun away, "other officers don't believe it because you have a knife to her neck. Prove to them that you don't want to hurt Bethany. Prove to them that you love her and put the knife down."

Shawn moves the knife away from my neck then Officer Lackett shoots his Taser at Shawn making him go down instantly, forcing him to let go of the knife and me. When he does, Uncle Michael pulls me away from Shawn and into his arms. I start crying hysterically as he holds me.

"Take a deep breath, sweetheart. It's over. Shawn's going to be fine and he won't come after you again. I promise you that."

After Shawn's in handcuffs, Chief Franks comes in and unties my dad and Uncle Chuck's hands. My dad rushes to me pulling me out of Uncle Michael's arms and into his.

"You're okay, baby girl. You're okay."

Chief Franks looks over at Detective Barbado. "Get his ass out of here!"

Detective Barbado responds. "I'll see you back at the station. Our boy here has a lot of questions to answer."

"Bethany." Shawn calls out.

My dad shoves me toward Uncle Michael as he turns towards Shawn.

"ANDY!" Uncle Michael yells making Chief Franks jerk around and grab my dad just as he gets in Shawn's face.

"If you ever come near my daughter again, I PROMISE YOU…I…will…kill…you!"

"I just want to tell her that I am sorry," Shawn pleads.

While holding my dad back, Chief Franks yells again. "Get Shawn the hell out of here, now!"

"We're getting him out of here. Let's go Shawn," says Barbado.

The detective and a couple of other officers take Shawn out of the house. Chief Franks nods toward the door.

"Let me know when they have Shawn in the squad please."

My dad tries to break lose from the Chief's grip. "You can let go of me now, Chief."

"No way. Not until I know Shawn is in the squad. I'm not giving you any chance to go after him."

"Wouldn't you if it were your kid?"

"Yes I would. Which is why I know you would too."

"He's in." Uncle Chuck informs.

Chief Franks taps my dad on the back. "Come on, buddy. He's gone and Bethany is safe. Okay. Go tend to your daughter.

My dad walks over to me and pulls me back into a hug as he looks at Uncle Michael. "You were supposed to make sure that bastard never came near her again! That was the damn deal in her helping you catch him to begin with!"

"Andy…" Uncle Michael tries to talk to my dad but my dad just walks away with me in his arms.

Chapter Twenty-Four

After Attorney Cesar Layton finishes meeting with Shawn, he calls Detective Barbado and Chief Franks into the interrogation room.

Layton motions to them to sit. "I spoke with my client. He understands that the original deal is now off the table. He also understands that the only deal he's being offered now is just reduced jail time. He says he's ready to cooperate."

"How much would it be reduced?" asks Shawn.

Layton responds. "That would depend on how truthful you are with them now and it depends on the judge."

Detective Barbado pulls out a chair and sits on the same side of the table facing Shawn. He doesn't like having a table between him and a suspect. He's always said that you can't read somebody properly if you have something between you and them. He likes to be able to watch their every body movement while interviewing them.

"Start talking. I want the truth this time. I want you to start from the very beginning from the time you first saw Joe."

"I met Joe about two months ago when he…"

"Wait." Barbado stops Shawn immediately. "You knew Joe before this incident happened with Bethany?"

"Yes, sir, I did."

"How, why and where did you guys first meet?"

"He found out from a kid at his school that I was selling drugs. The kid gave Joe my number. I don't know who the kid was, I didn't ask.

"What type of drugs do you sell?"

"I sell mostly heroin, cocaine, meth and LSD. Sometimes marijuana."

"What was Joe hitting you up for?"

"Whatever, it didn't seem to matter to him what he bought."

"What do you mean it didn't seem to matter? Don't drug addicts already know what they want?"

"Most of the time yes. But Joe didn't come to me as an addict. He was looking to become an addict. Joe said that he was having a hard time dealing with the loss of his mom. Said he couldn't talk to his dad because his dad was going through enough as it was and was having a hard time too. He was just looking for something to take the edge off and get her out of his mind. He was definitely a newbie to drugs."

"Why do you say that? Is that what he told you?"

"No, he was just asking a lot of questions. Questions that somebody who had done drugs before would have known the answers to. Things like how do the drugs effect you and how long do the effects last and which are the best ones to use."

"There were very well packaged hypodermic needles labeled 'Dragon' found in the glove compartment of Joe's car and in his bedroom. Did you sell those to him?"

Shawn looks at Layton waiting for the okay to answer the question. "Go ahead and answer him, Shawn. We're trying to make another deal here. The only way to do that is to be completely honest with them."

"Yes, I sold those to him. It was heroin."

"We know what 'Dragon' means. How is it that heroin became his choice of drug?"

"I suggested that he use heroin and since he was a newbie at it, I told him that he should start out with the preloaded first. Since the preloads are hard to get I only sell them to the newbies to get them started. That way all they have to do is insert and inject. There's no thinking about it."

192

Chief Franks jumps up and starts yelling. "You son of a bitch! You suggested heroin of all drugs to be his first drug? You couldn't suggest marijuana?"

"Hey man, I was in the business of making money! It made no difference to me what he took! I made the suggestion and he took it! I didn't twist his arm!"

"You piece of..."

Chief Franks takes in a deep breath to calm himself down before he's thrown out of the interrogation room. He looks at Layton, who surprisingly doesn't say anything yet.

Barbado puts his hand on the Chief's arm and proceeds to question Shawn. "How may preloads did you sell him? And did you sell him anything else?"

"Twenty and no, that was the only drug he bought from me."

"Eight were found in his bedroom and six were found in the glove compartment of his car. Which means he's done six so far." Chief Franks says, stating the obvious.

"How much did he pay you for them?" asks Barbado.

"Those preloads are hard to get but since Joe was a newbie I only charged him one thousand for all twenty. He's paid me five hundred so far so he still owes us the rest."

"When you say, 'us' who else are you referring to?"

"Me and my gang."

"That's expensive shit."

"I told you, they're hard to get."

"Have you ever given any or sold any to Bethany?"

"WHAT? Hell no!"

"Are you sure about that?"

"YES!" Shawn says defensively.

"How many times has he bought drugs from you?"

"It was only that one time and it's pretty obvious why since it sounds like he still had a lot left. I'm surprised he hasn't gone through the whole twenty yet. Most people finish all twenty within a couple of weeks if not less."

"When was the next time you saw Joe?"

"At his house when he found me and Bethany together in her room."

"What happened when he saw you?"

"He threw me up against the wall and threatened to kill me if I ever came near his sister again. At that time Bethany didn't know that Joe and I already knew each other. I told him that he better be careful who he's threatening. Then he kicked me out."

"That was it?"

"Yeah, that was it!"

"What happened next?"

"Later on that night I received a text message from Bethany asking me to meet her at our bridge so we can talk, so I met her there. We got into a big argument because she was trying to breakup with me and I didn't want to breakup. That's when she found out I was in a gang. She left upset. After a while I left too, and then I returned a little while later when I realized that I dropped my wallet somewhere."

"Is that why you went back to the bridge, to look for your wallet?"

"Yes. That's when Joe showed up which shocked the hell out of me. I asked him what he was doing there and how did he find me. He said he followed Bethany earlier that evening."

"What happened from there?"

"He went off on how he told me to stay away from his sister. Told me that he doesn't want her mixed up with me. That's when he started swinging at me. I swung back defending myself. Before

I knew it we were both rolling around on the ground throwing punches at each other. Apparently Bethany wasn't the only one that was followed that night."

"What do you mean? Who else was followed?"

"Me. Three members of my gang followed me to the bridge when I came back to find my wallet. They saw Joe and me fighting and jumped in to help me."

"Do these guys have names?"

"George, Arturo and Jose, I don't know their last names. Our gang doesn't exchange last names in case somebody decides to snitch."

"What happened once they jumped in?"

"Joe was trying to defend himself against four guys, not very good odds as you can imagine. Joe took George's knife from him and stabbed him with it several times in the stomach and chest killing him. Joe killed in self-defense but the other two guys didn't see it that way. That's when they really started beating on Joe. Arturo took the knife from Joe and started stabbing him with it. Joe just stopped moving."

Chief Franks tries with everything he has, to keep his anger inside. "Did they kill him?" Chief Franks asks as he swallows hard.

"No, but we thought they did. It was in the middle of the night so it was dark. It looked like he was dead, so they stopped beating and stabbing him and left him alone. Turned out, he was just unconscious. It's only because of Bethany that I didn't want Joe dead."

"How commendable of you." Barbado says sarcastically. "Why did these guys follow you to begin with?"

"They thought I was selling behind their backs. I assured them that I wasn't. Joe still owes us a lot of money so they didn't want me selling anything more to him. I told them that Joe and me were fighting over something personal."

"They didn't ask you what that was?"

"No."

"What happened next?"

"They started flipping out about what to do with George's body. I told them, that I got us into that mess so I would handle burying George and Joe's bodies. They agreed and Jose took Joe's cell phone and then they left."

"You said they didn't kill Joe."

"They didn't. Shortly after they left, Joe started coming around. I put George's body in the trunk of Joe's car and put Joe in the back seat where he ended up passing out again."

"What were you going to do with them?"

"I was going to dump George's body somewhere and later that night drop Joe and his car off in front of his house but that plan changed very quickly."

"What do you mean? How did it change?"

"After I put Joe in the backseat, Arturo and Jose showed up. Turned out they never left. They still thought I was doing something behind their backs. Arturo forced me into the driver's seat of Joe's car. Then he got into the front passenger seat. Jose got back into his own car behind us. They were taking Joe and me back to the gang. They were going to kill us both for sure, I have no doubt about that." Shawn pauses.

"Keep going," says Barbado.

"I floored the gas trying to lose Jose. Arturo started fighting me while I was driving trying to make me pull over. Then before I knew it, Jose was bumping into us with his car."

"What kind of car was Jose driving and what color was it?"

"An older red Buick. I don't remember what model."

Barbado looks at the Chief. "That explains where the red paint came from on the back of Joe's car." He then looks back at Shawn. "Go ahead, continue."

"Jose chased us to the warehouses near the boat docks. He started bumping into us again. I took a wrong turn and ended up on the break wall. At that point, I knew he was going to run us right into the lake so I braced myself and so did Arturo. I heard Jose's tires squeal behind us as he was trying to keep himself from going into the lake too. Too bad he didn't end up in it like we did."

"What happened once you were in the lake?"

"I was surprised that the car started sinking so fast, too fast. Electric windows don't work well under water."

"Yeah, I'm sure they don't," comments Barbado.

"Arturo started fighting me again so I took out my knife and stabbed him a few times to get him off me. Once I got him off me I tried to find a way out. I noticed that Joe had his moon roof partially open. Water started rushing in through it so I started to kick at it until it popped out. I grabbed Joe and pulled him out of the car with me through the moon roof, which wasn't easy. Arturo got out of the car too and started following us but then he disappeared. I didn't know where he went."

"He's one of the bodies they found in the lake," says Barbado.

"We waited under the docks to see if Arturo was going to come up from the water but he didn't. Then I looked around for Jose. I didn't know where he went either. I figured he must have gotten scared and left. I pulled Joe out of the water and down the dock a little ways then did mouth to mouth. Like I said, I didn't want him dead. I looked up when I heard something and saw that Jose was coming at me. I started to run but he caught up with me, then we started fighting. I was able to get his knife and stabbed him several times, making sure he was dead. Then I dumped his ass in the lake too."

Barbado looks at Layton. "So far your boy's telling us the truth. Shawn was in Joe's car, which is why we found his watch there. Jose's body was the second body we found in the lake and the third body was found in the trunk of Joe's car like Shawn said."

"The third body being George Desoto," confirms Layton.

"That is correct." Barbado turns back to Shawn. "What happened next?"

"I turned around to finish helping Joe and he was gone."

"What the hell do you mean he was gone?" Chief Franks asks.

"That's what I said, man! He was gone! I don't know where the hell he went! He wasn't even conscious when I pulled him out of the damn lake! I can't explain it!"

Barbado puts his hand on the chief's arm telling him to keep quiet. "You're sure he was unconscious when you pulled him from the lake?"

"I had to do mouth to mouth on him! I wouldn't have done that if he were awake! Maybe he woke up while Jose and I were fighting, I don't know. But he would have been too weak to run off anywhere! I tried looking under the docks but I couldn't find him. It was too dark outside. Shit! It was in the middle of the night when all of this went down and it was cold! He could have gone anywhere!"

"Did you go back in the water to look for him?"

"No, I didn't. It was too cold. I figured at that point he was on his own. It was dark, cold and the middle of the damn night. We weren't even supposed to be down at the docks that late. I didn't want to get caught."

"You said that Jose took Joe's cell phone, is that correct?"

"Yeah, he did. He took it before they left the woods."

Barbado looks at Chief Franks. "Now that explains the mystery of Joe's cell phone ending up on the docks nice and dry. It must have fallen out of Jose's pocket when he and Shawn were fighting." Barbado looks back at Shawn. "What happened next, Shawn?"

"I headed back to my gang. They didn't know anything about anything. I told them that there was a bad deal that went down and blamed it on another street gang. Told them I got rid of our guy's bodies. I didn't say anything about Joe."

Chief Franks shakes his head. "Great, so you just created more animosity among the street gangs to cover your own ass."

"Yeah, I suppose I did."

Barbado cuts in. "What kind of shape was Joe in? What were his injuries?"

"I don't know for sure but I can tell you that it looked like his face was messed up pretty bad. I think he had a broken nose, hand, black eyes, some stab wounds and probably some broken ribs."

"What happened next, Shawn?"

"You guys caught up with me so you know the rest from there."

"The last place you saw Joe was at the docks, is that correct?"

"Yes, sir it is."

Chief Franks stands. "Shawn, everything you just told us better be the truth this time."

"Am I still going to get reduced jail time?"

"If we find Joe and it's proven that you didn't kill him then you'll get reduced jail time. How much will depend on the judge. But if Joe turns up dead and I find out you killed him, then I will push for the chair for your ass." They all get up and leave Shawn alone in the interrogation room.

"This means that there's a chance Joe may still be alive," says Barbado.

"I sure as hell hope so," says the Chief, but I think that all depends on where he is and the extent of his injuries. It's the dead of winter so that makes his chances of surviving even less. I'm going to send some officers back to the docks and to the warehouses to search for him again just in case he is still around that area somewhere. I need to get a hold of the owners or security guards for the warehouses so we can get inside and do a search. Jeff and his dive team have already searched the lake several times for several hours. If Joe were in the lake they would have found him. We'll do a land search only this time."

"I'll come with you to help search. There's some containers at one of the warehouses too that have been there for a long time. We should search those as well," offers Barbado.

Layton surprisingly throws in his two cents as well. "Chief, maybe you should call Michael and have him help search."

"I don't want Michael on this side of the investigation."

"But if you guys end up finding Joe and he's still alive, you'll want him to see a friendly and familiar face. Not that yours isn't. But I'm talking family. If he's alive, he's probably scared shitless right now. It's just a search, Chief. It's not like he's talking to suspects and informants."

"True. Alright, I will call him." The Chief extends his hand out to Layton. "Thank you for your help."

"You're very welcome. Good luck and let me know if you find him."

"We certainly will." The Chief looks at Barbado. I'll call Chief Davis and have his firehouse on standby at the docks in case we find Joe."

Chapter Twenty-Five

Chief Franks calls Chief Mark Davis at the firehouse.

"Hello?"

"Hey, Mark. This is John. I think we may know where to look for Joe."

"Where?"

"We're going back to the docks."

"Jeff's dive team has already checked the…"

"Not the water, the warehouses and the containers over there. We need the fire department on standby in case we find Joe. If Joe's alive then time will be of the essence in getting him to the hospital immediately."

"We'll meet you there right now."

"Is Jeff working today? I haven't had a chance to talk to him."

"Yes, he's the paramedic in charge today."

"Excellent! We'll see you at the warehouses shortly."

"Hey, John!"

"Yeah?"

"Have you contacted the warehouse security yet?"

"No, I haven't. I'm was going to do that now."

"I'll call the head of security over there. He's a close friend of mine. He'll do whatever he has to do to help, even if that means opening up buildings so we can search inside."

"That would be great, thank you. See you in a few minutes."

Chief Franks then calls Michael. "Hello?"

"Michael, I don't want you to get your hopes up but we may know where to find Joe."

"Really? Where?"

"We're going up to the docks to search the warehouses and containers there. Jeff's fire department will meet us up there in case we find Joe."

"I won't say anything to Andy yet."

"That's a good idea. Where are you right now?"

"I'm at the lab processing some fibers."

"Drop what you're doing and meet us at the docks, we can use your help looking for Joe."

"Are you serious? I thought you didn't want me on that side of the..."

"It was suggested that you be there to help. It's not like we're searching for a suspect. We're searching for your nephew."

"Whose suggestion?"

"It was Layton's."

"Really? Okay. I'm leaving now. Thanks, Chief."

"Michael, be careful going out there, don't drive like a madman."

"I'll be careful."

When Michael arrives at the warehouses he sees that the warehouse head of security, the fire department, police, Chief Franks and Detective Barbado are already there. Chief Franks and Barbado are barking orders to the officers telling them where to start searching while the head of security unlocks the containers that are not already unlocked. As soon as Michael gets out of his car he sees Jeff standing next to the ambulance with Alexander. He immediately walks up to Jeff and shakes his hand.

"Let's hope this is it and we find Joe," says Michael.

"I'm sorry to say this...but I just hope he's still alive. I have to warn you, Michael, based on the injuries Shawn says Joe has and the cold weather conditions we've had, I don't know if there's much hope. Not to mention the withdrawals from the drugs he was taking. Sometimes that alone can kill someone. I don't think Joe has been on those drugs long enough for that to be much of a problem but then again that would depend on how deep into the drugs he was. You need to be prepared for the worst."

"Wonderful." Michael says sarcastically. "I've been preparing for the worst since this whole thing started, my friend."

Chief Franks hollers to Michael. "Michael, let's go! Let's get this search underway!"

"I'm coming! Are you coming, Jeff?"

"No, we have to follow you guys with the ambulance in case someone does find Joe."

"Okay." Michael quickly jogs to catch up with Chief Franks and Detective Barbado.

They search some of the buildings and cubbyholes around the warehouses then start searching the containers. The ambulance follows slowly behind them as they go from container to container. They've been searching for forty-five minutes when they hear Officer Welch yell out.

"WE FOUND HIM! WE FOUND JOE! OVER HERE!" Welch is standing outside a container waving his arms around trying to get the ambulance's attention.

"No way! They really found him?" says Michael.

Michael and Chief Franks rush to the container where Welch is standing. Several officers are shining their flashlights inside so they can see. Michael's the first one inside. He sees Joe sitting up against the wall of the container, hunched over with his arms dangling at his side and unresponsive.

"JOE! JOE!" Michael lifts Joe's head to look at his face. "JESUS CHRIST! JOE! COME ON, BUDDY!" He feels for a pulse in Joe's neck and screams. "HE'S STILL ALIVE! WHERE'S THAT DAMN AMBULANCE? HANG IN THERE, JOE! COME ON!"

"We're right here!" Jeff says as he and Alexander rush inside the container with medical equipment and a backboard. "Get out of our way, Michael!" Jeff scolds.

Michael immediately moves out of the way. Everybody helps provide light by shining flashlights inside the container. They all watch as Jeff and Alexander examine Joe.

Alexander check's Joe's eyes for a response to light and looks over his face and head while Jeff listens to Joe's chest and checks his blood pressure.

"It looks like he's got a broken nose, couple of black eyes and a small head wound. The head wound does not look serious," reports Alexander.

"His blood pressure is low," says Jeff.

They wrap a c-collar around Joe's neck then lay him down on the floor of the container.

"His pulse is weak." Alexander says as Jeff cuts Joe's shirt off.

Jeff continues to report what he finds. "There's a lot of bruising on his right side which tells me that most likely he's got some broken ribs. There's a stab wound to his right side, one to his left leg and one stab wound…two stab wounds to his left arm. This kid has lost a lot of blood, Alexander."

Alexander looks at Joes right arm. "The way his right arm is laying, it looks like it may be broken. Whoever got a hold of him did a number on him, that's for sure."

They wrap gauze around the stab wounds applying pressure to them then splint the broken areas to stabilize them. As Alexander is splinting Joe's arm, Jeff starts the I.V. David and Brian are standing nearby waiting to help with the backboard. Once Joe is stabilized they put him on the backboard and into the ambulance. Michael follows the ambulance as he calls Chuck.

"Hello?"

"CHUCK!"

From the tone of Michael's voice, Chuck knows something is up. "What's wrong?"

"We found Joe!"

"WHAT? Where? Is he okay?"

"No. Joe is in bad shape, real bad shape, bro. We found him in a container at the warehouses near the docks. I'm following the ambulance to the hospital now."

"Have you called Andy yet?"

"No, I thought maybe it would be best if you swung by and picked him up. I want him to get to the hospital safely and that won't happen if he drives right now."

"Got it! I'll leave my office now. We'll see you in a few. Bethany and Tony are at school, I'll have Linda go pick them up."

"No, let's wait and see how things go with Joe first. There's no sense in upsetting the kids more when we don't have all the answers yet. We can always have Linda go pick them up in a little while."

"Okay, sounds good. Bye."

Once they arrive at the hospital the doctor rushes Joe into a room to stabilize him further, and then sends him upstairs for an emergency body scan to check for any internal injuries. Michael signs off on the papers for them to proceed in treating him until Andy can get to the hospital. Shortly after they take Joe upstairs Andy, Chuck and Linda arrive.

Andy barely able to contain his emotions asks, "Where's my son? Is he okay?"

Michael gives his brother a hug. "They took him upstairs for a body scan. I signed the papers for them to proceed in treating him.

"Thank you for doing that. Why are they doing a scan?"

"You're welcome. They're doing…" Just ask Michael starts to explain the doctor approaches them.

"Excuse me, I'm Doctor Seeley. Are one of you Joe Phillips father?"

"I am. I'm Andy Phillips. These are my brothers Chuck and Michael and my sister in-law Linda. What's going on with my son? Why are you doing a body scan on him?"

"Right now your son is unresponsive so he is unable to tell us where all of his injuries are. He has a lot of bruising and a few stab wounds, therefore, we're doing a scan to check for any internal injuries."

"I can't believe this is happening."

"Let's not get ourselves too worried about the scan unless we find something, okay? Due to his condition, this is just a precaution."

"What injuries are you aware of so far?"

"I'm not going to lie to you, Mr. Phillips, your son is in pretty bad shape. His pulse was very weak when they brought him in and his blood pressure was low. He has a small head injury but it looks like it may just be a bump on the head but we'll know more from the scan. He has a broken nose and two black eyes. He has a broken right arm and four stab wounds, two to his left arm, one to his left leg and one to his right side. He has a substantial amount of bruising over the right side of his ribs which probably means he has some broken ribs as well."

"Holy shit." Andy rubs his face with his hands then starts snapping the rubber band on his wrist. The doctor notices the rubber band but doesn't say anything about it.

"Are you going to be okay, do you need some water or something?"

"That depends if my son is going to make it or not. Is he going to make it, Doctor Seeley?"

The doctor takes in a deep breath, as he was not prepared yet for this question. "I'm sorry but it's too early to tell yet. I'll have a better answer for you once the results from the scans come back. Mr. Phillips, I understand that your son has been doing heroin?"

"Yeah, we just found out about that a few days ago. We have no definite answer as to how long he's been on it or how much he's been doing."

"I must prepare you, that depending on how long and how much of it he's been doing, it will make a difference on whether he makes it through this or not. Sometimes the withdrawals alone from that crap can be worse than injuries. I've taken some blood, urine and hair samples from him to run some drugs tests and other blood tests to make sure everything else is working okay. I'll let you know the results of the drug tests as soon as I get them."

"Great! That's just great!" Andy says as he walks a few feet away. Jeff walks with him making sure he's okay.

The doctor looks at Michael and Chuck. "Is your brother going to be okay? I'm always concerned about the parents when they're going through something like this. It can really take a toll on them."

Chuck answers the doctor as he watches Andy pacing. "Yeah, we'll be here for him. We'll get him through it. He just lost his wife about a year ago to cancer."

"I'm sorry to hear that. I'll let you know more as soon as I receive the results back."

"Okay, doctor, thank you." Michael and Chuck shake the doctor's hand.

Doctor Seeley then turns to Chief Franks. "Due to the drug situation, if Joe Phillips pulls through this is he going into police custody?"

"No, he will not be."

"Okay, that's good to know."

"Do you have a private room I can use to talk to the family?"

"Absolutely, you can use the one right behind you."

"Thank you." After the doctor walks away Chief Franks calls Andy over. "Andy, come here. Let's all go in here and talk." Once the six of them are in the room Chief Franks closes the door. "Andy, said that if we found Joe you would put him in a rehabilitation facility. Is that something you still plan to do?"

"As hard as it will be for me to do it, yes absolutely. It would be for his own good," answers Andy.

"Okay, then I have an idea that may ensure that he sticks with the program. Right now he's seventeen so you have the legal right to force him into any facility you want. However, pretty soon he'll be turning eighteen, and then he can do whatever the hell he wants. My suggestion would be to have him sign an agreement stating that he will stick with the rehabilitation program even after turning eighteen. He would also need to agree to take a minimum of one drug test a month, two if the rehabilitation facility or family feel that he may be taking drugs again. If he fails just one test, then he will be arrested for consumption of an illegal substance.

"Like being on parole?"

"Kind of like it yes, but we're not going to let this go on file unless he fails a drug test. Then he'll have a record. Think about it okay? Talk it over with your family and let me know what you want to do."

Andy looks over at Michael and Chuck. They are both nodding in agreement.

"I don't have to think about it. I've already talked it over with my family. Just do it. Have the papers drawn up."

"Are you sure? Because once he signs them there's no going back."

"Yes. I'm desperate to keep him off of that shit. I'll do whatever I need to do."

"Okay, I'll have the papers drawn up this afternoon and will bring them by tomorrow morning."

"Thank you. We'll just have to get Joe to agree with it. If he pulls through."

"Oh, He'll agree to it. I'll make sure of it," says Michael.

Chuck puts his arm around Andy's shoulder. "Come on, we have to think positive that he'll pull through."

Chapter Twenty-Six

It's been three hours since they took Joe upstairs for a scan. Michael and Chuck watch Andy closely, they can tell he is becoming very antsy and inpatient. Suddenly Andy rushes up to the nurse's station.

"What the hell is taking so damn long with my son's scan? I want to see my son!"

"Sir, we're still waiting to hear from the doctor," says the nurse.

"GET HIM DOWN HERE, I WANT TO..."

"Andy, tests like these take sometime then the doctor has to read them." Michael says as he gently grabs Andy's arm.

Chuck takes Andy's other arm and they escort him back to the waiting area. "Start snapping that rubber band, Andy. Come on, bro. The doctor will be out soon." Andy glares at Chuck but starts snapping the rubber band on his wrist.

Just as they return to the waiting area the doctor comes walking quickly down the hall toward them. "May I please speak with you and your family in the privacy room?"

Everyone follows the doctor into the privacy room.

"What's going on with my son?"

"Andy, the scan shows that your son has a ruptured spleen, most likely from the blows to his abdomen. It looks like it just started bleeding into his abdomen within the past...maybe forty-eight hours. We have to operate and I mean now! If we don't he's not going to make it!"

"WHAT?" Andy immediately sits down in shock.

"Since he's under age, I need your permission to have the surgeon operate."

"YES! DO IT! OPERATE! PLEASE!"

"Okay. Wait here please. I'll go tell the surgeon and have the nurse bring the paperwork for your signature. I'll be back shortly. I still need to go over the rest of Joe's test results with you."

"Okay." The doctor leaves the room as Andy sits stunned trying to take this all in. Then suddenly he loses it, putting his hands over his face as he cries. "SHIT! He can't die on me! I can't lose my kid!"

Michael and Chuck stand next to him, their hands on his shoulders to comfort him. They look at each other with tears in their eyes. Linda rushes out of the room unable to watch a grown man breakdown and Jeff indicates that he has to head back to the station.

"I'll call Dakota on my way to the station."

"Okay, thanks," says Chuck. "We're going to help you through this, bro. We promise." Chuck whispers to Andy. A few moments later he leaves the room looking for Linda. He finds her pacing up and down the hallway crying. He pulls her into his arms and holds her tightly. "Are you going to be okay, sweetheart?"

"Yes, are you okay?"

"As good as to be expected I guess…who am I kidding? No, I'm not okay."

They see the doctor walking back to the room so they return quickly not wanting to miss the update on Joe.

"How are you doing, Andy?" the doctor asks.

"I'm not sure. I'm kind of numb and confused."

"I can understand that. Everything is happening so fast for you guys. I would like to go over the rest of Joe's test results now if you're up to it."

"Yes, please go ahead."

"First let me give you the best news of all. Joe regained consciousness before putting him under anesthesia and taking him in for surgery."

"Thank you, god." Andy whispers.

"The other good news is. The rest of the scans came back and it appears there's no severe trauma to the head. We also had some x-rays taken to confirm that he has some broken ribs and he does. He has three and they'll all heal in time."

"Okay, what about the blood tests?" Andy asks.

"Well, there's some good news with all of that, too. Joe's blood test showed no signs of heroin. However, heroin can leave the blood stream in as little as six hours."

"What about a urine test?"

"Generally, it can show up on a urine test for as little as two and half hours or even as much as two days but heavy drug users can fail a urine test for up to seven days whether they've continued using the drug or not. Nothing showed up on his urine test."

"Okay, I'm confused, does that mean he wasn't using heroin?"

"Not necessarily. Since it's very important for us to know what kind and how much drugs are in a patient's body when we need to treat them, we had the lab test some of Joe's hair follicles. It's become a very popular way to test for heroin as well as other types of drugs. Heroin will remain in the hair follicles for several months no matter how much or how often it was used.

"Have those results come back yet?"

"Yes, and I am sorry to say, that they do show signs of heroin in his system but honestly, I really don't think he's an avid long time user. I didn't see any other drugs in his system either, which is more good news."

"Yes, it is. Why do you think he hasn't done much of it?"

"His nose didn't show any signs that he's been sniffing drugs and when I examined his arms, legs and feet I found only a few track marks. I can tell you that he's not very good with a needle. Some people can shoot heroin for two years and not show any track marks. It depends on how you do it and on your health. As bad as he was with using a needle, if he were an avid user he'd have more track marks to show for it. His withdrawals should be very minimal. He's probably gone through them already."

"What kind of withdrawals?" Andy asks.

"Pain through out his body, sweats, nausea, vomiting and diarrhea to name a few. We've put him on some medications to help him through it but there's only so much we can do. His body just has to get rid of the drugs on it's own. He's got hypothermia so we had to cover him with as many warm blankets as we could to warm his body up. He lost a lot of blood, which is one reason why he was found unconscious. We're giving him some blood now. I've stitched up all four stab wounds and have put him on some very strong antibiotics."

"This is so overwhelming," says Andy.

The doctor taps Andy's back. "I know it is."

"Knowing what you know now, can you tell me whether you think he'll make it or not?"

"If the surgery goes well, and it should, then he should make it. The notes on his chart say that he was found inside of a container?"

Michael responds. "Yes, he was. The door must have been open for him to get in it. Either that or somebody put him in there."

"Regardless of how he got in there, that's probably what helped save his life. Had he been found out in the elements in this weather, you would be talking to a funeral director right now instead of talking to me." He then turns to Andy. "You have a very strong son. To go through what he did and still be alive says a lot about him."

"Thank you, doctor. Thank you so much."

"You are very welcome. The surgeon will come out after the surgery and talk to you and your family. The waiting room for his surgery is up on the fourth floor, east wing."

"Thank you." Andy shakes the doctors hand.

"You're welcome and I wish you luck with your son's surgery and recovery."

"Thank you."

Everybody goes up to the fourth floor waiting room to wait for the doctor. An hour and a half later he finally comes out and the expression on his face tells Andy everything is going to be fine.

"Family for Joe Phillips?"

The entire family stands. "Right here, doctor. I'm his father, Andy Phillips."

The doctor shakes his hand and everyone else's too. "I'm Doctor Stephens. I am very happy to tell you that Joe did great during surgery. We were able to repair his spleen."

"Is he going to be okay?"

"Absolutely! He should make a full recovery."

Andy plops down on the couch and rubs his face with his hands. "Oh, thank god! Thank you so much, doctor."

"You're very welcome. Joe is in recovery right now. In about an hour he should be awake then they'll move him to a room. The nurse will let you know when they do and what room."

"Okay." Andy stands. "My son has been missing for about a week. I haven't had a chance to see him. Can I please go see him just for a few minutes?"

"Nobody is really supposed to go back into the recovery area but considering the circumstances, sure. You can bring one person with you if you'd like. You can only stay for a few minutes."

"Thank you very much."

Michael and Dakota decide to let Chuck accompany Andy to see Joe. The nurse shows Andy and Chuck the way.

Andy picks up Joe's hand. "I have been worried, sick about you, Joe. I'm so happy to have you back. You're going to be okay now. You and I will need to have a long talk, buddy, when you wake up."

The nurse comes in and interrupts Andy. "Sir, I'm sorry but we can't allow you to stay long."

"I understand. At least I got to see him." Andy leans down and kisses the top of his son's head. "I love you, son. You can make it through this. We'll all be right here to help you."

Chuck pulls on Andy's arm. "Come on, bro. We've got to go."

"Okay. Thank you nurse."

"You're welcome. We'll let you know when we're ready to take him to his room."

"Okay."

They return to the waiting room, everybody is hugging and crying tears of joy. Chuck taps Andy's shoulder as he hugs him.

"See bro, everything is going to be okay. Joe is going to be okay."

Andy turns and looks at Linda. "I would like to be here when Joe wakes up. Would you mind picking Bethany up from school right away?"

"Sure, no problem."

"Thanks."

"I'll go with Linda," says Chuck. "Michael, do you want us to pick up Tony too?"

"Are you taking your kids out of school for the rest of the day too?"

"Yeah, I think we will. Family should really be here for Joe when he wakes up."

"If you don't mind, then yeah, please pick him up too."

"Sure."

Andy puts his hand on Chuck's shoulder. "I hate to ask you this but can you do me one more favor?"

"Of course, what do you need?"

"I don't want Bethany to be caught off guard when she sees Joe. Would you mind telling her what's going on with him before bringing her here? I would appreciate it."

"Absolutely."

"Thank you."

"You can let Tony know too," says Michael.

"Okay. We'll see you guys in a little bit."

Chapter Twenty-Seven

Chuck and Linda have a big SUV and are able to fit in all five kids. They've picked up their kids and Tony and are now picking up Bethany.

"I'll be right back," says Linda.

"Okay."

The principal calls Andy to make sure it's okay for Bethany to leave school then walks Linda to Bethany's classroom. Linda knocks lightly on the window of the classroom door to get the teacher's attention. The teacher opens the door to the principle and Linda.

"Yes, may I help you?"

"Yes, I am Bethany Phillips's Aunt and I am here to pick her up."

"Sure, one moment please." The teacher has Bethany gather her things and meet Linda out in the hallway.

"Aunt Linda, what are you doing here?"

"Bethany, they found Joe. He's in the hospital right now."

"What? Really?"

"Yes, come on, we have to go."

As we hurry outside I question Aunt Linda. "Where are we going?"

"I told you we're going to the hospital."

"You can go but I'm not going."

"Excuse me? What do you mean you're not going? Are you afraid of hospitals or of seeing Joe?"

"No, I just don't want to go. I don't want to see him."

"Why?"

"Because I don't want to, that's why."

"Do not take that tone with me young lady!"

Aunt Linda motions to Uncle Chuck that she needs his assistance. He gets out of the car and walks to the door of the school where we're standing.

Great, here comes Uncle Chuck.

"What's going on?" he asks.

"Bethany says that she is not going to the hospital to see Joe. Says she doesn't want to and she's giving me an attitude."

Uncle Chuck looks at me. "What? Why don't you want to see Joe?"

"The same reason I just gave to Aunt Linda. Because I don't want to, that's why. So if you will excuse me I need to finish out my class." I turn and start to go back into the school as I glance back at Uncle Chuck.

He raises his eyebrows and quickly grabs my arm yanking me back as he starts yelling. "I don't know what your problem is, but you're going to drop that attitude with me right now! I will not put up with it! Do you understand me? You may be able to get away with that with your father at the moment but I'll be damn if you're going to talk to us like that! What's going on with you, Bethany?"

"I don't want to see Joe because I am angry with him, okay! His stupid ass put our dad through hell these last several days! He put everybody through hell! Are you guys too stupid to see that?"

Uncle Chuck grabs my lower jaw. "You better watch what comes out of that mouth of yours or I will whip your ass right now! Don't you ever talk to me like that again! You've put your father through hell recently too with the shit you've pulled! I think you owe Aunt Linda and me an apology!"

I look at the ground realizing that I have really crossed the line with my Aunt and Uncle. "I'm sorry. I really do not want to see Joe."

"What the hell is wrong with you? You don't EVER abandon a family member when they need you the most! Your mother and father did not raise you to be like that! We're all angry with Joe but we are still going to be there for him! Because that's what a family does for one another! Your ass is going to the hospital and you're going to give your brother and father the support they need! Do you understand me?"

"Fine!"

"Excuse me?"

"Yes, sir!"

"That's better! Drop the damn attitude! Your father doesn't need it right now! Now get your ass in the damn car!"

Uncle Chuck backhands me hard on the ass as I walk past him.

"Ouch!" *I've really pissed him off now.*

"The next time I smack your ass I'll do it so you can't sit down!"

None of my cousins say anything to me when I get in the car. Uncle Chuck lowers his voice as he and Aunt Linda get into the car too.

"Linda, when we get to the hospital I'll pull Bethany aside and talk to her alone about Joe. If you can walk ahead a bit and fill in the rest of the kids, I'd appreciate it."

"Sure, honey."

Once we arrive at the hospital, Uncle Chuck pulls me aside to a nearby bench and allows the others to continue walking.

"Bethany, come here."

"I'm sorry, Uncle Chuck."

"I know. I let the others walk ahead of us so I could talk to you about Joe."

"What's wrong with Joe? Is he going to be okay?"

"You're dad wanted me to prepare you for what Joe looks like before you see him. He's going to be okay but he's in really bad shape right now. He just came out of emergency surgery for…"

"Surgery? When was he found? How long has he been in the hospital? Nobody told me he was in surgery!"

"Bethany, let me finish explaining, okay?" I nod my head. "Everything happened so fast. They found him earlier this morning. It wasn't long after they got him to the hospital that he ended up in emergency surgery. We didn't tell you kids right away because we didn't have any answers as to what was wrong with Joe and if he'd be okay or not. We didn't want to upset you and your cousins any sooner than we needed to. We didn't even get a chance to see Joe before they took him into surgery."

I start crying. "You haven't see Joe at all yet?"

"Not until he came out of surgery which was just before we came and picked you kids up."

"Is Joe going to be okay? What was the surgery for?"

"Yes, Joe is going to be just fine. He had a ruptured spleen but they were able to repair it. The spleen helps your body fight off infection. If they didn't do the surgery, Joe would have died. That's why everything had to happen so fast."

"How did it rupture?"

"He got into a fight with Shawn and a few of Shawn's gang members. The blows to his abdomen ruptured his spleen."

"I knew this was all my fault!"

Uncle Chuck grabs my hand. "Hey, don't go there, okay? This is not your fault. Joe has been involved in some serious shit that none of us knew about and he's been involved in it way before this incident with Shawn happened."

"How bad did they hurt Joe?"

Uncle Chuck takes in a deep breath and lets out a huge sigh. "He's got a few broken ribs, a broken arm, a broken nose, black eyes and four stab wounds."

"STAB WOUNDS?" I shout as I cry harder.

"Listen to me, he's going to be okay now. They found him in time."

"You said Joe was involved in some serious stuff. What kind of stuff?"

"He got himself involved with drugs."

"No way! Joe would never…"

"Bethany, they found drugs in Joe's car and we found them in his bedroom."

"Maybe somebody is framing him." *He's lying. Joe wouldn't do drugs!*

"I really wish that was the case but they did a drug test on Joe and it came back positive for drugs. The good news is that it doesn't look like he's been doing them for very long."

"Joe would not do drugs, Uncle Chuck."

"I know this is hard to believe but…"

"He wouldn't! There's no way!"

"Bethany, I'm telling you the truth, honey. I wouldn't lie to you about something like this."

"Where did they find him?"

"In a container…a trailer at the docks."

"I can't go see him, Uncle Chuck. I can't. I'm not turning my back on him but I can't look at him. This is all my fault!"

Uncle Chuck squints his eyes while tilting his head slightly. "Wait a minute. You're not mad at Joe are you? You're mad at yourself. Is that why you've had such an attitude lately?" I nod my head yes. "Why are you mad at yourself?"

"If I wouldn't have snuck around behind my dad's back this would never have happened. Joe wouldn't have gone to the bridge to confront Shawn about me! He should have stayed out of it! Shawn's gang wouldn't have beaten him up! He wouldn't have…"

"Stop it! This is not your fault! Yes, what you did was wrong. But Joe was protecting his sister, which is what he's supposed to do. I wouldn't expect anything less from him and neither would your dad." He puts his arms around my waist. "I want you to listen to me very carefully. The drug Joe was using was supplied by Shawn's gang."

"What? Oh, no."

"Joe owes them a lot of money. That's why he got himself into trouble. You had nothing to do with that. Stop blaming yourself. This was all him. Do you understand?"

"Yeah."

"Are you okay?" Uncle Chuck wipes the tears from my cheeks.

"Yeah. I'm sorry for my attitude toward you and Aunt Linda."

"I know."

"Are you going to tell my dad? I'm already grounded. If you tell him, then I'll probably get a life sentence."

Uncle Chuck smiles to himself, trying not to show his amusement. "We'll see. It all depends, if you continue giving people an attitude and talking back, especially to your father. He doesn't need the added stress right now."

"I won't anymore, I promise."

"Okay. Come on, let's go see Joe." We catch up with Aunt Linda and my cousins. "Did you talk to Tony and our kids about Joe?" Uncle Chuck asks Aunt Linda.

"Yes, I did. They had some questions that I couldn't answer."

"Like what?"

"How and why Joe ended up where he was found."

"Hmm."

"How did it go with Bethany?"

"Turns out the attitude is coming from her blaming herself for Joe's disappearance. She didn't know he's been involved in drugs."

"But it's not her fault."

"I know. I told her the same thing. She'll be okay."

Chuck holds open the elevator for everyone to get in.

Chapter Twenty-Eight

Andy and Michael head to Joe's room. Andy takes in a deep breath as they walk in, afraid of what they're going to see. Joe is hooked up to several IV's, a heart monitor, blood pressure monitor and an oxygen machine.

Andy calls out to Joe as he walks closer to the bed. "Joe?"

Joe opens his eyes and after a few seconds realizes who's standing in front of him. "Dad?"

"Yeah, it's me." He gently kisses the top of his son's head. "I can't tell you how it feels to have you back." Andy wipes tears from his eyes and becomes choked up as he continues. "I thought I...lost you. You really scared the shit...out of me."

"I'm sorry. I never though I'd see you again either."

Michael puts his hand on Joe's shoulder. "We were determined to find you. Are you up for a few questions?"

"He just got out of surgery, Michael!" scolds Andy.

"It's okay, dad. Go ahead, Uncle Michael, it's fine."

"You just got out of surgery!"

"Please, dad, it's okay." Andy motions to Michael to proceed.

"First of all, do you remember how you got into the container? From the docks to the container is quite a distance for you to walk in your condition. Did somebody help you? Shawn maybe?"

"I remember clearly how. Bruce."

Michael and Andy look at each other confused. "Come again? I'm sorry, buddy, I don't think I heard you right. I thought you said Bruce. You sure it wasn't Shawn?"

"You heard right, Uncle Michael. I don't know where Bruce came from. He just showed up out of the blue."

"Are you positive that it was Bruce?"

"I know for sure it was. It was dark so I couldn't see well. I kept trying to fight him off thinking he was one of the gang members but he kept telling me that he was Bruce and he was there to help me. When I caught a glimpse of his face in the dock lights I saw that it really was him. He carried me over to the containers. He and some other guy told me to stay in there until help arrived. Said I would be safer there. I was too weak to go anywhere anyways."

Andy looks at Michael. "What the hell was Bruce doing down at the docks?"

"That is a very good question."

"I don't know whether to be thankful that he saved my son or be pissed that he left him for dead. He didn't know how soon Joe was going to be found. He could have died by the time you guys found him!"

Michael turns his attention back to Joe. "You don't know who the other guy was?"

"No, it was dark and I didn't get a very good look at him. From what I could see he didn't look familiar to me."

"It might be one of Bruce's new guys. Was it just Bruce and this other guy or were there others there too?"

"No, just Bruce and the other guy."

"Did you see Shawn and Jose fight on the docks?"

"All I remember is what happened at the bridge and Bruce carrying me to the container. I don't recall anything in between. I'm sorry."

"That's okay, buddy. You've already told us something we didn't know. We'll talk more about it tomorrow when you're a little more rested up."

They hear a light knock on the door. Chuck, Linda and all of the kids come in. Chuck immediately walks to Joe's bed and shakes his hand. "Hey, buddy, how are you doing?"

"Hi, Uncle Chuck. I'm hurting all over the place."

"Well, you've got quite the injuries going on there."

Linda gives Joe a kiss. "Hi, honey. It's a relief to have you back with us."

"Thank you, Aunt Linda."

Each of the cousins walks up to say hello too. I stand at the foot of the bed just staring at Joe, tears rolling down my cheeks. *I never thought I would ever see him again. He looks terrible! I've missed him so much. I love him so much!*

My dad gently taps my arm breaking my trance. "Sweetheart, are you okay?"

Joe motions with his hand. "Come here please. I'm going to be okay, Bethany."

I swallow hard then slowly walk to the side of his bed trying to talk through my tears. "I can't believe that you're really here and you're...alive."

Once I'm within reach, Joe pulls me in for a hug. And that's when I finally lose it. My dad stands behind me rubbing my back as I cry on Joe's shoulder.

Joe hugs me back with his good arm. "Come on, baby sister, don't cry. I'm okay now. I promise."

"I'm so mad at you! But I'm so glad you're okay."

"I'm sure you are. I'm sure a lot of people are."

After a few moments my dad pulls me off of Joe. "You're going to hurt your brother more than he already is. Come on."

We get comfortable around the room and stay with Joe until visiting hours are over. Everyone is exhausted.

Chapter Twenty-Nine

The next morning Chief Franks arrives at the hospital shortly after Andy does. "Hey, buddy. How do you feel this morning?" he asks Joe.

"Other than a whole lot of pain, I'm feeling a little better. At least I've gotten something to eat now."

"Good." Chief Franks then turns to Andy. "Here are the papers."

Joe looks at Chief Franks and his dad confused. "Papers for what?" Joe asks.

Andy looks at the Chief then at Joe and sighs. "There's something I have to talk to you about, Joe."

"Okay, this can't be good."

"We need to talk about the drugs you've been taking."

Andy watches as Joe rolls his eyes and throws his head back on his pillow putting his arm over his forehead.

"Shit!" He says barely in a whisper.

"Yeah…shit…you can say that again," says Andy.

"I'm so sorry, dad."

"You kept some very…very…dangerous secrets from me and from everyone else. We promised never to have any secrets, Joe. You broke that promise. How can I trust you again?"

"I'm so sorry." Joe pleads.

"I'm angry with you right now, Joe. You brought that shit inside my house! With your sister there! You kept a secret from me! We were NEVER to have secrets from each other! And you didn't come to me for help!"

"I know and I'm sorry!"

"I hate having to do this but you've left me no choice. When the doctor releases you from the hospital you won't be coming home with me."

Suddenly Joe removes his arm from his eyes and looks at his dad. "What do you mean? Where am I going? Am I going to jail?" He asks frightened.

"I'm putting you into a rehabilitation facility for while."

"WHAT? You're locking me up?" Joe says in shock.

"I'm not locking you up. I'm trying to get you some help for your drug addiction. But since you're going to be turning eighteen soon I need you to sign these papers stating that you'll stay in the rehabilitation program even after you turn eighteen."

"Dad, I don't have a drug problem!"

Chief Franks takes a step closer to Andy, afraid that he will spin out of control again. Anger sweeps across Andy's face as he starts snapping the rubber band on his wrist and hollers at Joe.

"You have been doing heroin, Joe! And you're telling me that you don't have a drug problem? Are you kidding me right now? Have you fried all brain cells up there?" He asks as he taps Joe's head.

Chief Franks puts his hand on Andy's arm. "Joe, it's in your best interest to sign these papers. Your father and I are doing this for you."

"I'm not signing anything! I'm not getting locked up!"

"Damn it, Joe, we're not locking you up! We're getting you some help!" Andy yells.

They continue for another hour trying to get Joe to sign the papers but he still refuses.

"Can I come home anytime I want?"

"No, you can't. You have to stay there until they say you're ready to leave."

"Then I'm getting locked up! I'm not signing any damn papers!"

"I'm trying to help you!"

"I'm not signing them!"

"God bless the brainless!" Andy says as he storms angrily out of the room.

Chief Franks walks out of the room as well but stops to call Michael as Andy paces up and down the hallway.

"Hello?"

"Michael, this is John."

"Hi, John."

"I am really sorry to ask you this but we are at a point where we now have no choice."

"What are you talking about? Ask me what?"

John let's out a huge sigh. "You need to work your nephew over. He won't sign the papers."

"Are you freaking kidding me? My own nephew?"

"I'm sorry, buddy. Andy and I have been trying for the past hour and he just won't budge. He just won't sign the papers."

"Shit! Do you realize what I put kids through to get them to agree to those deals?"

"I know. I've seen you in action before and I sure as hell would never want to be in their shoes. But it needs to be done. You have a better track record than anybody getting through to young drug addicts." Silence falls between them. "Michael, I wouldn't ask if this wasn't…"

"I know. Alright…I know."

"When can you come to the hospital?"

Michael sighs. "I'll get some things together and be there in about twenty minutes. I just want to get this over with. Don't tell Andy yet. He may not understand why I'm doing this."

"I wasn't planning on it. I'm sorry, Michael. But you are the best at this."

"Yeah, that seems to be my curse. Who would ever think that I would have to do it to my own family some day?"

"I'm sorry, son. It has to be done."

"See you in a few."

Shortly after Chief Franks leaves the hospital, Chuck and Linda arrive to visit with Joe. Chief Franks had already called Chuck and filled him in. Andy still hasn't returned to Joe's room, so Chuck finally decides to go and check on him.

"Andy, are you okay, man?"

"I've been trying to calm myself down before going back into that room but I am having a very difficult time doing so because I am so angry with him."

"I completely understand. I don't blame you one bit for being angry."

Michael arrives holding three envelopes in his hand and asks Andy. "Chief Franks called me and said that Joe wouldn't sign the papers. Has there been any change? Has he signed them yet?"

"No. He still refuses."

"I was afraid of that. Where are the papers he needs to sign?"

Chuck watches Michael closely as Andy hands the papers to Michael.

"We've tried, Michael. Good luck if you think you can get him to sign," says Andy.

"I just have one question for you, Andy?"

"Sure."

"Do you trust me?"

"What the hell kind of question is that, Michael? You're my brother. Yes, I trust you."

"That's all I wanted to hear. I just need about a half an hour alone with Joe."

"Okay, that's fine. What are you going to do?"

Michael taps Andy's shoulder as he walks past him. "Something that I wish I didn't have to do. Don't worry, I've got a plan."

"Shit! I know that look." Chuck says almost under his breath.

Andy turns to looks at Chuck. "What's going on here, Chuck?"

"Let's just say that Michael is one of the best around for getting young addicts to agree to just about anything."

"What do you mean? How?"

Chuck looks at Andy. "You don't want to know. You just have to trust him."

"Yes, I do want to know."

"Okay. Be careful what you ask for." Chuck starts filling Andy in.

Michael knocks lightly on the door of Joe's room then enters.

"Hey, Uncle Michael."

"Hi, Joe."

"Hi, Michael," says Linda.

"Hi, honey. May I have some time alone with Joe please?"

"Sure."

"Can you close the door behind you on the way out?"

"Sure."

"Thank you."

"What's going on, Uncle Michael?" Michael tosses the papers down near Joe's hand on his bed. "I am not signing anything. I've already told my dad and Chief Franks. I'm not getting locked up."

"They're not trying to lock you up."

"I don't have a drug problem."

"Excuse me?" Michael tugs on one of his ears. "I'm sorry but I thought I just heard you say that you don't have a drug problem." Joe doesn't say anything. "Let me ask you something. After you shot up for the first time what was it like?"

"What do you mean?"

"Just what I asked, Joe. What was it like? How did it make you feel? What did it do for you?" Joe doesn't answer right away. "Answer me! What did it do for you?"

"At first it made me sick but then it helped me forget about things!"

"Things like what?"

"Things like my mom and the pain I see in my dad's face because she's gone! It helped me forget about all of that!"

"Why would you want to forget about your own mother? She was a damn good mother!"

"Because it hurts too much to think about her, that's why!"

"So you take drugs to forget about her? There's better ways than drugs, Joe!"

"I just couldn't deal with it anymore. It was bad enough that I had to see the pain in my dad's face everyday and know that there was nothing I could do to help him."

"What do you think happened when he found out about you taking drugs? That almost killed him, Joe! Your dad is seeing Doctor Schiller now and he's been in a much better state of mind since. So you don't need to worry about him. I guarantee you that your mom's very disappointed in you right now! Do you really think she'd want you to forget about her?"

"No, she wouldn't."

"How did the heroin make you forget the pain? What did it do?"

"I don't know. It made me feel high and feel good I guess. It made the loss of my mom feel like it was no big deal. It made me forget about the sad look that I'd see on my dad's face everyday. I don't know it just made life seem easier."

"Drugs don't make life easier, Joe, they make life more complicated! I think you just figured that out the hard way! What happened when you didn't take it?"

Michael continues to ask Joe questions hoping that Joe is paying attention to what's coming out of his own mouth, hoping he'll realize himself that he's got a problem.

"I started thinking about her and started getting depressed. So then I'd take more."

"When did you start using?"

"At first I was too scared to shoot up so I wasted the first three syringes. I finally got the courage to shoot up about a week before my fight with Shawn."

"So you haven't been doing it for long?"

"No. I've only shot up three times so far."

Even though Michael is relived to hear that, he still maintains his composure. "Do you hear yourself? You just said, 'so far'. You said that you have to take the drugs to forget about your mom. Do you know what they call that, Joe? Addiction! They call that being addicted to drugs!"

"I'm not addicted! I can stop anytime!"

"No, you cannot stop at anytime! You have a damn problem and you need to start recognizing that! Think about everything you just told me! How it makes you feel, what happens when you don't take it and why you take it!"

Michael takes the breakfast plate off of the table in front of Joe then opens the first envelope laying down some pictures in front of him.

"What are these?" Joe asks.

"Take a good look. Does this room look familiar to you?"

Joe looks at the pictures then says in shock. "That's my bedroom! Did my dad do that?"

"Your dad, me, Uncle Chuck, Uncle Jeff and Chief Franks did that! We were looking for drugs in your bedroom, Joe! This was after drugs were found in your damn car! Still don't think you have a drug problem? Do you love your father, Joe?"

"Why would you even ask a question like that?"

"Just answer the damn question! Do you love your father?"

"Hell yes, I love my dad!"

"For somebody that loves his father, you sure as hell hurt him really bad!" The tone of Michael's voice and his words have tears forming in Joe's eyes and that makes Michael come down harder, knowing that he's now finally getting through to him.

"I didn't mean to!" Joe's voice quivers. "I would never hurt my dad!"

"Well you did! You hurt everybody in our family!" Michael then spreads out pictures of Joe's wall.

"You guys put holes in my wall?"

"That's what your father did, Joe! Out of anger! You really hurt your dad! And that really pisses me off! You hurt your entire family! All of us! We were worried sick about you! Your sister spent many nights sitting in her room crying because of you! You never thought once about how your doing drugs would affect anybody else in your life! You don't give shit about anybody else but making yourself feel better!"

"THAT'S NOT TRUE! I didn't mean to hurt anybody!" Tears are now streaming down Joe's cheeks.

"Well you did! Your father has been seeing Doctor Schiller, Joe! Because of you!"

Michael knows that's not the real reason why Andy has been seeing Doctor Schiller, but feels it would help him get through to Joe if he makes him think that.

"What?"

Now, I've got his attention. Michael opens up the second envelope of pictures and spreads them out on the table. Joe reacts immediately when he sees them.

"Oh, my god, those are gross, Uncle Michael! Why are you showing me these? Who are these people? What happened to their faces?"

"DRUGS, JOE! All of these people are drug users! This is what drugs do to you! You need to understand that drugs do not just affect the inside of your body, Joe, they affect the outside too!"

"That's really disgusting, Uncle Michael!"

"Yes, it is! And if you don't stay off of drugs, this is EXACTLY how you're going to end up! I promise you that! You WILL look just like these people! Disfigured, drawn out, missing teeth, discolored skin, scabs all over your body, sometimes hair loss! Is this how you want to end up?" Joe stares at the pictures not saying anything until Michael yells making him jump. "ANSWER ME!"

"NO! IT'S NOT!"

"These people's families don't even talk to them anymore! Do you want that?"

"NO!"

"I understand from Uncle Chuck that you and your girlfriend broke up several weeks ago. Why?"

"I broke up with her. I didn't want her knowing about me using or getting involved with drugs. I couldn't explain to her why I was acting different without her figuring out it was drugs. I was afraid she'd tell you guys."

"You two have been dating for two years, Joe. She was good for you."

"I know."

Andy, Chuck and Dakota are waiting out in the hallway when they see four police officers escorting a convict in shackles and cuffs down the hall and right to Joe's room.

Chuck watches in amazement. *Shit, Michael is going to break Joe down hard.*

Andy immediately starts walking toward Joe's room but Chuck stops him. "Why are they bringing a prisoner into Joe's room?"

"Andy, its all part of Michael's plan."

"Plan? You said he breaks kids down, shows them pictures, you didn't anything about visiting convicts!"

"Please, trust him. It's all part of the plan."

There's a knock on the door. Michael gets up to see who it is. The convict named Tim walks in with the four officers.

"Tim, thank you for doing this," says Michael.

"Hey man, if it will help these kids, I'm all for it."

The man in shackles and cuffs is a big, tall, bald white man that looks like he takes no shit from anyone. The officers lead him to Joe's bed, making Joe very nervous.

Michael makes the introductions. "Tim, this is my nephew Joe. Joe, this is Tim.

"Why is this man in my room, Uncle Michael?"

Michael motions to the convict. One of the officers sits Tim down in a chair next to the bed.

"I'm here to talk to you," says the convict.

"Why? I don't know you."

"Oh, but you will and you'll get to know a lot of other guys like me too if you continue down the road you're on."

Joe looks at Michael. "I don't understand. Why is this man here?"

Tim answers for Michael. "I'm here to talk to you about me."

"Why would I care about you? I don't know you."

"Shut up and listen to him, Joe!" Michael scolds.

Tim continues. "Because someday you're either going to end up like me or end up dead. I understand that heroin is your drug of choice."

Joe doesn't answer and looks away from the convict.

"Answer the man, Joe!" Michael says in a stern voice.

Joe answers in a soft tone. "Yes, it was."

"That was my choice of drug too, but now I'm serving thirty years in prison, that's if I don't die in there first." Joe doesn't say anything. "Hey, man. It's rude not to look at somebody when they're talking to you!"

Joe looks up at the man. "What do you want from me?"

"I want you to look at me when I'm talking to you and I want you to listen to what I'm telling you kid! I'm trying to help you! If you don't want to talk that's fine but you will listen to what I have to say!"

"Look at him when he's talking to you, Joe!" Michael scolds again so Joe keeps his eyes on Tim.

"I'm three years and five months clean and serving a thirty year sentence for murder, burglary and for selling drugs to a cop."

"That's your problem."

"Hmm, a kid with an attitude. What a surprise. Look, I know what that shit does to you, man. I've been there. I loved how it made me feel too. How did it make you feel?"

"Why don't you tell me since you seem to know."

"Okay. You stop me if I'm wrong." The convict starts to explain in a very slow and deliberate manner. "You feel it burn, but in a good way as it travels up into your veins. You know when it's in your head when you start feeling like you're spinning out of control. You're spinning so badly that it makes you vomit. But for some reason…one that you can't explain, it still makes you feel good. Am I right?"

Michael scolds again when Joe doesn't answer. "I won't tell you again, Joe! Answer his questions!"

"Yeah, that's how it feels!"

"Do you know what happens next?"

"No."

"Yes, you do. At some point you disassociate yourself from everyone you love because they don't like your habit and can't possibly understand it. You start sleeping all the time. Eventually you start stealing from your loved ones and robbing stores to get more and you will kill for it, over and over and over again."

You can hear Joe getting choked up as he tries to speak. "You're right. I do sleep a lot and I don't hang with my family and friends as much anymore. I've even broken up with my girlfriend."

"Have you robbed or killed for it yet? Have you stolen from family or friends yet?"

"No. I haven't done anything like that."

"You will. Because let me tell you, when you run out of heroin you will become sicker than you have ever felt in your life and you will be in more pain than anyone could ever imagine. Your heroin will become a necessity for you to survive. Your life will depend on it. I ate maybe three times a week. The only water I had around was to fill my needle. My heroin became my food and water. It was my lifeline. I couldn't think or function without it. My body craved it every minute that I was awake. I didn't shower for weeks at a time and I had no energy or desire to. Did you know that your organs slowly stop working?"

"What do you mean they stop working?"

"Well, let me enlighten you. I had to rub ice between my legs to give myself a jolt just so I could piss something out. I didn't shit for almost two months. Hell, I didn't even know I had to. I didn't feel like I had to. I have stage three Cirrhosis of the liver. That means one more stage and I pretty much die. I got hepatitis C from my own dirty needle. My blood pressure went through the roof. I was in the hospital for several months and almost died because my body started shutting down. They had a very difficult time getting an IV in me because my veins had so much scar tissue and were collapsed...are you listening to me, man?"

"Yes!"

The convict looks at one of the officers. "Can you please roll up my sleeves?" One of the officers obliges and rolls up his sleeves revealing his arms. The convict then looks back at Joe. "Look at my arms! Look at them! They're all marked up from drugs! I see your arms don't have many marks on them yet because you're still a newbie, but give it some time and they'll look just like mine. Look at my face, what it did to me. I look like I'm eighty years old and I'm only in my forties."

Joe finally looks away from the man not wanting to see or hear anymore.

"So much more has happened to me in my life, that your tiny little sheltered brain would not be able to grasp or believe and it's

239

all because of drugs. Now…knowing what I've been through does it still make drugs appealing to you?"

"No, it doesn't."

The convict sighs. "Time will tell I guess. Don't end up like me, man. It fucks up your whole life and you'll never get it back."

"That's enough, Tim. Thank you. I think Joe's gotten the point." Michael says as he motions to the police officers to take Tim out of the room.

"You're welcome. I just hope it helped."

The officers take the prisoner out and, Michael turns to Joe seeing even more tears in his eyes. *This is killing me having to put my nephew through this but I have to finish this.* Michael takes out the last set of photos and puts them down in front of Joe.

Joe responds stating the obvious. "These are the same people that are in the last photos you showed me."

"Yes they are, Joe! Except they're dead in these photos!"

Joe looks up at Michael. "Why are you showing these to me? Why are you doing this to me, Uncle Michael?" Joe asks as tears stream down his cheeks once again.

"Because I love you, Joe, and I am trying to get through to that damn thick ass skull of yours! I'm trying to show you what happens to people who use drugs! You're either going to end up like Tim or end up like the people in these photos! Is this how you want to end up?"

"NO, IT'S NOT!"

"Then prove it and sign the damn papers! Right now you're under the age of eighteen so your dad can force you into rehab but once you turn eighteen, by law you can do whatever the hell it is you want. We are trying to make sure that you stick with the rehabilitation program all the way to the end. This agreement says that you agree, even after you turn eighteen to stay in rehab until the rehabilitation facility feels you're okay to check out. That you agree to a minimum of one drug test every month, maybe more if the rehabilitation center or any of us think you may be using drugs. If you fail just one drug test then you will be arrested for consumption of an illegal substance, and then you will have a police record. You once told your dad that you want to become a police officer like grandpa and me."

"Actually, a detective like you."

Michael's voice now becomes soft and gentle. "Well that won't happen if you have a record. This agreement also says that you will volunteer in the drug addiction wing for as long as the rehabilitation center feels is necessary. There you will see first hand what drugs do to people. Is this agreement clear to you and do you have any questions?"

"Yes it's clear. Can I have visitors?"

"Not for the first four weeks, after that only family is allowed to visit."

"Can I at least talk to family on the phone or write letters during the first four weeks?"

"No, you can't. That's because you have to focus on yourself during the first four weeks and not worry about anything or anybody else. The facility will provide us weekly updates on your progress." Joe lies there and cries as he stares at all of the photos lying in front of him. "Joe?"

"What?"

Michael puts the agreement on top of the photos. "Sign. Now. You need to do this for yourself."

Joe signs the papers, Michael takes the agreement, kisses the top of Joe's head, and starts to leave the room. "I'm sorry, buddy, for putting you through all of that but I had to get you to sign the papers."

"I know. I'm sorry, Uncle Michael. I am really sorry for everything I did."

"I know, but you did the right thing signing this agreement, buddy."

"Uncle Michael, wait, you forgot the pictures."

"No, I didn't. I want you to keep them as a reminder of what you're going to end up like if you go back to drugs. Oh, I have two more questions."

Joe looks up from the photos. "What?"

"Why have you been avoiding Uncle Jeff and I? We thought you were mad at us for something but it seems clear now…that wasn't the case was it?"

"No it wasn't. You're in law enforcement and Uncle Jeff is a paramedic so I was afraid that you guys would figure out that I was using drugs, so I just stayed away from you both."

"That's what we thought. I just wanted to hear it from you."

"What's your other question?"

Michael lets out a deep sigh. "Have you ever listened to anything I've told you about gangs? About getting involved with them?"

"Yes, I have. I'm sorry, I know that I have disappointed you."

"Yes, you have. A lot of people actually."

Michael leaves the room closing the door. He stands outside the room with his hands on his hip shaking his head looking at the floor, almost wanting to cry himself. *I am mad at that kid for making me do this to him.*

Andy approaches Michael. "How did it go with Joe?"

Michael hands him the agreement. "It's signed. He completely understands the agreement and agrees to it."

"Chuck filled me in on what you were doing in there with Joe. Is Joe okay?"

242

"No, not really. But he will be."

"Are you okay, Michael?"

Michael shakes his head in disgust. "I had to break him down. It broke my heart to do it to my own nephew but I had to do it. I just want to go home and see my own son right now."

Andy, Chuck and Linda look at each other then head towards Joe's room. Dakota goes after Michael.

"Michael!"

He stops but doesn't turn around. She walks to him and gives him a hug. "It's going to be okay. You did the right thing. As hard as it must have been for you to do it, you still did the right thing."

"Thanks, baby sister. Right now I just want to go home and spend some time with my son."

"Okay. Call if you need anything."

Michael gives her a kiss on the head. "Thanks. Love you baby sister."

"Love you too, Michael." Dakota then joins Andy and the rest of the family as they go back into Joe's room.

Andy's the first one to walk in and sees his son crying.

"Hey, buddy. Are you okay?"

Through his tears, Joe pleads with his dad. "Please forgive me, dad. I'm so sorry. I am so damn sorry. I didn't mean to hurt you or anybody else. Please forgive me."

"I'll be able to forgive you if you go for help and stick with it."

"I promise I will."

Andy sees the pictures laid out. "Whoa! What in the world are those? They're disgusting!"

"Pictures. Uncle Michael brought them. They're pictures of people on drugs and pictures of them dead. Said he wants me to keep them as a reminder of how I will look and end up if I stay on drugs."

"Oh, that's gross!" says Linda as she covers her mouth and looks away.

Chuck gags too. "That's enough to keep anyone off of drugs, but I guess that was the whole point of this to begin with."

"You said earlier that Michael uses pictures to get through to kids? Is this what you meant?" Andy asks Chuck.

"Yeah, I've seen him in action twice and it's not pretty."

"What do you mean?"

"The tactics he uses to get through to young drug addicts is rough but it works. He's one of the best at it! Anytime somebody needs to get through to a kid they call Michael. Except this time he brought in a convict and that is something he doesn't normally do. I can guarantee you that this was a lot harder on him than it was on Joe. Having to tear down a family member is totally different than having to do it to a stranger. You don't have an emotional connection to the stranger."

"Is Michael going to be okay?" Andy asks with concern.

"In time. This one will take some time." Chuck taps Andy's shoulder as he responds.

"Uncle Michael hates me now doesn't he?" Joe says ashamed.

Chuck leans over the railing of the bed. "Absolutely not! It was just his way of trying to get through to you. That's all."

Andy sits on the bed next to Joe. "He's just angry with you right now, son. Honestly, all of us are."

"I know and I am so sorry. Please forgive me, dad. I know I've lost everyone's trust and respect and I know I'll have to earn that back."

"And you will if you stick with the program and keep yourself clean."

Chapter Thirty

Joe wakes up to find Tony sitting next to his bed watching television. "Hey Cuz."

Tony looks over from the television. "Hey Joe. How are you doing, man?"

"Doing better each day."

"That's a relief to hear. I'm glad you're getting better."

"Thanks. Me too. What time is it?"

Tony looks at his watch. "Almost one o'clock in the afternoon."

"Wow, I slept a long time. Where's my dad? He was here this morning."

"I don't know. He wasn't here when I arrived and I've been here for about half an hour."

"Maybe he went to grab a bite to eat. Where's your dad?"

"My dad has been at the lab most of the day so I haven't had much time to talk to him but he said he was going to come by later this afternoon to visit."

"Cool."

"Have they found out who's responsible for your house yet? Don't get me wrong; I don't mind your sister and dad staying with us. I was just wondering that's all."

Joe looks at Tony confused. "What are you talking about?"

Tony then realizes that Joe knows nothing of what's happened since he's been gone. "Shit! I didn't realize that they haven't said anything to you."

"What are you talking about, Cuz? Why have they been staying at your house? What happen to our house?"

"There was a drive by shooting at your house, Joe."

"JESUS! What? When?"

"It happened the day after you had disappeared. I'm sorry, I thought maybe your dad told you."

"No, he didn't! Nobody said anything to me about it! Shit! I have to get out of here."

"You can't leave the hospital, Joe."

"Tony, you don't understand. It's me they want not my family." Joe starts disconnecting himself from the machines. "I still owe that gang five hundred dollars."

"What are you doing?" Tony jumps up and tries to stop his cousin from leaving. "Joe, you can't go anywhere. You're not in any shape to go anywhere, Cuz! Stay in bed." Tony is bigger and stronger than Joe, so he is able to hold him back until the nurse comes in.

Two nurses rush in and force Joe back into bed. "Let go of me! I have to get out of here!"

"I'm sorry, Joe, but you're not allowed to leave the hospital until your discharged." The nurses hold Joe down while tying his arms to the bed.

"WHAT ARE YOU DOING?" Joe screams as they continue tying him down.

"WHAT THE HELL DO YOU THINK YOU'RE DOING TO MY COUSIN? GET YOUR DAMN HANDS OFF OF HIM!" Tony yells as he physically tries to stop the nurses.

"Tony, get your hands off of me and back off or I will have security take you out of here!" Nurse Daphne scolds as she finishes tying Joe down. The other nurse leaves the room to call Andy. "I may be your dad's fiancé but that doesn't give you the right to be disrespectful to me like that!"

"I was trying to stop you from doing what you don't have permission to do! Why are you tying Joe to the bed?"

"We do have permission! It was his dad's request that we do this if Joe attempted to leave the hospital!"

"What? My dad told you to do this to me?" Joe asks.

"I'm sorry, Joe. Your dad signed some papers last night giving us permission to tie you to the bed if you tried to leave. He's afraid of something happening to you."

"I can't believe my dad would do this to me."

"I'm sorry, honey." Daphne gives Tony a dirty look and leaves the room.

Tony takes out his cell phone. "Are you calling my dad?" asks Joe.

"NO, I'm calling mine. This is crazy. I can't believe your dad is doing this to you."

Joe throws his head back on his pillow. "Your dad can't do anything about this, Tony. It was my dad's decision."

"You know my dad better than that, Joe. If he knows nothing about this then he won't let your dad do this to you."

"I'm telling you, it's not up to him."

"We'll see."

"Hey, buddy, have you left the house yet?"

"Hi, dad. Yes, I'm at the hospital with Joe. When are you coming up here?"

"I'm at the hospital now, right down the hallway from Joe's room."

"Joe's dad signed some…."

"I know, son. I just received a call from Uncle Chuck, which is why I'm here now instead of later. Uncle Chuck has court today. I've already left a message for your Uncle Andy to call me. Joe's not in restraints right now is he?"

"Yes he is. They just put them on him."

"I'll see you in a few seconds." Michael hangs up.

"My dad is just down the hall." Just as Tony says that Michael walks into Joe's room. You can see the anger in his face.

"What your father is doing to you is bullshit, Joe! Uncle Chuck was here earlier when you were asleep and found out about the papers your dad signed." Uncle Michael says, as he tosses his keys down onto the bed and starts to untie the restraints.

Nurse Daphne then rushes into the room. "Michael, stop it! You can't untie Joe's restraints!"

"You want to bet! There's no need for my nephew to be tied down like a damn criminal!"

"It was Andy's wish that we do this if Joe tried to leave the hospital! He signed the papers giving authorization for us to do it! If I don't follow his wishes then I can get into trouble with the hospital administrator!"

"You followed his wishes and did what you were told to do. Now, I'm untying him. Why didn't you call me?"

"I thought Andy had already discussed this with the family."

"Well, he didn't!"

"Michael, he has to stay in the…"

"Daphne, please honey. I love you dearly but please stay out of this now, okay. I am going to be talking to my brother about this. I've already left him a message to call me."

"We already called him when Joe tried to leave a little while ago."

Uncle Michael looks at Daphne. "I will handle it from here, okay. I will take full responsibility for whatever happens if Joe takes off." He then looks at Joe with warning. "But he won't be taking off, will you, Joe?"

"No sir."

Daphne leaves the room and Uncle Michael follows with his cell phone in hand. He starts to dial Andy but then sees him coming down the hallway. Michael goes to meet him halfway and immediately starts yelling.

"What the hell are you thinking having your son tied up?"

Andy starts raising his voice. "Michael, don't start…"

Daphne walks up to them. "Guys, you are disturbing the other patients. If you must yell then use that room over there."

Daphne points to a consultation room that the doctors use to talk to family members. Both Andy and Michael immediately go into the room and close the door as Andy now starts raising his voice.

"Michael, don't start with me! I almost lost my son once and I'll be damn if I'm going to let that happen again! I had a feeling that he may try to leave the hospital and apparently I was right."

"Are you out of your damn mind once again? You're treating him like some damn criminal!"

"No, I am not!"

"Yes, you are! That is what we do with convicts when we bring them into a hospital. They are restrained to the bed. I understand why you're doing this but it's not right, Andy, and I will not tolerate it!"

"Who the hell are you to tell me what you're going to…?"

"Do you have any idea what kind of damage you're doing to Joe right now?"

"What are you talking about? Those restraints will not harm him!"

"Andy! Joe is depressed, which is why he's in this mess to begin with! You having him restrained will only depress him even more!"

Andy becomes silent and paces for a moment. "Shit! I didn't think of that."

"That's why you should have spoken to family first. We can help you think things through before jumping into something! Your head is overwhelmed with so much shit right now, you can't do this all on your own."

"I tried talking to Chuck but we had a blow out over it. Apparently he doesn't agree with my decision either."

"You had a blow out with him because you are too damn hard headed!"

Andy stops pacing and looks at Michael. "Knowing you as well as I do, I assume you've already taken the restraints off of Joe?"

"You bet your ass I did! I wasn't going to stand by and watch you do that to him."

"What would you have done then?"

"I would have asked Chief Franks to post an officer outside his door."

"Can you do that then? Ask the Chief to put an officer outside Joe's door?"

"I will do it as soon as we're done here and I will stay here until the officer arrives. I'm sure he's not going to have an issue with doing that for us."

Feeling like a huge fool, Andy lets out a sigh. "I'll go talk to Daphne. She called me and told me that Joe tried to leave. I'll have her void out the authorization to restrain him."

"Okay, come on." They leave the room and walk over to the nurse's station. "Daphne, sweetheart?" Michael calls out.

"Yes?"

"Andy wants to talk to you." Michael walks a few feet away to put in a call to the Chief to have an officer put outside Joe's door.

Daphne looks at Andy. "Hi Andy. How are you doing?"

"Hi, honey. Michael is going to have an officer posted outside Joe's room. Can you please tear up or void the papers I signed giving permission to restrain Joe?"

"You don't want him restrained anymore?"

"No, I don't."

"Okay. I'll do that right now."

"Thank you." Andy looks back at Michael as he hangs up. "Do you know why Joe tried leaving?"

"No, I don't. I haven't had a chance to talk to him about it yet. Chief Franks will get an officer here tonight."

Andy takes in a deep breath. "Okay, thank you. I guess we need to go talk to Joe."

Andy and Michael walk into Joe's room as Tony and him are talking. Andy moves a chair next to the bed and puts his hands up. "Before you say anything...I am really sorry for the whole restraint thing."

"Why did you do it, dad?" asks Joe.

"I almost lost you once and I am so afraid of that happening again. I guess I just want to know that you're safe and you're where you're supposed to be and...that was my way of doing that."

Tony jumps into the conversation right away. "I am really sorry, Uncle Andy. It's my fault. I didn't know that no one told Joe about the drive by shooting at your house. I just assumed you guys told him and I asked him if they've been caught yet."

Andy answers like a kid caught with his hand in the cookie jar. "Ah, shit. That's okay. We should have told him."

"Why didn't you, dad?" asks Joe.

"It's not something that you need to worry about right now, Joe. Getting you out of here is more important than worrying about the house at the moment."

"But it's my fault that they took those shots at our house! I owe them five hundred dollars! It's me they want! I need to get the money and pay them so they'll leave our family alone!"

Michael sits next to the bed. "Your heart is in the right place but your head is not. If you attempt to meet with them, they will kill you, Joe."

"Better me than my family."

"Stop thinking like that!" Andy scolds.

Michael asks in an interested tone. "Are you saying that you may know who took shots at your house?"

"It had to be Shawn's gang. They're the only ones I've ever bought drugs from and they're the only ones I owe money to."

"Anyone specific that you think may be responsible for the shooting?"

"No, it could have been anyone of them. Hell, it could have been Shawn for all I know."

"I don't think it was Shawn but I do think it was somebody from his gang. I kind of figured that from the beginning."

Tony starts apologizing again. "I'm so sorry, Uncle Andy, for saying something to Joe."

"Don't worry about it, buddy. It's all right. We should have told him anyways."

Tony points to the hallway. "Dad, can I talk to you out in the hall?"

"Sure, buddy. Come on."

As soon as they walk out into the hallway Tony takes a deep breath. "I need to tell you something. Maybe we should go somewhere more private."

"What did you do, Tony?" Michael gently grabs Tony's arm and brings him into the consultation room. "Okay, let me have it. What's going on?"

"I apologize because I got a little out of line with someone."

"Tony, stop beating around the bush and tell me what's going on."

"When Daphne and the other nurse came in and started tying Joe down I tried stopping them."

"Okay, so what's so bad about that?"

"I guess it's how I did it. I grabbed their arms and tried pushing them away from him."

"Tony, you were trying to protect a family member. You didn't attack them or mean anything malicious. You didn't hurt either one of them right?"

"No, sir. I didn't."

"Then it's okay. As long as you didn't hurt one of them in the process then what you did is okay."

"Okay. I guess I should apologize to them anyway."

"No, apologies necessary. You did what you needed to do to protect family. Okay? Thank you for coming to me and telling me. I appreciate that."

"Your welcome. Thanks for being so understanding. I'm sure Daphne will talk to you about it."

"I will handle it if she does. Don't worry about it."

After two weeks of being in the hospital Joe is finally discharged to a rehabilitation facility for drug addiction.

Chapter Thirty-One

Andy and his kids are still staying with Michael until their house is fixed from the shooting. Michael's in his study working on his other case when his cell phone rings. He grabs it to answer it and notices that it's one of his informants.

"Raymond, what do you have for me?"

"Detective, I have some big news for you but if the gang finds out it was me that leaked this out they'll kill me."

"They're not going to find out. What do you have for me?"

"Well, you were right. The location of the deal has changed but you're not going to like where it's going to be now."

"I knew they would change it. Where is it going to be now?"

"Pagosa Springs."

"WHAT? That's on the other side of the county line in Archuleta County! Are you positive that's the new location?"

"Absolutely, without a doubt. I overheard them talking about it myself."

"Why would they travel over an hour and over sixty miles for a deal? Don't mind me, Raymond; I'm just talking out loud. Where in Pagosa, when and what time?"

"Tonight at ten o'clock just outside the county limits at the old abandoned train yard."

"I know exactly where that is." Michael looks at his watch. "Shit! That's six hours from now! Are you positive about this? If you're wrong and we go...."

"I am one hundred percent positive, Detective. I wouldn't steer you wrong."

"I know, I know. I just can't believe they're going all the way out there for a deal. Can you stall them without making it obvious?"

"No, I can't. I overheard them vote me out as a tag along so I won't be going on this run with them."

"All right. Would you happen to know what route they plan to take? I don't want to end up on the same road."

"I can tell you that they will not take any major roads or highways. They'll take all back roads even if that means it takes them two hours to get there instead of one."

"How many guys will they bring along?"

"They usually bring the entire gang except four guys. The leader always likes to keep a couple of guys back just in case something happens."

"That doesn't tell me how many will be going, Raymond. How many guys will they be bringing?"

"Most likely fifteen. We have twenty in our gang including Shawn but nobody knows where Shawn's at."

Michael says nothing, but knows exactly where Shawn is. *Hopefully this guy comes through for me because god knows Shawn hasn't given us crap.*

"What type of weapons will they be bringing?"

"Pistols and one guy, has a machine gun that dumps a lot of rounds. Word of advice…have somebody take that guy out first or you won't stand a chance because he's quick and he's good."

"Good to know. Thank you. How many vehicles will they have?"

"The drugs are going to be delivered in a small box truck. It's going to be loaded from nose to ass and from top to bottom with drugs and just a little room for three guys."

"So they'll have three guys inside the back of the box truck?"

"Yeah and two guys in the cab. There will be one guy driving a black Riviera. The guy with the machine gun usually rides shotgun in the Riviera. The leader usually rides in the back. Three guys will be in a dark brown Chrysler LeBaron and the rest will travel in a dark grey 87' Cutlass Supreme Coupe. All of them will be armed with guns and knives. The group my gang is selling to are not people you want to mess around with either. They're...."

"I already know about that group. I want you to delete my number from the history in your cell phone and don't call me again until after this deal is done, unless something changes. I'll talk to you soon...and thank you, Raymond."

"You're welcome. I'll delete your number now. I know it by heart anyways."

Michael hangs up and calls Detective Brantley who's been working with him on this case.

"Hello?"

"Hey Chester, this is Michael. We've got a time and place for the drug deal. Except we have to act fast and I do mean real fast or we're going to miss our chance."

"Finally, we get a damn break. How soon are we talking?"

"Ten o'clock tonight at an abandoned train yard just inside Pagosa Springs."

"Way the hell out there? That's out of our jurisdiction! We can't make a bust in another county! Shit!"

"Oh, yes we can. I have a way around it."

"Of course you do. Why am I not surprised?"

Michael chuckles. "We really did catch a break this time. I am friends with the head of the police department in Pagosa. We went through the police academy together. He's always said that if I needed a favor to pick up the phone. Let me call him and I'll call you right back."

"Okay. In the meantime I'll get our team together and have them meet us at the station with their gear."

"That's a great idea. I'll call you right back. Bye."

Michael starts pacing the floor as he hangs up with Chester and calls his Pagosa contact.

"Pagosa Springs Police Department."

"I need to speak with Steven Hubbard please."

"Sir, Chief Hubbard is in the middle of an interrogation. Can I..."

"Pull him out of it please. This is an emergency."

"Sir, may I ask who is calling?"

"Detective Michael Phillips from Durango. He'll know who I am."

"One moment please."

A few minutes go by before Chief Hubbard comes to the phone.

"Hey, Michael! How are you doing, buddy? What's the emergency?"

"I'm alright, Steven. Look, I seriously need your help. I am on the verge of a huge bust and I mean huge, the only problem is, it's within your jurisdiction."

"My jurisdiction? Okay, tell me what's going on and what do you need from me?"

"The largest drug cartel in my county is going to be making a huge deal tonight in Pagosa Springs at the old abandoned train yard. I'm talking millions of dollars in drugs." Chief Hubbard whistles at Michael's comment. "They usually do their dealings within our own county but this is supposed to be their biggest deal ever, which is probably why they're crossing over the county line to do it."

"That's the case you've been working on for a few years now."

"Yeah it is and we finally got a break."

"What do you need from me? To come into my county and make the bust?"

"Yes. I need permission for me and my swat team to come into your jurisdiction, do the bust and extradite them back to our own county to prosecute."

"You got it! You're more than welcome to take them the hell out of my county. I don't want those kinds of problems here. Since it is in my jurisdiction I will need to have some of my officers present during the bust. It's your show, your bust so you call the shots. We're just going to be there for backup and nothing else."

"I understand. Thank you very much. I really appreciate the cooperation."

"You got it. When and what time is this supposed to go down?"

"Tonight at ten o'clock. I literally just got word a moment ago myself so I apologize for the short notice."

"No apology necessary, I understand how this stuff works. Sometimes you have no control over when information comes through. You've got our support and blessings to come on over. We'll be there for backup. Let me round up a team of officers and I'll call you back in about a half hour to an hour for the details of your plan."

"Great! Thank you very much for this. I owe you one. A big one."

"No, you don't. We do things for each other all the time. I'll talk to you within the hour. Bye."

Michael then calls Chester back. "Michael, what's the word?"

"We're in. We even have backup if we need it. He's going to call me back within the hour for details of our plan."

"Michael, does your knowledge of people you know…know any bounds?"

"Nope. My dad always told me to keep a lot of friends because you never know when you may need them."

"He was a very smart man."

"Yes, he was. Thank you. Hey, did you get a hold of the team?"

"Yes, they're all on their way to the station now. We'll get geared up there."

"I'm going to be leaving my house in five minutes. See you then. Bye."

Michael rushes into his bedroom while calling out Andy's name. "Andy! Andy!"

"What's all the yelling about?" Andy asks.

Michael is quickly changing his clothes. "I won't be home for dinner and I am not sure how late I'm going to be."

Andy's eyebrows shoot up. "I know that type of clothing. Are you going out on a bust?"

"Yep. You know that big case I was telling you about?"

"Yeah."

"Well, it's coming to a head tonight."

"Shit! Are you serious?"

"Damn straight, brother. The biggest bust our town or even county has ever seen."

"What do I tell Tony when he gets home?"

"Tony and I have promised a long time ago that we'd have no secrets. Tell him the truth and tell him that I love him."

Andy becomes worried after hearing Michael's comment. "Don't talk like you're not coming back."

"I'm planning on coming back but you never know."

"Michael, I don't want to hear that shit. We'll see you home later however late that may be."

"Okay. Okay." Michael gives Andy a brief hug then unlocks his gun cabinet grabbing his AK-47, the rest of his tactical gear and rushes out of the house.

Michael arrives at the police station and sees that everybody including Chief Franks is out in the parking lot waiting for him. He gets out of his car and brings everybody up to speed according to what Raymond told him.

"Does anybody have any questions?" They all shake their heads no. There's one more thing that I want every one of you to remember. Have each other's backs…we want everyone to go back home tonight to their families. Good luck. Let's do this!"

The officers put on their armor vests and gather their helmets and kneepads. They each test their tactical radios making sure they're working. Then grab their night vision goggles, binoculars and smoke grenades sticking them inside the pockets of their pant legs. They each check their weapons making sure their M-16 rifles and semi-automatic AK-47's are fully loaded and ready to go then head out in six undercover dark colored vehicles.

They meet up with the Pagosa Springs police department behind some industrial buildings about two miles down the road from the old abandoned train yard.

Michael gets out of the car and meets with his old friend Steven Hubbard. "Steven, I can't tell you how much I appreciate the support." Michael says as he shakes Steven's hand.

"You're welcome. I don't want that shit in my town or my county."

"Have your men been briefed?" Michael asks as they walk toward Chief Franks.

Steven shakes Chief Franks hand. "Chief."

"Steven, it's nice to see you."

"Yes, they're up to speed on everything." Steven says in answer to Michael's question.

"Great, thank you."

"Let's go get these guys," says Chief Franks as he walks back toward his car. Steven heads back to his car too.

Michael waits until Chief Franks is out of earshot. "Hold up guys." Michael says to everyone else. He takes out his cell phone, pulls up a picture and shows everyone. "When you see this guy and you will see him. He's mine. Everyone understand?"

Everyone nods. One of the guys from Steven's group asks Michael. "Why? Do you know this guy?"

"Let's just say that our paths have crossed before and this is my chance to finally bust him. I've been waiting for this moment for a long time."

They all agree, returning to their cars and head back out on the road.

It's been forty-five minutes and everyone is still hiding in trees, weeds, and bushes and on rooftops waiting for the drug cartel and their buyers to arrive. Michael hears Chief Hubbard in his ear.

"Detective Phillips, are you positive this is where the deal is supposed to go down? They should have been here by now."

"I have one hundred percent trust in my informant. So yes, I am positive." *Shit, Raymond better be right about this or I'm going to look like an idiot!* Just as Michael has that thought he hears the familiar sound of tires rolling over gravel. "They're here." Michael whispers into the radio.

A car pulls in turning off its headlights and a small box truck with two cars pulls in after it. They quietly watch the cartel get out of their cars and prepare for the arrival of their buyers. They open the back door of the box truck letting out three guys that were riding in there, and then closes the door back up. Fifteen minutes later, two cars and another small box truck come rolling in turning off their headlights as they pull up. Everyone gets out of their vehicles and shakes hands with one another. Two of the cartel members open the door to their box truck revealing the drugs inside.

"Shit, they don't waste any time. Wait for my queue." Michael reminds everyone on the radio.

Four of the buyers check the drugs, even testing some, then retrieve three large duffle bags from one of the vehicles handing them to the drug cartel. The leader of the cartel opens the bags and inspects the money then motions to his others guys to proceed with the transfer. They start transferring all drugs from one box truck to the other.

"The one with the limp is mine." Michael says on the radio then hollers. "GO! NOW!"

Police officers and detectives start swarming around the drug cartel and their buyers. Suddenly somebody on the cartel side starts shooting. The shoot out doesn't last long but when it's finally over there are three drug cartel members dead, one dead buyer, one police office from Durango and two officers from the Pagosa Springs Police department injured but thankfully nothing life threatening.

Michael sees the buyer with the limp trying to make a run for it so he chases him and corners him near a fenced in area. "STOP RIGHT WHERE YOU ARE!" Michael says while pointing his AK-47 semi-automatic at the suspect.

With his hands in the air and a weapon still in one hand, the suspect turns around then drops the weapon to the ground. "Michael, long time, no see," he says calmly.

Michael tilts his head as he squints his eyes in curiosity. "You don't seem surprised to me. Why is that?"

"I'm no fool. No one can hide from you forever. I knew someday I would get busted and knew you would be the one to bust me. I just didn't think it would be this soon."

"You underestimated me, Bruce."

"Oh, see that's where you're mistaken. I know better than to underestimate a Phillips boy."

"Why this? Why did you go this route, Bruce?"

"Come on, Michael, I've never been on the right side of the law, you know that. I've been breaking the law and getting into trouble since I was a kid."

"That may be true but you used to help out the law now you're working against us."

"Sometimes there is no other choice."

"Pick up your weapon."

Bruce raises his eyebrows in surprise. "My weapon? You want me to pick up my weapon? I told you, Michael...I'm no fool. I know what you're doing. I pick up my weapon then you shoot me dead and say it was self-defense. I'm not going to give you that satisfaction."

"PICK UP YOUR WEAPON!"

"If you want me dead then you'll have to just shoot me unarmed which I know you won't do. We used to be like brothers, man. Why do you want to kill me?"

Michael becomes stunned and at the same time agitated with Bruce's question. "You son...of...a...bitch! My sister was almost killed...twice, because of you and that damn club! And you left my nephew for dead, Bruce!"

"For the last time, I had nothing to do with your sister almost getting killed! As for Joe, I saved his life!"

"Leaving him in a fucking container already half dead is not saving his life!"

"If I hadn't put him inside that damn container he would have already been dead by the time you found him!"

"Because of his injuries, he almost died! Why didn't you drop me a line telling me where he was, Bruce? Why didn't you let me know he was in trouble or drop him off at home? Something…instead of just leaving him for dead! The disappearance of Joe almost destroyed my brother! This is my family you're fucking with again and I'm tired of it!"

"I'm sorry, Michael, but I couldn't take the chance of you catching on to my connection with Shawn's gang!"

"So you leave my nephew for dead? Is that why you wouldn't help Andy find Joe?"

"I didn't leave him for dead. I knew you'd find him. And yeah, once Andy mentioned Shawn's name we knew we couldn't get involved in looking for Joe. We would have ruined our relationship with the cartel."

"How did you know that Joe was at the docks?"

"I didn't know. Nick and I were near the warehouses making a deal with someone else when we saw Joe's car go over the wall. We saw Shawn pull Joe from the water. Then Shawn got into a fight with one of his cartel members. We didn't know what Shawn was going to do with Joe so when he was fighting we took Joe and hid him inside one of the containers where it was safe."

"You left him for dead!"

"We were trying to help him! Look man, we used to be like brothers! Why would I leave him to die? I knew you'd find him in time!

"You and I have NEVER been like brothers! I've got two brothers and they would never leave a family member for dead! Pick up your weapon, Bruce!"

"You're going to have to kill me unarmed."

Suddenly, a hand is placed over the top of Michael's gun. "Michael, don't do it, son."

"Chief..."

"He's not worth it, Michael. He's not worth losing your career over."

"He almost killed my sister six years ago, almost destroyed my brother now and almost killed my nephew. He needs to be stopped."

"He's going to jail for the rest of his life, or at least for a very long time. Let the law take care of his ass. Your famous words, remember?"

"Yeah."

"You're angry right now so you're not thinking clearly and I don't blame you, but he's not worth ruining your life over. Hasn't your family suffered enough because of him? If you take him out then you'll be no better than he is. Not to mention you'll spend time in the pen too. I can't cover this one up for you, Michael. Too many witnesses around."

"I'm just tired of my family getting hurt because of these guys."

Chief Franks gently pushes down on Michael's gun. "Come on, son. He's not worth it. You know that. If you really wanted to take him out, you would have already when Andy went to them for help."

Michael takes in a deep breath then lets it out. "You're right." Michael stares Bruce in the eyes. "He's not worth it."

"Besides, you have a much bigger fish to fry right now." Chief Franks says as he takes Michael's gun out of his hand and taps his back.

Michael glances back at the Chief. "What do you mean?"

"You'll see when we return back to the others."

Michael looks back at Bruce. "Turn around and put your hands behind your back. You're under arrest."

"I really was trying to help Joe, Michael." Bruce tries to convince Michael that his intentions were good.

"I don't want to hear it, Bruce."

They return to the others and Chief Franks has Detective Brantley take Bruce to the squad and read him his rights.

"Apparently there are a whole lot of people following each other these days. It seems that we had ourselves a little tail coming up here. One that was hiding in the bushes but his car kind of gave him away since it wasn't hidden very well."

"What are you talking about?"

"I'm not going to tell you to stay calm because I already know how you're going to react and I can't say that I blame you. I've already laid into him pretty good myself and I do mean good."

"Laid into who?"

"Your son." Chief Franks steps back a little so that Michael can see Tony standing near his car.

"What the hell is my son doing here?"

"Apparently he was curious as to what we do when we make a bust so he followed us."

"WHAT?" Michael walks over to Tony. "WHAT IN THE HELL ARE YOU DOING HERE, TONY?"

"I was on my way home when I saw you guys outside the station getting your gear together. I knew you must have been getting ready for a bust. I wanted to see what happens on one so I followed you guys here."

Everyone except for Chief Franks and Officer Welch walks way from Michael and Tony. "ARE YOU OUT OF YOUR FUCKING MIND! WHAT THE HELL IS WRONG WITH YOU! THIS IS DANGEROUS SHIT HERE! YOU COULD HAVE GOTTEN YOURSELF KILLED COMING HERE! THIS WAS A STUPID ASS THING TO DO!"

"I'm sorry, dad, I was just curious!"

"I'VE TOLD YOU WHAT HAPPENS AT THESE BUSTS!"

"You've never told me that there are shootouts on these busts! You could have gotten killed, dad!"

"YOU COULD HAVE GOTTEN KILLED TOO! GOD DAMN YOU, TONY! THIS IS MY JOB! THIS IS WHAT I DO! YES, SOMETIMES THERE ARE SHOOTOUTS AT THESE THINGS BUT THAT'S PART OF THE DAMN JOB!" Michael is so angry, his face is beet red and the veins in his neck and head are popping out.

"Why didn't you tell me that there could be shootings at these busts?"

"Because I don't want you worrying about me every time I go out on one! You're my kid, I don't want that burden on your shoulders!"

"News flash, dad, I already worry about you! You've been a cop my whole life! With the exception of my aunts, uncles and cousins, you're all I have. I don't have a mom. All I've got is you!" Michael's speechless as he paces a few times back and forth shaking his head. "I didn't think there would be any harm in tagging along!"

"That's the problem, Tony, you didn't think! Give me your damn keys!" After taking Tony's keys, Michael points to the passenger seat. "I will finish dealing with you later! Park your ass inside the car and stay there until I come back! Do you understand me?"

"Yes, sir." Tony responds as his father walks away.

Chief Franks walks with Michael. "Are you okay?"

"I'm pissed off! But right now I have a job to finish!" Michael stops and turns toward the Chief. "Can you do me a favor please?"

"Sure, what do you need?"

"Can you call Andy and let him know that Tony is with me and what's going on? Tony was supposed to be home a long time ago, so Andy is probably going out of his mind wondering where he is. My brother has been through enough already. I want him to know that Tony is okay. He should be back from taking Joe to the rehab center."

"Sure. I'll call Andy right now."

"Thank you, Chief."

Michael helps take inventory of all drug packages before any of it is hauled away. After several hours, they finally finish and he advises Chief Franks and Chief Hubbard of the final count.

"This is huge, boys." Michael says smiling as he walks up.

"How much?" Chief Franks asks with curiosity.

"Seventy three pounds of heroin, on the street it's worth eighteen million dollars and twenty kilo's of cocaine worth ninety thousand on the street. I'd say...with the exception of my son...this turned out to be a pretty damn good night."

Chief Franks whistles loudly then shakes Michael's hand. "Great job, Michael! You really did a great job. This is the biggest bust our county has ever seen."

"That goes for our county too. Congratulations, Michael," says Chief Hubbard.

"Thanks guys, but it's not just my celebration." He looks over at his team watching them lock the truck up. "It's our celebration. I couldn't do this without my team."

Steven points to Tony. "You have a strong minded son and he looks just like you, Michael. And from what I understand he's just as stubborn too," says Steven as he chuckles.

Michael chuckles too and looks over to see Tony standing outside the car. "Speaking of my son…I need to finish having a conversation with him. Excuse me gentleman."

Chief Franks taps Michael on the shoulder. "If you need anything let me know, Michael. Go easy on him."

"Go easy on him? You know that's not going to happen." Michael shakes his head as he turns and walks to Tony. "You were told to stay in the damn car!"

"Yes, sir."

Tony quickly turns to get back into the car but Michael grabs him by the arm.

"Give me your wallet first?"

"My wallet?"

"Give me your damn wallet, Tony."

Tony hands over his wallet. Michael takes a card out of it and sticks it inside his own wallet.

"Dad, what are you doing? That's my driving permit!"

"No, that WAS your driving permit! Your driving privileges have now been revoked! You'll be lucky if you get them back next year! We'll discuss the rest of your punishment on the way home!"

"Dad! I have to get so many hours in to get my license! I need my permit to do that!"

"You're not getting your license anytime soon!"

"Dad!"

"Don't argue with me! Get back in the damn car!"

"I'm sorry, dad."

"I will not tell you again to get back in the damn car!"

Chief Franks quickly walks up and turns Tony toward the door of the car. "Boy, you better move your ass while you still have one." Tony gets inside the car and Chief Franks closes the door.

Michael looks at the Chief and shakes his head. "I'm sorry, Chief. I can't believe my son did this. I just can't believe he came out here. I don't know what the hell was in that crazy mind of his."

"Tony was curious, Michael. You need to fill him in on whatever details he wants to know. Explain to him in detail what happens when we make a bust or what could happen. I know you don't want him worrying about you but it's better than him putting his own life in danger coming out to these things. He'll get himself killed. You've got a damn good kid here, Michael."

"I know. With the exception of tonight, he has been a good kid. This is going to be a long ride home for him. I'll have the report for this bust done tomorrow."

"That's fine. Get some rest, we've had a long night."

Chapter Thirty-Two

Seven months later-

The entire family, except Dakota is at Tony's baseball game watching him pitch. Chief Franks arrives to watch his grandson play; he's on the same team as Tony.

Linda leans over Chuck and taps Jeff's leg. "Hey, Jeff, how's Dakota doing?"

"She's good. She's frustrated that the doctor has put her on bed rest for her last four weeks."

"Poor thing. Who's with her right now?"

"My mom and Natalie."

"Oh, good."

"Damn, he's got a fast arm! It never ceases to amaze me how fast he can throw." Chuck says to Michael.

Michael laughs as he responds. "Indeed his does. He sure doesn't get that from me."

"I think he got that from Andy. Andy has always had a good arm. Has Tony ever been clocked?" Chuck asks as the players take a timeout to huddle.

"Yeah, last year. The coach was curious too because Tony is the fastest pitcher on his team. They clocked him at ninety-six mph."

"What? Are you serious?"

"I'm not kidding you, bro."

"Holy shit! That's almost major league!"

"Yeah, it's almost a shame that he wants to become a detective like me instead of a pro baseball player. He'd be amazing at it."

"Yes, he would be. I hear you finally gave him his driving permit back."

Michael lets out a huge sigh. "Yeah, I gave it back to him last week. He's lucky I didn't hold onto it for longer."

Chuck turns to Andy and nods his head in Joe's direction. "How's Joe been doing out on the job site with you? Still good?"

"Oh yeah. Joe's loves it. He's fitting right in and picking it up quick. Everybody there loves him. I'm tickled pink that Joe wants to learn the family business and take it over some day. I'm so proud of him. I tell him that everyday. He's kicked his drug addiction and is doing great. He's got himself back on track again. Although, I think he's getting tired of hearing it."

"He's come a long way. Tired of hearing it or not, don't stop telling him that you're proud of him."

"I won't believe me. Bethany just finished her sessions with Schiller yesterday. She's doing great too."

"Yeah, she told me that when I saw with her yesterday. You're doing great too, bro. Now that you've finally dealt with the demons inside."

Andy looks at Chuck confused. "What do you mean?"

"Dealing with the loss of Melanie and your temper."

"Oh. It was rough, but my kids and I are finally, back to normal. Well, as normal as can be without my wife."

Chief Franks cuts in on their conversation. "Oh, I have an update on Shawn and his gang."

"I don't understand why court cases have to take so long, especially when they're open and shut cases. It's obvious they're all guilty," says Andy.

"That's the court system for you. We're lucky it didn't take longer. So what's the verdict? How much time did everyone get?" asks Chuck.

"The judge only reduced Shawn's jail time by two years and that's because he wasn't completely cooperative and truthful with us. He's serving about twenty-five years but will probably only do twenty. The rest of his gang are getting life without parole due to the drug charges and murder charges against them."

While looking at the Chief, Andy leans forward putting his arms on the railing in front of him. "Good, they deserve it...them bastards. What about Bruce and his gang?"

"Well, as you know Bruce's record goes way back."

"Yeah, we know," replies Michael.

"He and his guys are getting the same sentencing as Shawn's gang. We won't have to worry about seeing them again. They're in jail for the long haul."

"Good. He's done enough damage to...." Chuck's attention is suddenly distracted when he sees a woman that looks familiar on the other end of the bleachers. "What the hell?" Chuck says real slowly as he stares at the woman.

Michael looks at Chuck then follows Chuck's stare. "What's wrong? What are you looking at?"

"You guys are going to think that I've lost my mind but I know what I'm seeing."

"What's going on? What are you looking at?" Michael asks again.

"Mom."

"You're right, you've lost your mind."

Just as a batter on Tony's team hits a home run ending the game, eight to one, the woman notices Chuck staring at her and runs to her car. Chuck starts chasing after her. Andy and Michael hear the Chief whisper under his breath.

"Shit!"

"CHUCK!" Michael yells as he, Andy and Jeff now run after Chuck.

Chuck doesn't catch her but notices her license plate number. Michael, Andy and Chief Franks finally catch up with Chuck.

"I know what I saw, guys! That looked just like mom!"

Michael agrees. "I would have never believed it either if I hadn't seen her with my own eyes just now."

"I saw her getting into her car and you're right, she did look like mom!" Andy comments as he continues to stare in the direction the car went.

Chuck looks at Michael. "What the fuck is going on here, Michael? That was mom! It had to be! It looked just like her! You guys said so yourself!"

Andy starts to yell too. "Dad had an open casket but we were told that mom was too messed up to have an open casket! We didn't get a chance to see her before she was buried! You were at the hospital before any of us got there, Michael!"

"I know what you're implying and I don't appreciate it! I never saw mom either!"

"So when you got to the hospital you didn't see her?" Andy tries to confirm.

"No, they would let me see her! They said she was too messed up for us to see her!"

"Who wouldn't let you?"

"Chief Franks and the...hospital." Michael says as he starts to put it together in his head. He turns to look at the Chief. "Something is not right here, Chief Franks! That looked just like our mom but a little grayer! What the hell is going on?"

Andy starts questioning the Chief too. "Michael and I heard you whisper 'shit' when Chuck said he saw our mom. Now, it's one thing when one person thinks they know somebody but when you have three people that think they know somebody then something must be up! What do you know about this?"

"Did you catch the license plate number?" Chief Franks asks as if they should be able to figure it out at this point.

Michael and Andy each respond. "No." "No, I didn't. Did you?"

Chuck replies too. "Yeah, I did. It said 'MACD4'."

"I'll have the plate run and see where it takes us," says Michael.

"Michael, think about the initials." Chief Franks prompts him to stop and think for a moment.

Suddenly Michael's face falls as he says out loud. "Michael, Andy, Chuck, Dakota, 4?"

"Yes," replies the Chief.

Chuck throws his arm up toward the parking lot. "Still think I'm crazy?"

Michael turns to the Chief. "You need to start explaining!"

Chief Franks takes out his cell phone and makes a call. "It wasn't time yet but now we have no choice. Please come back."

Michael, Chuck and Andy look at each other completely confused. Within moments the car comes back and slowly pulls into a parking spot. The woman gets out of the car and slowly walks toward them. As she gets closer Andy reacts first.

"Jesus that is her! How is this possible?"

Chief Franks replies with remorse. "I'm sorry to have kept this from you guys. This isn't the time or place to discuss this. I think we should meet somewhere and talk."

Chuck continues to stare at this woman who looks like their mother. "I don't give a shit if it's not the place but it is certainly the time!"

"I agree!" says Michael. "What in the hell is going on, Chief Franks?"

Joan stops within six feet of her boys putting her hands to her face as she cries. "Oh, my god. I have missed you kids so much."

"Shit! If my wife were here right now she'd go into instant labor for sure," Jeff says in shock.

Joan looks at Jeff. "You've been very good to my daughter. She deserves the best and I think she's met her match. Thank you." Jeff says nothing in return.

You can hear the anger in Michael's voice as he speaks to her. "Don't you dare talk about my sister like you've..."

"She's my daughter!"

Michael turns to Chief Franks. "What the fuck is going on here, Chief?"

Linda walks up behind Chuck with the kids. "Oh, my god. She looks just like your mom in the pictures."

"Apparently, she is our mom."

"WHAT?"

"Sweetheart, can you please take the kids to our house? We'll meet up with you there shortly. And please don't call Dakota yet."

"Sure, honey. Come on kids."

After she leaves and the park is now cleared out they continue their conversation.

"Start explaining, Chief Franks. Were our parents even really involved in a car accident?" asks Chuck.

The Chief looks at Joan and takes in a deep breath. "Yes, they were. Your mom and dad witnessed a triple murder. Obviously you guys remember Scott and Logan?"

"Yes, unfortunately. Scott was Dakota's abusive boyfriend and Logan, his brother tried to kill Dakota. What do they have to do with this?" Andy asks.

"The killer that your mom and dad saw was their father. His name was Tristan."

276

"WHAT?" Michael screeches. "Tristan was in Shawn's gang. He was the leader of the cartel. Are you telling us that Scott coming into the picture was no accident?"

"No it wasn't. I'll get to that shortly. A few days before your mom and dad's accident, they witnessed the triple murder behind the grocery store down the street from where you lived. You guys didn't know this, but your mom and dad started receiving death threats. Tristan knew who your father was because your father had busted him before on other charges. So it was kind of a bittersweet thing for Tristan to take your dad out. It was a matter of time before Tristan would act on his threats. The threats were never toward you kids, only to your mother and father."

Chuck responds. "What did that have to do with their accident?"

"Their accident was a perfect time to take your parents out of the picture for a while until we had these guys in custody. It was the only way to protect them. Unfortunately, your father…as you had witnessed for yourself did not survive the accident."

"And her?" Michael asks as he points to his mother. "How? We thought our mother died too!"

"She was immediately transferred to a private hospital where she was treated then put into protective custody."

Michael starts to pace back and forth while Andy sits down on the bleachers. "I'm confused." Says Michael. "Who did we bury then? We received life insurance money for both our father and mother! Their retirement money! Everything! Even the house was transferred to me!"

Chief Franks let's out a huge sigh as Joan answers for him. "Honey, Chief Franks and the FBI set up a fund for you kids. All of the money you received was from your dad's savings, the FBI and Chief Franks. The FBI put together all the paperwork. I still have my retirement money and everything else. As for the house, I added your name to the mortgage, you just didn't see my signed copies."

"But grandma helped me with all of that!"

Chief Franks continues to explain. "After your father died, we had called a secret meeting with your grandmother and filled her in on everything. She…"

"SHE KNEW ABOUT THIS? ARE YOU KIDDING US?" Chuck yells. "Do you have any idea what we all went through losing our parents? Or we thought we did!"

"Yes, we do. We needed your grandmother's help. Doing it this way was the only way to protect your mother. The casket that you thought you buried your mother in was empty."

"Why didn't you guys just tell us?" Asks Chuck.

"Because we needed to protect you kids as well. Even though they weren't after you kids, the less information you knew the better it was for everyone. We just couldn't take the chance of any of you knowing about any of this."

"What about when I sold the house?" Asks Michael.

Joan replies. "I signed the papers for the house to be sold. You just didn't see the copies with my signature. I made sure all of the money from the house went to you kids."

"And now, twenty three years later? I don't get it. Why turn up now?" Michael asks.

"Because, Tristan was never caught until now."

"What do you mean until now? We've always known where he was. We just needed the evidence against him."

"Remember the big drug bust you did seven months ago?"

"Yeah."

"As you already know, Tristan was the leader of the drug cartel and as you know the leader was shot and killed at the bust. His last

278

surviving son was one of the cartel members. We found out that he was the one responsible for the drive by shooting at Andy's house. We had to wait until the trial was over before we could take your mother out of protective custody. We weren't sure what kind of time he was going to get. He's in the pen for good. Now that it's finally over your mother can have her life back with her family."

"And Scott?" Chuck asks.

"Scott went after Dakota after he found out about what your parents witnessed. He was trying to protect his father. Logan only went after Dakota when he found out about Scott and the last surviving son is now in the pen for the rest of his life. It just became a vicious circle."

"This is fucked up!" Michael shouts as he starts to pace back and forth.

Joan starts crying again. "I'm really sorry, boys. Please know that I have always kept tabs on all of you kids and my grandkids. Thanks to Chief Franks, I have albums and albums full of pictures of you and your families. Please believe me that I have missed all of you so much! I've been to all of your weddings and Melanie's funeral."

Suddenly Andy moves to within a couple of feet from her. "What? You were at my wife's funeral?"

"Yes. I was. I was disguised with a wig and everything. I am so sorry that you lost her, sweetheart. And I have attended all of my kids weddings…well, the church portion of it anyways."

Andy looks at the Chief. "Is this really happening? I mean other than a little grayer she looks just like her." He says still in shock.

"Yes, this is your mother."

Suddenly, Andy grabs her, pulling her close and they both start crying. Michael and Chuck then join them.

After several emotional happy minutes, Michael finally breaks loose from their hug. "You already know who Jeff is but I think a proper introduction is in order. Jeff, this is our mom, Joan. Mom, this is Dakota's husband, Jeff."

They shake hands and she pulls him into a hug. "It is so nice to officially meet you. You've been so good to my daughter."

"Nice to meet you too."

"Shit!" Andy whispers.

Chuck looks back at Andy. "What's the matter?"

"How are we going to tell Dakota about mom? She's already on bed rest for the remainder of her four weeks of pregnancy. This just may throw her into labor now."

"We don't tell her yet," Michael replies.

Jeff becomes angry, which is unusual for him. "Bullshit! I will not keep this from my wife! I will NOT keep something this big from her!"

"Just until she's had the twins. She's..."

"NO, Michael! We are not keeping this from her!"

"Then how do you suggest we tell her?"

"I will tell her. Let's go to my house right now and I will tell her. I have a game plan."

Once they arrive, Jeff pulls his mother and sister outside and fills them in on what's happening. They go back inside and everybody stays in the living room while Jeff goes to the bedroom to talk to Dakota.

"Hey, baby. How are you doing?"

"I'm really good, honey. I was just sitting here watching a movie with your mom and sister. Did they leave?"

"No, they're out in the family room. They'll be back in here in a minute."

"Is everything okay?"

"Yeah, baby, it's great actually. I was just thinking about our conversation last night about your mom and how you miss her."

"You're going to get me all emotional again."

"I know, I'm sorry. I just feel so bad for you though."

"I wish she could meet our kids and you."

Well, she's already met me. "Yeah, I know. It's too bad that it couldn't be one of those situations where she was just in protective custody all of these years and now she'd be free to be with her family again."

"Wow, he's good." Natalie whispers out in the family room.

"Shhh!" Andy scolds her as he nods his head agreeing with her.

"That would be great! At least we would have our mom back," Dakota says responding to Jeff's comment.

"You wouldn't be upset with her if something like that had happened?"

"Not if she was in protective custody. If she had just abandoned us that would be a different story but I know my mom would have never abandoned us. Hmm…protective custody…that would be a dream, come true."

"Well, your dream has come true, baby."

Dakota looks at Jeff confused. "Did you get hit in the head by one of Tony's fast balls? You're not making any sense at the moment. Are you okay?" Everybody in the living room tries to keep from laughing at her comment.

"I'm fine, baby. I want you to take in a deep breath."

"What?"

"Trust me. You're going to need it."

"What's going on?"

"Take in a deep breath. Your dream has come true. What I am about to show you is one hundred percent real and I promise you that you will get an explanation to it all." She looks at Jeff with shock and does what he says, taking in a few deep breaths. Then he hollers out. "Michael, Andy, Chuck…Joan."

All of them walk into the bedroom and Chief Franks, Jeff's mom and sister follow behind. Dakota's eyes pop wide open once she sees her mother.

"OH, MY GOD!" Her hands instantly fly up to her mouth.

"Take in a deep breath, baby. I know this is a shock but you have to take it easy. Breathe!" Jeff coaches.

She continues doing what Jeff says. "Is that really my mom?" She asks as she starts to cry.

Chuck replies. "Yes, it really is. I promise you it is."

Dakota looks at Jeff. "That whole protective custody thing you were babbling about really happened?"

"Yes."

"Oh, my god. My dad?"

"Unfortunately, baby sister, dad really is gone. Just mom survived that accident." Chuck replies again as he's now standing next to her.

Dakota holds out her arms so Joan rushes to her. They cry in each other's arms for several minutes making everybody else in the room cry again too. After what seems like an eternity, they finally pull apart. Joan brushes Dakota's hair behind her ears just like she used to do when Dakota was a child.

Dakota looks at her brothers with anger. "How long have you guys known about this?"

Michael replies. "We just found out a couple of hours ago."

Chief Franks and Joan retell the story from beginning to end filling Dakota and Jeff's mom and sister in on everything.